the peculiar case of the petersburg professor

A Michelle Kilpatrick Mystery

Book One

sharon kay

hale & thornton press llc

This book is a work of fiction. Any references to historical events, real people, or real places are used fictitiously. Other names, characters, places, and events are products of the author's imagination, and any resemblance to actual events or places or persons, living or dead, is entirely coincidental.

Copyright © 2022 by Sharon Kay

Book Cover Design by Kay Meadows
www.kaymeadows.com

ISBN: 978-1-960581-00-6 (paperback)
ISBN: 978-1-960581-03-7 (paperback—Amazon)
ISBN: 978-1-960581-01-3 (eBook)

the peculiar case of the petersburg professor

chapter one

October 14, 1974

The sound of Bad Company's "Can't Get Enough" jarred me from my deep sleep, but I refused to open my eyes. Even the sound of dishes clanging in the kitchen couldn't motivate me to get out of bed.

Mornings on the farm started early during the harvest season for everyone in my family except me. Despite my parents' disapproval, my responsibilities on the farm were put on hold so I could focus on my classes at the University of Petersburg. One year down, three to go.

With my eyes closed, I rolled over and hit the nightstand until I found the off switch on the clock radio. *Just a few more minutes, please.* As I snuggled between my flannel sheets and pulled the down comforter closer to my chin, Gidget, my silver-haired Persian cat, started her journey from the foot of my bed, up my calves to my shoulders. With each step, her paws sank deep into my skin until she stopped in front of my face, ending my quest to fall back to sleep by persistently tapping my cheek.

"Okay, okay, you win," I muttered, half asleep. There was

no sense arguing with my furry feline friend. It was time to face the day.

I put on my glasses, glanced at the Monet calendar hanging on the wall—October 14, 1974—and smiled. Fourteen was my favorite number and had been since junior high. Maybe today was my lucky day, in spite of it being a Monday *and* having Professor Ladd's journalism class later this morning.

Although I dreaded going to her class, I knew the professor could be my ticket out of Petersburg. With her help, becoming a first-rate journalist was within the realm of possibilities. Of course, the way the quarter was going, she just as easily could be the judge who condemned me to a life within these four walls. The jury was still out on which role she would fill.

With trepidation, I sat up in bed. To delay any longer would not stop the inevitable. I had to face the beast I called Professor Ladd.

To thwart any thoughts I harbored of lying back down, Gidget moved to the still-warm spot on my pillow, curled up, and squeezed her eyes shut.

I slipped my feet into the fuzzy pink slippers beside my bed and headed to the closet. Looking back at my clock, I realized time had been marching on, even though I had not. Behind schedule, I hurriedly thumbed through the clothes in front of me, pulled three skirts and four shirts out of the closet, and flung them on my bed. I moved the pieces around several times until I had a combination I liked. Once dressed, I gave my image in the white Cheval mirror a critical once-over.

"Guess that's as good as it gets," I uttered. Gidget raised her head, annoyed I had disturbed her sleep. "Sorrrrry… didn't mean to wake you." I stopped. Did I seriously just apologize to a cat?

Hopefully, no one overheard me, but if they knew Gidget

the way I knew Gidget, they would have apologized too. She, like most cats, considered herself superior to us mere mortals and was obstinate, opinionated, and vocal—very vocal—about her likes and dislikes. One minute she could be a sweet, cuddly ball of fur, and the next a hissing, angry miniature lion. But we were soulmates. We understood each other.

Gidget peered at me through her slivered eyes as I adjusted my olive green and brown plaid skirt. She raised her head, uttered a drawn-out sleepy meow, and returned to the pressing matter at hand—sleeping. *She must like the ivory blouse with this skirt.* I grinned. Had she not approved, I knew the feline fashion expert would have jumped off the bed in disgust.

After fluffing my blond shag, I slipped the silver chain with the Eiffel Tower charm around my neck and glanced back at the clock. It was 8:10 a.m.—ten minutes before T.J., my best friend, would be here to pick me up. We both had 9:00 a.m. classes at the University of Petersburg, and Monday was his day to drive. I hoisted the pile of textbooks off the nightstand and raced downstairs. As I landed on the last step, T.J.'s horn blared in the driveway.

"Michelle," my mother yelled. "T.J.'s here!"

"I know, Mom," I answered as I opened the front door.

"But your breakfast!"

I spun around and saw my mom in the hallway, drying her hands on a yellow dishtowel. As usual, her golden blond hair, courtesy of drugstore hair dye, was styled and her makeup flawless. Out of habit, she only left her bedroom in the morning after she was presentable, in case anyone dropped by the house unannounced. She looked picture-perfect in her yellow and orange floral house dress that perfectly matched the colors in the living room.

I ran back and gave her a quick kiss on the cheek. "No time to eat. See you tonight."

As I stepped onto the porch, the crisp autumn air greeted

me and reminded me to reach back and grab my brown jacket hanging on a hook next to the door. I threw the jacket over my books, closed the door behind me, and bounded down the concrete steps. T.J. again hit the horn of his green Nova.

"I'm coming. Hold your horses." I laughed as I picked up my pace and put on my jacket while shifting my books and purse from one arm to the other.

T.J. rolled his window down and blasted The Rolling Stones' "It's Only Rock and Roll (But I Like It)" from his radio, providing upbeat background music as I tried to find my clip-on sunglasses in my jacket pocket. Unfortunately, they weren't there, which meant they were probably in my purse. There was no way I could carry my books, rummage through my purse, and dodge the glare of the morning sun all at the same time without falling flat on my face. The clip-ons would have to wait.

T.J. leaned out his window and flashed a smile while motioning for me to hurry up. Although not what most people would call handsome, T.J. always had an endless stream of girls vying for his attention. I knew him as a funny, intelligent, and loyal friend, but what did they see? The way he dressed? I doubted it. T.J. was, in a word, predictable. He always wore pressed shirts—either a striped shirt in warm weather or a plaid flannel shirt when it was cooler—with wrinkle-free jeans.

Although most guys on campus wore their hair long, T.J. kept his hair short, with a side part and a slight swoop of the bangs—the same way he had worn it for years. However, the one thing that set T.J. apart from everyone else was his smile. It was genuine, full of life, and infectious. A girl could get lost in that smile.

As I climbed into the passenger seat, T.J. glanced at his watch and then turned the volume down on the radio. "I can't believe you're late again. Really, Michelle," he said in his pretending-to-be-annoyed voice.

4

I elbowed him and pointed to the clock on the dashboard. "You, dear sir, are five minutes early. Is someone in a hurry to get to class?"

His cheeks turned pink.

"Oh, my word, you are. You want to get there early so you can sit next to Meg." I couldn't help but smile. He had been talking about Meg for the last couple of weeks.

"No," he protested. "I just want to be there early. No big deal." With each word, his face turned a brighter shade of pink.

"Right."

"If I want a good seat in class, what's the big deal?"

"If by 'good seat' you mean sitting next to the girl of your dreams, go for it, man."

He said nothing. Maybe I had teased him too much. I was relieved when he shook his head and laughed.

T.J., short for Timothy James, and I go way back. His family, the Wilsons, bought the farm across from ours when I was six years old. I remember the day my mom and I went to welcome them to the area. She took one of her homemade apple pies, and T.J. and I bonded while eating it. We've been inseparable ever since. We've shared our secret crushes, comforted each other when things didn't work out, and talked about our hopes and dreams for the future. He's been my confidant, my cheerleader, my best friend.

The wind rushed through the car's open windows and blew my hair into my eyes. I rolled up my window and nudged T.J. to do the same. *It must be nice to have such short hair.* Not one light brown strand was out of place. Peering at me over his aviator sunglasses, he smiled as I tried to put myself back together again.

The twenty-minute drive from our homes in rural Petersburg to the university wasn't a bad commute. It was nice having someone to talk to on the way home and to be able to unwind from the day's classes. While not ideal, commuting worked for me, but I worried if T.J. felt the same.

As we approached campus, a wave of melancholy swept over me. I blurted out, "Do you ever regret not living on campus?"

"Why? Do I look like I regret it?" Laughing, he looked in the mirror, making faces.

I nudged him with my elbow. "Be serious. Sometimes I feel guilty. You always planned to live on campus, but you're still commuting because I can't afford to move out."

"I'll tell you now what I told you then. We're in this together. If you commute, I commute." T.J. reached over and put his hand on my arm. "And no, I don't regret it." He returned his hand to the steering wheel, shook his head, and grinned. "You worry too much."

I was about to reply, but then "Brandy (You're a Fine Girl)" by Looking Glass came on, and T.J. and I began singing as loud as we could. We laughed so hard at our off-key singing that tears streamed down our faces. All my thoughts of guilt disappeared.

Our laughter continued as T.J. turned into the university's Commuter Lot 1 but ended when he couldn't find a parking spot. According to the clock on the dashboard, it was 8:42. T.J. was fidgeting, visibly nervous about not being able to get to his class early.

"How 'bout Lot 3?" I suggested. "There are usually some spots over there."

Nodding, he drove in that direction. As he turned into the lot, he saw an empty parking spot. Another car was coming around the corner in the opposite direction. Not wanting to lose his spot, T.J. turned on his blinker and slid into the prized location before the other car could claim it.

"See you 'round noon." He closed his car door and, not waiting for my reply, headed toward the row of brick buildings in a steady, focused jog.

"Yeah, see ya," I answered, even though he couldn't hear me above the sound of the Air National Guard jets flying overhead. But it didn't matter. We would meet at the Commuter Lounge for lunch like we always did.

I made my way to Sheffield Hall and climbed the stairs to the fourth floor. My heart sank when I read the note taped to the door saying class was canceled. *Why can't the department's secretary call us and let us know when there's no class?* I chuckled, thinking about Betsy Braxton, the journalism department's secretary, making thirty-five phone calls. She'd probably break a nail dialing all those numbers and then have to take the day off.

Since my next class didn't start until 10:30, I headed for the Commuter Lounge in Whitley Hall—the home away from home for all the campus stepchildren, also known as "the commuters."

I heard Lawrence's voice as I walked down to the basement, and it didn't take long to find him. Sitting at the table along the back wall, he was engaged in a heated discussion with Tasha.

"Hi," I whispered to Rick as I pulled out the seat next to him and laid my textbooks on the table, trying not to make any noise.

Rick quietly asked, "How's it goin'?"

"Okay, how 'bout with you?"

The layers in his brown hair moved slightly as he nodded. "Okay."

I leaned closer to him. "What's up with them?"

"The war. Communism. Socialism. You know, the usual. She got the old man riled up today." Rick grinned.

I understood. The Vietnam War vet and the "make love, not war" hippie were at it again.

Lawrence jumped to his feet, pushing his chair to one side. He leaned on the table, shaking a finger at Tasha. "If we leave Vietnam before the job's finished, the entire region

7

will fall to communism! But I suppose you'd be cool with that."

Lawrence's inflammatory tone did not faze Tasha. Her parents—both professors at the university—moved from Romania to the United States when she was three. They encouraged her to express her opinions and debate political issues, so it was no wonder she thrived on arguing with Lawrence. With his three years of service in the Army, she loved to question his trust in the United States government and his support of its involvement in the Vietnam War.

Tasha brushed a wayward strand of her waist-length chestnut brown hair off her face and calmly replied to Lawrence while motioning for him to sit down. "Do we have the right to be involved in another country's civil war? How many people have to die? And for what?"

I was so focused on Lawrence and Tasha's "discussion" that I didn't see Alice, the middle-aged woman who ran the Commuter Lounge, until she appeared behind Lawrence.

She tapped him on the shoulder and said, "Can you keep it down, please? What's this all about?" Then she looked at Tasha sitting across the table. "Oh, I see. Again…really? You guys are how old?"

Lawrence pushed his John Lennon-ish, wire-rimmed glasses back up his nose as his lanky frame sank into his chair, and he muttered an apology. He was smart enough to know not to start a fight with Alice.

Although barely reaching his shoulder when standing next to him, Alice was the supreme leader within the walls of her domain. She made the rules. We followed them. If not, we lived with the fear she would banish us from our home away from home. We had never seen her kick anyone out of the Commuter Lounge, and we certainly didn't want to be the first.

"What have I told you about being so loud? Don't make me tell you again." Alice placed her hands firmly on his shoulders and stood there for a moment. "Be good, you two." And, with that, she walked away.

Perhaps it was nervous energy, but after she returned to her office, the four of us looked at each other and broke out in laughter.

Once Lawrence regained his composure, he looked at Tasha. With a slight smile, he asked her, "Why do I always get in trouble with Alice, and you don't?"

"Guess it's 'cause I'm better looking." She grinned, fluffing her long, dark locks.

The tension between the two of them vanished. Tasha began reading her copy of John le Carré's *Tinker Tailor Soldier Spy,* and Lawrence picked up his newspaper. All was well in the Commuter Lounge world once again.

I glanced at the clock on the wall and breathed a heavy sigh.

"What's wrong?" Rick asked. "You don't sound happy— your next class?"

"Yeah—my investigative journalism class. I've got Professor Ladd, and I can't do anything right in her eyes."

"What do you mean? You write good enough...I mean, you've had a lot of stuff published in the *Daily News*."

"Thanks, but apparently, pleasing the editor of the university's paper is easier than pleasing Professor Ladd. The paper's standards are obviously much lower."

"Low standards at the *Wildcats' Daily News*?" He laughed sarcastically.

"Yeah, I know. Hard to believe, right?" I rolled my eyes. "Professor Ladd always compares my writing to Craig Miller's, and I always come up short."

"Craig Miller, the mystery writer? He's a grad student here, right? I don't understand why a successful writer would go to grad school?"

"I guess he's one of those guys who likes the world of

academia, and, lucky me, he's in my investigative journalism class."

Rick shook his head in dismay. "Why would he take an undergrad journalism class, and why here? Didn't he go to Columbia for his bachelor's? I mean, let's get real. Petersburg is a good school, but it's not prestigious like Columbia."

"Ladd said he's working on his next book and wants to learn more about investigative reporting. Guess when you're in the MFA program, you can take a few classes outside your department, and as fate would have it, he picked the one I'm taking."

"That's weird. If I had a promising career like his, no way would I go to grad school."

"Isn't that the truth? He doesn't need another degree to get a book on a bestseller's list. Rumor has it his publisher paid him a sizable advance for his next book. Must be nice." I sighed. "Doesn't matter. He's here, and he's making my life miserable. I mean, he writes fiction for a living, and I'm just trying to write the who, what, when, where, and why of a story." I shook my head in disgust. "I have no idea how he does it, but his finished product always sounds better than mine, and Professor Ladd loves nothing better than pointing it out to me."

"That's a bummer," Rick said.

I threw my jacket over my arm and picked up my books. "Oh, well, off to class. Guess I'll go see how much the good professor hated last week's assignment. Fun, fun."

chapter two

I fought the urge to skip class with each step toward Sheffield Hall. It was such a gorgeous day. The sun was shining, and it was now warm enough for me to take off my jacket. *Who knows how many more days like this we'll have? Do I really want to ruin a beautiful fourteenth day by going to Professor Ladd's class?*

After all, I still had my three unexcused absences I could use, and it would be no problem to borrow the notes from Melody. What did I have to lose? Ultimately, my drive to get good grades prevailed over my justified reasons for skipping.

Taking a deep breath, I begrudgingly opened the door to the bane of my existence. A stack of graded papers on Professor Ladd's desk caught my attention, and I found mine near the bottom.

Rattled, I stuffed my paper with a red 7/10 written next to my name into my textbook and headed for a seat. I didn't care where I sat, as long as it was close enough to the front to read the overhead transparencies on the screen and far enough back not to feel Professor Ladd's disapproving gaze. I reminded myself to stay calm. *Everything will be alright.*

I rubbed the miniature Eiffel Tower hanging around my neck between my fingers. *Tomorrow Professor Ladd has office hours. I'll go talk to her and get this figured out.* Struggling to get

Cs and Bs was a new experience for me, and I didn't like it one bit.

I adjusted my jacket on the back of my chair, resulting in my sleeve hitting the pen on my desk. It rolled onto the floor and under the desk next to mine. I looked. Craig Miller was sitting there. *Really…of all the people. Just my luck!*

According to his bio in the school paper, Craig Miller was the crowned golden boy of mysteries. Not many people write a bestseller while they're working on their bachelor's degree, but he did. Every book he wrote got rave reviews. No wonder Professor Ladd liked his writing.

Asking him to get my pen would be the simplest thing to do, but I didn't want to talk to him. I reasoned that if I could find another pen, I could leave that one on the floor. So, I rummaged through my fake leather shoulder purse but came up empty.

With sheer determination, I leaned over and stretched across the aisle, attempting to retrieve my wayward pen. No dice. My arms weren't long enough. I sat up, preparing to think of a new plan, when, out of the corner of my eye, I saw Craig reach under his chair and grab it.

"Is this yours?"

Despite being halfway through the quarter, I had never actually looked at Craig. I had been too annoyed with him to notice how good-looking he was. But today there was no denying it. Sandy brown hair. Golden tan. White teeth, I mean, *really* white teeth. He looked like he should be on the cover of a magazine. Although only a few years older than me, he seemed so mature and confident.

I took my pen from his hand, and he smugly pulled back his tweed blazer and pointed to the pen guard in his front pocket. "Rule Number One: A successful writer always carries spare pens."

What a jerk! Who cares about perfect teeth and movie-star

good looks? Craig Miller might be a first-rate author, but he was a snob. I hoped I never sat near him again. Ever.

My internal ranting and ravings about Craig were paused as Professor Ladd walked into the room, which immediately went quiet. She assumed her position in front of her desk and, while looking at us over her large black-rimmed glasses, launched into a lecture on conducting interviews. I took notes, trying to copy all the information on the transparencies. She was a fast talker, making it challenging to keep up with her.

I often wondered if she always talked so quickly, or if it was a habit she picked up when she lived in New York City. I didn't know a lot about her except that she grew up in Petersburg and after high school attained a degree in English from Barnard College and a Master's in Journalism from Columbia.

I once overheard some students say that Professor Ladd's family connections opened the doors for her to get her first newspaper job. Regardless, it was her hard work at the *New York Times* and the *Washington Post* that earned her a reputation as a first-rate reporter. No one could deny Professor Ladd knew her stuff, and, although I disliked her as a teacher, I knew I could learn a lot from her.

As the lecture drew to a close, Professor Ladd announced, "For your final project, which is due at the end of the quarter, I have assigned two-person teams. You'll find the list posted outside the door. Remember, the assignment is worth 60% of your grade. Make sure you understand the requirements and the deadlines, which are in your syllabus."

After class, there was such a large group gathered in front of the list that I couldn't see anything, so I moved down the hall. While waiting for the crowd to disperse, I listened to the various reactions of my classmates as they read their team assignments. Some were happy, and others not so much.

Once the coast was clear, I walked over and ran my finger

down the list of names until I came to mine. *Oh, no…not Craig Miller.* I wanted to scream. There was no way I could work with that snob. Every bad thought I had about him rushed through my mind.

I blurted out, "Why does she hate me?"

Melody came up beside me. She brushed her long dark bangs to the side of her face. "What's wrong?"

I shrugged. "Every which way I turn, she's sabotaging me. She assigns me a partner I can't stand, gives me the most boring assignments, and hates my writing. What am I going to do? I've got at least two more classes with her before I graduate. I wish she would quit or disappear or *anything*, just out of my life."

Melody studied the sheet hanging on the wall. "Oh…I see. You got Miller. I don't envy you. He's a bit of a pain, isn't he?"

"That's an understatement."

Melody thought for a moment. "I don't get why she's so hard on you. Have you ever talked to her about it? Maybe find out what's going on?"

"You're right. I've been putting it off, but I need to talk to her, and the sooner, the better."

After picking up some cherry vanilla yogurt for lunch at the student union, I walked back to Sheffield Hall. Professor Ladd's office was a few doors down from the journalism office on the second floor. When I reached her door, I heard voices coming from the other side. I recognized one as belonging to Professor Ladd, but the other one belonged to a man whose voice I didn't recognize.

As I waited, their shouting grew louder and more heated. The man said something about an affair and then Professor Ladd said something about a divorce. I didn't need to listen any longer; she and her husband were fighting. Now was not the best time to talk to her about my grades or partner assignment or anything. Tomorrow would be soon enough.

* * *

"Wow, somebody had a bad day," T.J. said, leaning on his car.

I said nothing as I walked over to the passenger door, embarrassed that my mood was so transparent. T.J. slid into the driver's seat, leaned over to my door, and, with one swoop, unlocked it.

I climbed in, buckled myself, and took a deep breath. "Professor Ladd—"

"Your favorite journalism teacher?" He asked sarcastically, with a slight smile, as he put the car into reverse.

"Yeah, that's the one. Honestly...I think she hates me, and the feeling is becoming mutual."

T.J. slammed on the brakes and pulled the car back into the parking spot. Hearing me complain about Professor Ladd was nothing new, but I think he sensed it was more serious this time.

"She gave me a seven out of ten on my last assignment. Can you believe it? I worked so hard on that piece. The only thing she wrote, besides a big fat seven out of ten, was that I needed to be more passionate about my writing." I took another deep breath. "I could be the world's greatest writer, and I still don't think that would help me be passionate about interviewing the campus groundskeepers about the disease affecting the trees on the green. Really? She has got to be kidding!"

"Not into trees, huh?" T.J. flashed a wide grin. "Maybe next time you can interview me about the big, bad computers that will someday rule the world. Now there's a story to get passionate about!"

I couldn't help but smile and shake my head. T.J. and his crazy computers.

He placed his sunglasses over his eyes and looked into the mirror, adjusting a lone stray hair. "I know what you need to get your mind off your troubles," he said, reaching for a cassette and popping it into the cassette player. "You need some music!" He turned around, looked out the rear window, and started backing up.

"When did you get a cassette player?"

"I dropped it off at Bob's garage after my class this morning and had him install it. I picked it up a few minutes ago. Now I can listen to whatever I want when I'm driving. Cool, huh?"

"Definitely cool. The next time my car is due for an oil change, I should drop it off between classes. I always go in on Saturday. Don't know why I never thought of doing it while I was at school." I smiled. "Sometimes you are one clever dude."

"You got that right." He laughed.

Within a few minutes, we were singing along with The Moody Blues and their "The Story in Your Eyes." T.J. was right; the music lightened my mood.

As I looked out the passenger window, I had a hard time finding any green leaves hanging from the tree branches. Instead, trees covered in brilliant shades of red, orange, and yellow dotted the landscape. Fall had arrived, and with all my fuming about Professor Ladd, I had almost missed the beauty of the season.

T.J.'s voice broke the silence. "So, whatcha gonna do about it?" I must have looked puzzled because he added, "About Ladd?"

"I need to talk to her about the paper...and Craig."

"Why Craig?"

"Professor Ladd assigned us as partners for the final project."

"Isn't that a good thing?" T.J. turned and looked at me. "I mean, having a professional writer on your side sure couldn't hurt, could it? You might pick up a few pointers." He quickly added, "Not that you need any or anything."

"The only person Craig Miller is going to help is Craig Miller. He's arrogant, rude, and…a first-class jerk." I recounted the events of earlier in the day, emphasizing Craig's impoliteness. By the time I finished ranting, T.J. agreed that Craig and I working together was not in my best interest.

"When are you going to talk to her?"

"I thought tomorrow morning during her office hours; they start at 9:00. Would you mind if I picked you up a little after 8:00 tomorrow? I'd like to be at her office by 8:30, so I can be the first one to see her."

"Sure. No problem." He nodded.

After T.J. dropped me off at my house, I ran up to my room, where I grabbed my photography textbook. Mae Emerson, the owner of Mae's Gift Shop, had called the night before and asked if I could come to work after class, even though it was my day off. She needed me to run the cash register so she could unpack the shipments coming in this afternoon. With Mae in the back room, I could study for my midterm if there weren't many customers.

Before leaving, I went into the kitchen to kiss my mom goodbye and picked up a banana nut muffin off the counter to eat on my way to work. I hurriedly walked out the front door and hopped into the Orange Bomb, as I lovingly referred to my orange '68 Plymouth Roadrunner.

With no traffic to slow me down, I made every green light, a feat I rarely experienced, and pulled into the parking lot behind the strip mall that was home to Mae's Gift Shop.

From where I parked, I observed Mae closing the large industrial door to the back of her shop as a semi drove away. I was excited to see the new items Mae had ordered at the Gift Mart in Chicago.

Over the summer, there had not been any deliveries, and keeping the shelves from looking bare had been challenging. Conscious of the store's appearance, Mae often told her customers, whether or not they asked, how upset she was that shipments were being delayed because of shipping problems. The truth was the store was barely making payroll and rent, and Mae refused to put any more of her money into a losing venture.

Ordering new merchandise was out of the question. By the end of summer, she was thinking about selling the store, but then, despite slow sales continuing, the shipments started again.

With my purse slung over my shoulder and my photography textbook in my hand, I walked from the parking lot, around the corner, and down the street to the gift shop's front door. A glance at my watch told me I had made it to work by 4:59—one minute early.

Through the storefront window, I saw a woman in a red coat waiting by the brass antique cash register. She turned toward Mae, who was smiling and laughing.

The old saying, "You can never be too rich or too thin," described Mae's philosophy of life. Tall, thin, and rich. With her blond, shoulder-length hair, customers often commented that she could be a twin to Angie Dickinson from that new show, *Police Woman*.

Mae, a believer in having regular facials, looked at least a decade younger than her forty-five years. She had a quick smile that put everyone she met at ease. However, those of us who worked with her knew a very different side of Mae. Many times we were witnesses to her all-consuming wrath that spared no one. As a result, we lived on the edge when Mae was in the store.

I pulled the front door open and crossed my fingers that tonight would be a good night.

"Hi, Mae! I'll drop my stuff off in the back room and be right out." I stopped, backtracked toward the door, and told the woman leaving the counter, "Here, I'll hold the door for you."

She beamed as she juggled her purse, shopping bags, and the large box Mae had gift-wrapped. "Thank you!"

Out of habit, I closed the door to keep the cool autumn air out of the store. My father was a stickler for closing open doors. He said, depending on the season he was talking about, that open doors let the cool air in or the warm air out. Both were bad. I guess he trained me well.

As I walked to the back room, I greeted Mrs. Winterfield, one of our regular customers, as she was looking at the birthday cards, her cane propped up against the card rack.

"Finding everything, Mrs. Winterfield?"

"Oh, yes, dear. I wanted to pick up a few cards to have on hand. Winter will soon be here, and I don't like to drive in the snow and ice."

"I know what you mean. I don't like to drive in it either."

In the back room, I hung my purse on the chair by the table and noticed an envelope on the floor. I stooped to pick it up. The front had the words "PAST DUE" stamped on it in bright red ink. It was from an art glass company that was one of Mae's suppliers. Business had been slower than usual the last two weeks—the local car plant had laid off the second and third shifts—but with the deliveries starting again, I had hoped Mae's money problems were behind her. But perhaps not.

I placed the envelope on the table behind the other bills in Mae's stack of mail, hoping she wouldn't realize I had seen it. If she knew, Mae would be so embarrassed. Her money, her looks, and her reputation meant everything to her.

As I came out of the back room and went to tidy the candle display, I saw Mae talking to Barb Goodright, whose husband, Steve, was related to Mae. As president of the Peterson Lumber company, Steve, and his wife, Barb, were at the forefront of Petersburg society, and Mae loved nothing better than being seen out and about with them.

"How's Steve doing?" Mae asked.

"He's fine, but…"

Mae crossed her arms and tilted her head.

Barb's platinum blond locks swayed as she shook her head. "Oh, Mae, I don't understand what's going on with him. He hasn't been sleeping. I find him in his office at all hours of the night. He claims he's too tired to go out and, if he keeps this up, I fear we will be written off the holiday social calendar. That would be the death of me."

Mae nodded sympathetically, and Barb's diamond rings twinkled as she pulled the belt tighter around her black leather coat.

Mae glanced in my direction and, probably realizing I was within earshot, moved their conversation to the corner at the back of the store. I continued restocking the candles until Mrs. Winterfield headed for the cash register with a handful of greeting cards. We were at the counter when Bob, the local auto repair shop owner, entered the store. At first, he looked like he might stop by the register, but rushed by when he caught sight of Mae and Barb. The smell of gasoline trailed behind him.

"Barb," Bob's voice carried through the store, "you can tell that husband of yours if he doesn't pay me for that Fleetwood job I did for him, I'm going to get the police involved."

From where I was behind the counter, I could see the horrified look on Barb's face. Curious, I left my post after ringing up Mrs. Winterfield's purchase and pretended to check for empty slots in the card racks. I noticed Mrs. Winterfield lingering by the teacups.

"I don't know what you're talking about," Barb said. "Why would you work on his Fleetwood? He has his own mechanic to take care of his cars."

Even I knew that. The father of one of my friends from the Commuter Lounge worked as the mechanic for Steve Goodright and the Peterson Lumber Company.

Bob's stance became more rigid, but Mae interjected, "Bob, this is not the time or place."

"Stay out of this," Bob growled. "Barb, you tell Steve to get me the money or hire a lawyer." He turned toward Mae. "He's going to need one anyway if that sister of yours has her way. She's got no qualms about taking him down—even if he is family." He stormed out of the store, waving his grease-stained hands in the air, muttering, "I'll get my money if it's the last thing I do." And with that, he disappeared out the door and down the sidewalk.

Mae threw her arms around Barb, who was sobbing uncontrollably, and led her to the back room, closing the door behind them.

I returned to the cash register and rested my elbows on the counter, perplexed. Mae had never mentioned having a sister. In fact, Steve and Barb were the only family she ever talked about. Who was this sister and why had Mae kept her a secret?

chapter three

When I got home, my mom and dad were watching TV in the living room, each claiming their space in opposite corners of the couch. My dad's head leaned against a pillow folded in half, while my mom was wrapped up in a cocoon fashioned from an afghan she had crocheted.

"There's a plate of food for you in the refrigerator," Mom said, not taking her eyes off the small screen. When a commercial came on, she turned her perfectly coiffed head toward me. "This movie is great. Lucille Ball and Henry Fonda are in it. Why don't you bring your food in here and watch it with us?"

"Sounds good, but I have a lot of studying to do. I'll just take my food up to my room, and I can eat while I'm reading."

"I'll be glad when school is over, and you can get your life back and have time to help us around here." She sighed, turning back to watch the TV.

As I walked toward the kitchen, Gidget bounded down the stairs. She uttered a loud "meow," indicating she was hungry too, as she scurried in front of me and raced me to the kitchen. Her tail thumped on the tiled floor as she watched me put my plate into the microwave. When our eyes met, she led me to the pantry, looking back to ensure I followed her.

"Are we hungry tonight?" I grinned. She rubbed against my leg, purring as I reached for the bag of dry cat food and poured it into her dish. "Yeah, me too. What a day!"

She ate her food, one morsel at a time, dropping pieces of cat food onto the floor that did not meet with her approval. All it took was a bowl of her favorite cat food to make her troubles vanish. How I wished my life was so simple a plate of food could solve all my problems!

In my room, I sat down, but rather than enjoying my plate of warm food, I pushed the pile of string beans from one corner of my blue and white dinner plate to the other. The mashed potatoes drenched in gravy would have been hard to resist any other day, but not tonight—not with Professor Ladd on my mind. I forced myself to eat half of my slice of ham, but I was too upset to eat more. Admitting defeat, I gave up and headed down to the kitchen with my plate in hand.

As I passed the couch, my mom turned around, saw my plate of food, and gave me a questioning look. "Dinner was delicious," I told her. "Guess I'm not as hungry as I thought I was. I'll wrap it up and put it back in the refrigerator."

"I hope you're not coming down with something." She walked over and put her hand on my forehead, checking for a fever.

"I'm fine. I'm just tired. A long day."

"Okay. I worry that you're running yourself ragged between school and work." Mom swept a strand of golden blond hair behind her ear, revealing her pearl stud earrings.

"Everything's fine, Mom. It's normal tired…no big deal." I knew she didn't think getting a degree was worth all the stress. After all, neither my brother, Mike, nor sister, Crystal, had gone to college, and they were both doing fine. There was more than enough work on the farm to support three, even four, families. My mom's concern was well-intended, but I didn't have the patience to defend my life choices tonight.

"Can you two be quiet? I can't hear a thing with all your talking," Dad yelled.

"Sorry," I muttered.

"He's tired. He and the boys worked all day in the apple orchard," Mom whispered. By boys, she meant Mike and Crystal's husband, Mel. Despite both being in their twenties, they were "the boys" and probably would be forever in her eyes.

Mom's attention returned to the figures moving across the small screen as she walked back to her spot on the couch. I hurried into the kitchen, wrapped my plate of food in plastic wrap, and placed it in the refrigerator. My parents were so engrossed in watching their movie they never noticed me walking behind them on my way back to my bedroom.

If it took three more crazy years of juggling school and work to make my dreams come true, I was willing to go that route. I wanted to see the world and make a difference, and I was going to make it happen, whether or not my family supported me.

Kicking off my shoes, I plopped on the pink rosebud comforter covering my bed. Gidget, too, had snuck upstairs and was nestled next to the pillow shams. I rubbed her head and glanced around my room. "Maybe, Gidget, if we try hard, we can pretend we're already in Paris."

Gidget turned up the volume of her purr as I rubbed under her chin, which she moved from side to side, encouraging me to hit all the right spots. I gazed at the posters decorating my walls—the Eiffel Tower, Claude Monet's *Water Lilies*, and Edgar Degas's *The Ballet Class*.

"Someday, we're going to get there for real," I told Gidget. I leaned against a pillow. "I will walk the streets of Paris, dine at sidewalk cafés, and view the great art at the Louvre. And you, my fine furry friend, will watch all those lovely French birds from our apartment window. It'll be great!"

I pulled the silver Eiffel Tower charm and its chain away from my neck so I could see it. "Writing is our ticket out of here. But first..." I sighed. "But first, I need to figure out how I'm going to deal with Professor Ladd and Mr. Know-It-All Craig Miller."

With Gidget as my audience, I rehearsed what I would say to the professor in the morning. "How 'bout this? Professor Ladd, I think...no believe...that sounds more confident, don't you think? I believe you have been grading me unfairly, and I'd like to know why." I stopped and thought about what I had said. "Or is that too confrontational? Maybe something more like asking her how I can improve my writing. Oh, Gidget, what am I going to say?"

My furry friend stared at me with her green eyes, offering no suggestions. While I gently rubbed under her chin, I consoled myself, thinking that perhaps inspiration would hit me when I walked into Professor Ladd's office in the morning.

If I spent all night thinking about my meeting with her tomorrow, I would never finish studying for the photography midterm, so I opened my textbook and refocused my energy. But after an hour of reading, I took my glasses off and rubbed my burning eyes. Despite knowing I should study more, my heart and attention span were not in it. My stomach growled, and Gidget flashed me a disapproving look.

"Let's go get something to eat."

Not one to be told what to do, she closed her eyes in defiance. She had no intention of going downstairs with me. Sleep was the only thing on her agenda. I, however, had a hankering for something sweet.

As I descended the stairs, I tried to be quiet as the sounds of the *11:00 Nightly News* came from the TV.

"Need something?" my mom turned and asked.

"No, I thought I'd bake something."

"It's a little late for baking, isn't it?" She yawned.

"Yeah, but I thought it would help me unwind." *Plus, it couldn't hurt to take something sweet to Professor Ladd in the morning to get her in a good mood.*

"Remember to clean up. I don't want to wake up to a sink full of dirty dishes."

My father chimed in. "Yes, young lady, don't make more work for your mother like you do for the rest of us."

I rolled my eyes as I closed the kitchen door, careful not to let it slam shut. Of course, I wished I had more time to help around the farm, but with school and work, I couldn't. I did what I could, but there was no sense explaining myself to them now. Dad was in a bad mood, and no amount of talking would change that. I thought about going back to my room to avoid any possible confrontations, but then I spied a bag filled with bread crusts on the counter, and the thought of warm bread pudding covered in cinnamon sugar won out.

Suddenly, I heard clawing at the kitchen door. I smiled as I opened it wide enough to let in a hungry Gidget. Even for her, milk and eggs trumped getting to bed early.

After getting the carton of milk from the refrigerator, I grabbed a saucer from the cupboard. Gidget let out a loud screeching meow, letting me know she thought I was taking far too long to deliver her tasty treat. She cocked her head and followed the milk-laden saucer with her eyes as I lowered it to the floor and set it in front of her. She lapped the milk so quickly that had I not known I fed her earlier, I would have thought she was starving. With my partner in crime now purring away, I assembled the bread pudding.

The kitchen door creaked open as my mother popped into the kitchen. "What are you making?"

"Bread pudding bars. I'm going to take some to my professor in the morning."

"That's sweet. I'm sure she'll like that." She then added,

"Your father and I are going to bed. Don't stay up too late, and try not to make too much noise. You know how your father is a light sleeper, and he's got another full day in the apple orchard. Crystal is coming again, so she can help me with the canning. Any chance you can help?"

"I have to work after class. Sorry."

"Me too. Some extra help sure would be nice. Your father and I aren't as young as we used to be."

"I know," I said, feeling guilty.

"Well, goodnight. See you in the morning." She closed the door.

The sound of the TV in the living room stopped, and I heard my mom and dad go upstairs to their room. With the kitchen all to myself, it took no time to clean it up, leaving me enough time to go upstairs and get dressed for bed while the bread pudding baked.

I carefully crept on the outer edges so the stairs wouldn't creak—a trick I learned from my brother, who had done his share of sneaking in after a late night out. As I entered my room, I spied Gidget, who, unbeknownst to me, had slipped out of the kitchen and gone upstairs. She was now curled up at the foot of my bed, sound asleep.

I quickly changed into my jammies and returned to the kitchen, where the aroma of warm cinnamon filled the air. Pure perfection met my eyes—bubbling cinnamon and golden-brown bread pudding—as I removed the pan from the oven. Although I'd have to wait until morning for it to be firm enough to cut and wrap for Professor Ladd, I didn't have to wait before eating it. Warm, slightly runny bread pudding didn't bother me one bit. In fact, it sounded delightful.

I took my late-night snack to my room, crawled into bed, and stacked the pillows behind my back. Pulling the covers up as far as I could, I savored the warm, gooey goodness from the comfort of my bed. Everything, for a moment, was perfect.

When I finished, I set the bowl aside and turned off the light. "Goodnight, Gidget." She didn't move except for turning one ear in my direction. It was time for sleeping, not talking.

I snuggled in for a good night's sleep. Unfortunately, sweet dreams were nonexistent. Thoughts of Professor Ladd invaded my sleep, causing every muscle in my body to tighten. In a split-second, I went from comfy cozy to an absolute bundle of nerves. Nightmare after nightmare was about Professor Ladd. In one dream, Craig Miller and I were standing in front of her while she was waving a gun in the air, yelling, "There's only room for one journalist in the world." She turned the gun toward me. "And it won't be you, Michelle."

Tuesday, October 15th

As she pulled the trigger, I waited in terror for the bullet to pierce my heart. Instead of meeting my demise, the sound of my alarm saved me. I sat in bed for several minutes, drenched in sweat and tangled in my blankets, as I tried to steady my nerves.

Completely out of character, Gidget had not awakened me with her usual morning antics, so I jumped out of bed and frantically searched for her. She wasn't on my vanity or on the windowsill. But as I reached for my slippers, I found her curled up on the floor under the nightstand. Gidget raised her head and glared. At first, I didn't understand why she was angry, but I understood when I looked at my disheveled bed. I must have kicked her out of bed, and she wasn't in a forgiving mood.

"Rough night, wasn't it, Gidget?" I yawned. "I'll

straighten things out with Professor Ladd this morning. Tonight will be better, I promise."

My explanation seemed to appease her. She crawled out of her hiding place, jumped onto the bed, and sat beside me, allowing me to pet her. "As tempting as you make it to sit here next to you, I've got to get going, girl. It's time to get this Tuesday started."

I stumbled to my desk chair, grabbed the clothes I had set out the night before, and took a quick shower. After putting on my makeup and having a final once-over in my bedroom mirror, I dashed downstairs.

"Michelle," my father yelled, "slow down. You sound like a herd of elephants."

I wondered what a herd of elephants sounded like and if my father had ever heard that many elephants, or even one elephant, coming down the stairs. Wisely, I concluded, now was not the time to ask.

"Sorry." *I'll be so glad when I can run down the stairs, and it's nobody's business but my own. Someday…*

I did my best to walk past my father in the living room without making a sound. He was standing beside Mike, who was on the phone. Once in the kitchen, a loaf of zucchini bread on the counter caught my attention. "What's up with Mike?" I asked my mom as I cut a slice and wrapped it in a paper towel.

"He's trying to find some people to help in the orchard. The next several nights are going to be below freezing, and your dad and Mike have got to get those apples picked. We need more help."

Although I didn't have time to stand there and be the victim of another guilt trip, I didn't want to appear like I didn't care. "I'm sure he'll find some people. Mike is good at getting people to help him." I quickly wrapped a few squares of the bread pudding and blew her a kiss. "Gotta run. I've got a meeting this morning. See you after work tonight."

The hum of my old trusty Roadrunner's engine alerted T.J. to my arrival as I turned into his long driveway. I watched him get up from the rocking chair on his front porch, pick up the stack of his books perched on the ledge above the railing, and walk to the edge of the driveway, where he stopped and waited for me. The trees in his front yard swayed in the breeze, yet not one strand of his hair moved.

As he tugged on the seat belt and buckled himself in, I looked in the rearview mirror. I brushed my bangs back into place and rubbed a smudge of lipstick off my teeth, along with a few bread crumbs around my mouth, before maneuvering out of his driveway.

While waiting for two cars to pass, I turned on the radio. But when I heard B. J. Thomas singing, "Raindrops Keep Fallin' on my Head," I couldn't handle it. I turned the radio off.

T.J. flashed a quizzical look my way. "Since when don't you like that song?"

I laughed as I backed into the road and threw the car into drive."Oh, I like the song, just not today. I want to complain and not feel guilty about it."

Changing the subject, I teasingly asked, "Soooo, I forgot to ask you if you got the seat you wanted yesterday morning?"

He started blushing. I couldn't believe it. Could this be love? Could T.J. have lost his heart this quarter…already?

"I don't know what you mean." He smiled and looked out the passenger window.

I didn't want to keep teasing him. T.J. would tell me more about what was happening with this mystery girl named Meg when he was ready.

This time, he changed the subject and asked, "You ready for your meeting?"

"As ready as I'll ever be." I took a deep breath. "Professor Ladd grades me harder than she does anyone else in the class, and I don't understand why. My papers are just as good as the ones other people are turning in, but to look at my grades, you'd never know it.

T.J. looked sympathetic, and I could tell he was searching for the words to encourage me, but what could he say?

"Sometimes, I feel like the odds are against me," I said with a slight shrug.

T.J. winced. "Oh, come on. What do you mean?"

"There's this internship with the *Chicago Tribune* this summer, and I want to apply for it, but I need a letter of recommendation. I had hoped Professor Ladd would write one for me."

"You think she will?"

"I'm not even sure I should ask. She thinks I'm a horrible writer," I said, feeling dejected.

"But you need to try." T.J. put his hand on my shoulder. "You'll regret it if you don't."

"I guess I'll see how it goes this morning, and then maybe I'll ask." I paused and took a deep breath. "One step at a time."

After driving around the commuter parking lot for ten minutes, I found a spot in the back. "Why is it so busy this early in the morning? Who in their right mind takes an 8:00 class?"

"Apparently, quite a few people!" T.J. chuckled.

We both shook our heads. Although we lived on farms, neither of us was an early riser. We vowed long ago never to take a class that started before 9:00 a.m., and we intended to keep our promise.

Before heading to the Commuter Lounge, T.J. walked over to my side of the car. He gave me a hug, assuring me that everything was going to be alright. I stood by my car and watched the Air National Guard jets fly overhead. After they disappeared, I trudged toward Professor Ladd's office. I felt like one of the dogs from Disney's *Lady and the Tramp* taking the fateful long walk. I reached for my Eiffel Tower charm and focused on fighting for my future.

According to the black-rimmed clock in the hallway outside Professor Ladd's office, it was 8:35. There was plenty of time to get a can of pop before meeting with the professor. Still, I reasoned studying was more important, so I sat on the floor cross-legged and started reading my journalism law class notes.

Betsy Braxton, the journalism department's secretary, walked toward me with a cup of coffee. I assumed she was on her way to her desk in the office. Our paths had crossed several times in the journalism office over the last thirteen months. A few years older than me, Betsy was the picture of pure professionalism, dressed in her crisp white shirt, straight skirt, and black pumps. But today, she seemed ruffled. Her skirt had a large dark wet spot on the front. After seeing Betsy with her feathered, long blond hair and perfectly fitting clothes, having a lousy day, I felt better about my own appearance.

"Looks like you're having one of my days," I said.

Betsy stopped. "Yeah, I spilled coffee on my skirt. I tried to get it out, but I think I just made a bigger mess. Anyway, I got myself another cup. Hopefully, I won't spill this one." Her hand was shaking.

"I'm sure when it dries, it'll be fine."

Betsy looked at me, puzzled.

"Your skirt." I pointed to the wet spot.

"Here's hoping." She glanced at Professor Ladd's door, and then her eyes darted toward me. "What are you doing here so early?"

"I need to talk to Professor Ladd." I shrugged. "You know, sometimes she can be such a pain."

"I hear that quite a bit. I think a lot of people have a hard time dealing with her." Betsy's trembling hand raised the cup to her mouth.

"I can see why. I get the worst assignments, and the way she grades is a nightmare. Between you and me, she's destroying my GPA." I fumed. "I don't know what to do. She infuriates me. Something has got to change."

"Good luck. I hope you can straighten things out. Goodness knows she's not the easiest person to talk to." Betsy shrugged her shoulders as if there wasn't much hope.

I watched Betsy walk down the hallway until she disappeared behind the door to the journalism office. She was right. To say Professor Ladd was difficult was an understatement. I glanced at the clock. *I think I'll get that diet pop after all. It might calm my nerves. Besides, walking a little will do me good.* I jumped up, brushed the dirt off the back of my skirt, and headed to the vending machines around the corner.

I scrounged around the bottom of my patchwork bag for a quarter, then dropped it in the slot, made my selection, and smiled as the can appeared. I pulled on the tab but stopped when the building began shaking as several Air National Guard jets flew overhead. *Is this what it was like when planes flew over London during WWII?*

With my unopened can, I turned the corner to return to Professor Ladd's office when Craig, who was busy reading and not paying attention to where he was going, walked into me. Thankfully, I was a few feet away from the landing, or else I might have tumbled down the stairs.

We both scrambled to pick up the papers he'd dropped and then he rushed downstairs after muttering an almost inaudible, "Sorry."

After he was out of sight, I realized I had one of his papers in my hand. I set my drink down, folded the paper, and put it in my purse. The next time I saw Craig in class, I would give it to him, but I was in no hurry to see Mr. Rude again.

Opening my can of pop, I took a few sips and felt invigorated. I walked confidently back to Professor Ladd's office, ready to do battle.

I pulled the bread pudding squares out of my purse and knocked on her door. There was no response. I knocked a little harder, and the heavy wooden door inched open.

The sunlight shining through the window in Professor Ladd's office blinded me. I had to blink my eyes several times before the room became clear again. I saw the back of her oversized office chair, but Professor Ladd didn't turn around. She continued looking out the window. It didn't bode well for my mood that she didn't even have the courtesy to acknowledge my existence.

I closed the door behind me and called out her name. "Professor Ladd?"

Silence.

"Professor Ladd, do you have a few minutes to discuss my paper? I have a few questions."

No response. *Seriously? She's going to ignore me?*

I walked toward the desk, calling her name again, hoping to get her attention without startling her. But, still not getting a response, I moved to the front of her chair. The sun was shining on her face. Her eyes were closed. Her head hung down. Blood covered her white blouse.

I nudged her shoulder, hoping for signs of life, but there were none.

My body swayed, and the bread pudding squares fell to the floor as I leaned on the desk to steady myself. I needed help—fast.

I willed my feet to run into the hall. "Help! I need help! Someone shot Professor Ladd!"

My knees collapsed, and the hard, cold floor rose to meet me.

chapter four

The sound of muffled voices and shuffling footsteps hovered around me. I was caught between two worlds—one telling me to keep my eyes closed and continue to slumber, the other beckoning me to join the chorus surrounding me. Something slid under my head and gently raised it as a foul smell shook my senses, forcing my eyes to open and see the crowd of blurry faces gathered around me.

"Here, let me help you get up," said a man in a white shirt with a long dark tie. "Are you okay? Do you need a doctor?"

Out of habit, I said, "No," but my head was reeling. I was unsure where I was, why I was being helped into a chair, and even *who* I was at the moment. I looked around the hallway and it all came back to me, memories engulfing me like a mighty wave from which there was no escape. Images of the office, the chair, the blood, and Professor Ladd's slumped body flashed before my eyes.

"She's dead, isn't she?" I asked, hoping that, somehow, I had gotten it wrong. But from the look on the man's face, I knew I had not.

"Let's get you into the office where you can sit down. The police are on their way."

I leaned on the man as the woman with the long blond

hair opened the door to the room opposite Professor Ladd's office.

From my chair, I stared at the door that had opened to this nightmare. As I tried to process everything that had happened, I heard more footsteps coming down the hall, heavier than those I'd heard earlier. A man in a dark suit and two police officers walking behind him entered Professor Ladd's office.

After several minutes, the man in the dark suit emerged. He looked at the man with the tie and the woman with the long blond hair, who I now recognized as Betsy Braxton, as they huddled outside my door. He pointed at me and growled, "Is that the girl who found her?"

They nodded.

The man in the suit stepped into the office where I had been deposited, stopped in front of me, and asked, "Are you going to be okay if we leave you here alone for a few minutes?"

"Yeah." I shrugged. My gut instinct told me he would do whatever he wanted, regardless of my answer.

He turned back toward Betsy and the man with the tie and said, "I'd like to ask you both some questions." He started to close the door to the office where I was sitting but stopped, leaving it partially open. I heard him address the crowd gathered in the hall. "If you saw or heard anything that might relate to Professor Ladd, Lieutenant Grogan here will take your statement. Otherwise, you can go back to work." And with that, he pulled the door shut.

Alone with my thoughts, I relived the horror of finding Professor Ladd's body. I tried closing my eyes to make the image disappear from my mind, but it only became more vivid. In an attempt to create my own mental diversion, I looked at the ceiling and counted the white and black speckled tiles. After that, I counted the bricks on the wall by the window and realized there was, indeed, something thera-peutic about counting objects that didn't matter.

However, before I got to the floor tiles, the door opened, and my current obsession with numbers ended abruptly.

The man in the dark suit walked to where I was sitting and stood in front of me with a notepad and pen in hand. Etched on the bronze-colored tag hanging on his suit jacket were the words "Detective Douglas."

"Can you please state your name?" he asked.

"Michelle. Michelle Kilpatrick," I muttered, as I tried to steady my voice.

An officer with "Lieutenant Grogan" on his name tag came into the room. He left the door open, revealing an empty hallway except for the man in the white shirt and long tie standing with his arms crossed in front of the wall.

Lieutenant Grogan took a few steps into the room, his eyes focused on the detective. "Sir, the secretary said the dean won't be in until this afternoon, so you can use his office. It's in the journalism office down the hall on your left."

Detective Douglas turned toward me. "Michelle, I need to ask you a few questions. We'll go down to the other office. It seems the professor who uses this office does not like being displaced." He sounded miffed. "But first, Lieutenant Grogan is going to take your fingerprints and wipe your hands. That is, if the good professor can wait a few more minutes," he said, directing his remarks to the man standing in the hallway. He then turned back toward me and, reading the confusion on my face, explained the test was for gunpowder residue.

"But why would I have—" I stopped mid-sentence as it occurred to me that the detective might think I was the one who shot Professor Ladd. I shook my head. *Surely not. This is only standard procedure, I'm sure.*

After Lieutenant Grogan wiped my hands, Detective Douglas asked me to follow him. Our entourage had only taken a few steps down the hall when the door to the office we had been using slammed shut. The detective glanced over his shoulder and shook his head in disgust.

As we entered the journalism office, Betsy jumped up from her desk chair and led us to the back office. She unlocked the door with the brass nameplate "Dean Bradley Brown, Journalism Department."

Detective Douglas looked straight ahead as he walked into the office, and without looking back at Betsy, said, "Thank you. I'll let you know if I need anything." He pointed to one of the two brown leather chairs in front of the dean's desk. "Have a seat, Michelle. I have a few questions for you."

"Sure." I gulped as I sat down, unsure what to expect, but I had a bad feeling.

"Why were you in Professor Ladd's office this morning?"

I studied his face, but there were no outward signs whether he was friend or foe—only the look of impatience as he waited for me to answer.

"I stopped by to talk to her about a paper I had written."

The scowl on his face told me my answer did not satisfy him. "What time was that?" His brown eyes narrowed.

"Around 9:00 a.m. That's when her office hours begin." I shifted in my seat to avoid looking at him.

"And that's when you got there? You didn't get there any earlier?"

"I'm sorry, I misunderstood. You want to know when I *got* to her office? That was around 8:30, but I didn't knock on her door until 9:00."

He looked up from his notepad. "And why again were you meeting with her?"

"I wanted to talk to her about an assignment."

"Was there a problem with it?"

"No, I mean, yes. The assignment was okay, but..." I paused, trying to think how to explain my situation without incriminating myself.

The detective leaned over and moved closer to my face. I breathed in the sweet smell of cinnamon and nutmeg coming from his cologne.

"But what? I understand you've had some problems with Professor Ladd."

"A few…I thought I deserved better grades."

No sooner had the words left my mouth than I saw the detective's gaze become more intense. He jotted a few things down, and I immediately wished I could take my words back. He loosened his tie before continuing with his line of questioning. "So, you were upset with Professor Ladd, and you came here to—"

"To discuss why she graded my papers so hard and what I needed to do so I could do better in her class."

"You were having trouble in her class?"

"Yes. No…not that bad. I just wanted to do better."

He scowled. "According to witnesses, they say you believed Professor Ladd was standing in the way of your writing career. Is that right?"

"What witnesses? I didn't kill her, if that's what you're getting at," I said defiantly.

"No one is accusing you of anything, unless—"

"I went to see her during office hours…just to talk to her. I knocked on her door, and it opened. She didn't say anything, so I walked in and then I…I saw her…in her chair…and the blood. That's what happened."

I fidgeted in my seat, trying to find a comfortable position and get the image of the professor's dead body out of my head. The detective walked over to the window and began fervently writing in his notepad. Now and then, he looked at me but said nothing.

"How long have you known Professor Ladd?"

"I don't know…this was my first class with her." I paused. "No, I take that back. She taught a section on writing for newspapers in my Intro to Journalism class last year, but I didn't have anything to do with her."

"Why not? Did you have a problem with her?" he asked, his eyes narrowing.

"N-No," I stammered, trying to find the right words to formulate my answer. "There was no reason to talk to her…it was only for a few weeks. It was a survey class."

"So, why did you take this class with her?"

"Because I need it for graduation." All these questions were making my head hurt. I rubbed my forehead. "Can I go now?"

"Do you have someplace more important you need to be?" he asked, glaring.

"No, I just need some fresh air."

Detective Douglas frowned. "In a minute, but first, do you own a gun?"

"No."

"Do you have access to one?"

I said nothing while I, again, considered how to answer his question without giving him reason to suspect me of murder. "If you mean does anyone in my house own a gun? Yes, but I didn't take it. My father keeps 'em locked up."

As he wrote in his notepad, I continued. "If I shot Professor Ladd, wouldn't I still have the gun on me? I mean, where would I have put it? I called for help as soon as I discovered her body."

"Yes, that's what you've said." He glanced down at his notes and then back at me. "You can go for now, but leave your address and phone number with Lieutenant Grogan. He should be right outside the door. I may need you to come down to the station to answer more questions." He sternly added, "And don't leave town."

I was a nervous wreck. Between discovering Professor Ladd's body and talking to Detective Douglas, it was almost too much. *I know he's just doing his job, but while he's questioning me, the actual killer is out there. He might even be on campus looking for his next victim.*

Somehow, I made it from Sheffield Hall to Whitley Hall. After walking between the two buildings so many times over the past year, I could have done it with my eyes closed. Perhaps I did. The closer I got to Whitley Hall, the faster I walked, and, once inside, I ran down the stairs to the Commuter Lounge in the basement.

The fog lifted from my head as my feet hit the tiled floor, and the gravity of the situation engulfed me. I wanted to stand there and cry out, but I willed myself to remain calm as I made my way to our group of tables—just a few more steps and I would be safe.

T.J. and Rick were engrossed in a game of cards with Todd and Amy, while Lawrence regaled Billy with his favorite Vietnam War stories for the one-hundredth time.

I collapsed into the chair next to T.J., where he immediately took one look at me and raised his eyebrows. "Michelle, what's wrong? You look horrible."

"Professor Ladd is dead."

"Dead? Ladd?"

I nodded. Everyone at the table froze.

"Somebody knock her off for being a jerk?" Todd threw his head back and rubbed his scruffy beard. He grinned, convinced I was kidding.

Amy shook her head in disgust, her big brown eyes glaring at Todd. "Shut up, Todd. This isn't funny." She paused. "That explains why I heard the journalism building was closed. I thought it was a maintenance issue."

Todd laid his cards on the table and said, "I guess not." All traces of joking were gone from his voice.

I started again. "Somebody shot her. At least, I think they shot her. I went to her office, and she was dead. There was blood all over her. When the police got there, they asked me a bunch of questions."

T.J. reached over and put his hand on top of mine. "I'm sorry. That must have been rough." He paused. "You don't suppose they think you had anything to do with it, do you?"

I pulled my hand away. "Why would they think that? I'm the one who found her, not the one who shot her."

"That's not what I meant. Of course, you didn't kill her." He gently touched my shoulder. "I only want to make sure you're okay, that's all."

A calmness came over me as I looked into his brown eyes. "Sorry, I didn't mean to snap at you. It's been a long morning."

Lawrence pushed his textbook to the side and leaned on the table, staring at me through his round, wire-rimmed glasses. He worked part time at the police station as a police records technician, and he lived for a good crime story. "Do they think the killer is still on campus? Remember that case earlier this year when that high school student shot and killed the athletic director at his school? I think it was somewhere in Indiana. I still don't think they've uncovered a motive for that one."

"From what I've heard about Professor Ladd, I don't think it would be hard to find a motive for shooting her. I can guarantee the police have a long list of unhappy students," Rick pragmatically said as he tugged at his brown paisley shirt sleeve.

We all sat at the table for a few minutes in silence, until Lawrence asked, "Do the police know you were unhappy with your grades?"

"Yeah, I told them, but like Rick said, I'm sure I'm not the only one who had problems with Professor Ladd."

Lawrence leaned further over the table so he could look at me straight on. "But you *are* the only one who was with her dead body."

I straightened up in my chair. "True, but that doesn't mean

anything. Anybody could have found her this morning. It just happened to be me."

Lawrence barely let me finish my sentence before adding his own thoughts. "Let's just hope that's how the police see it. Did they take your fingerprints? Check for gunpowder residue?

"Yes," I said, crossing my arms. "But they won't find anything. Would you quit looking at me like that? I didn't kill her."

"I believe you," Todd proclaimed. "There's no way you would kill anyone."

I smiled. "Thank you." It was good to have someone in my corner.

Lawrence got up and sat down on the chair next to me. "Listen, I don't mean to upset you, but I work with these guys, and I understand how they operate. They're going to be under a lot of pressure to find the killer fast, because it happened at the university."

I was confused. "Why? Don't they always want to find the killer fast?"

"Yes, but when any crime involves the university, it gets tricky. The board doesn't want it out that the campus is dangerous. It's not good for enrollment."

"That makes sense." I leaned on the table and cupped my chin in my hand.

"Can I ask you a few more questions? Then I promise I'll leave you alone."

I bit my bottom lip and took a deep breath as I looked around the table. All eyes were on us. "Fire away."

"Do you remember seeing anyone by Professor Ladd's office before you found her this morning?"

"Like I told the police, I got to her office before office hours, so I studied. Betsy, the journalism secretary, walked by while I was waiting. We talked for a few minutes. She was upset because she had spilled some coffee on her skirt and had a huge wet spot on it from trying to get the stain out."

"Okay. Then what?"

"After talking to her, I went to get some pop from the vending machine, and on my way back, I ran into...no, *he* ran into me."

"He?"

"Craig Miller. Thank goodness I hadn't opened my pop yet; otherwise, I would have spilled it all over the floor. He dropped some papers, and I helped him pick them up. Then, in typical jerk fashion, he went down the stairs without even saying thank you."

Amy fumed. "What a jerk!"

Lawrence flashed her a look that said *be quiet* and then continued with his line of questioning. "And then what?"

"I went to Professor Ladd's office and knocked on her door. When she didn't answer, I went in and found her dead. That's pretty much it."

"Do you remember the officers' names? The ones who questioned you?"

"A Detective Douglas and a...give me a minute...a...a Lieutenant Grogan. I think that was his name. He took my fingerprints and wiped my hands."

"Did Douglas say anything after your interview?"

"He said not to leave town and that I might need to answer more questions later."

Lawrence leaned back in his chair. "One more question. I need you to think back to when you found Professor Ladd's body. Was it warm to the touch?"

"Uh, I don't know. I...I don't remember. I touched her. Her body moved a little—"

"But she wasn't stiff?"

"That is so gross! No, she wasn't stiff. She was dead." After I composed myself, I continued. "Why? What difference does that make?"

"Just trying to approximate the time of death. The body keeps its warmth and stays soft to the touch for the first three hours after someone has died. So, if what you're telling me is accurate, someone murdered Professor Ladd between 6:00 a.m. and 9:00 a.m. Which, unfortunately, places you in the crime's vicinity during the latter part of that time frame."

"Well, you certainly know how to make a girl feel better." I shrugged, feeling more upset than I had already been.

"It's nothing personal," Lawrence stated. "It's what I've learned from the guys in homicide." His eyes veered to the clock on the wall. "Listen, I've got to get to class, but I'll ask around at the station and see what I can find out. If you're a suspect, I'll let you know."

"Thanks, but I'm sure everything's okay. I've got nothing to hide." I looked into his eyes for confirmation that I was right, but there was none.

T.J. leaned over to me. "If you want to go home, I'm sure I can catch a ride with somebody after class."

I cocked my head. "You know, I'm surprised they haven't canceled *all* classes today. I mean, the killer could be loose on campus for all they know."

Lawrence interjected while slipping his jacket on. "My guess is they're trying to keep things quiet, so it doesn't—"

"Hurt enrollment," I said, shaking my head. "Mustn't let student safety get in the man's way of making a profit."

I looked back at T.J. "I should probably go to my political science class this afternoon, but I really need to go for a walk. I'll meet you at the car after class, okay?"

"You sure you're alright?"

"I'm fine."

And with that, T.J. and I grabbed our jackets and books and headed outside.

As I walked around the campus, I rehashed the questions Lawrence and the detective had asked me and the answers I had given them. I knew I was innocent, and there was no reason for the police to suspect me, but Lawrence didn't seem convinced. *What if he's right? What if the police think I killed Professor Ladd? Surely not.*

I brushed off the thought and went to the library, where I found a copy of one of my favorite books, *Désirée,* by Annemarie Selinko. I lost myself in the world of Napoleon, leaving my worries behind.

chapter five

T.J. talked non-stop as I drove to his house. He'd fire off questions about the murder, and, as much as I wanted to be obliging, I couldn't bear to keep rehashing everything. My one-word answers forced him to perform his own monologue on the many motives and suspects in the professor's murder.

I turned the corner to our street and let out a deep sigh. "I sure wish I didn't have to go to work tonight."

"Why don't you call Mae and tell her you can't come in? I think you have every right to take the night off after the day you've had."

"I know, but I need the money, and I can't risk making Mae mad. She might fire me, and then what would I do?"

T.J.'s dog, a German Shepherd named Sandy, barreled off the front porch to greet her owner, and my mood lightened. I chuckled as I watched her tail wag faster and faster the closer she got to the car. For fear of hitting her, I stopped the car halfway down the driveway. "Guess this is as close as I can get you to your house today."

T.J. reached for the door handle and then paused, leaving Sandy utterly confused. "How long have you worked for Mae? It seems like forever. What's it been? Two years?

"More like three. I started shortly after her husband died."

T.J. shook his head and climbed out of the car as Sandy obediently sat and waited for him. "You're a better person than I am. I could never have put up with Mae that long."

"Maybe I'm a glutton for punishment." I shrugged.

With Mae's lack of patience for anything less than perfection, I was always on edge working at her store, but the money I made wasn't bad for part-time work—$4.00 an hour, which was $2.00 above the minimum wage. My twenty hours a week brought in just enough money to cover my tuition and books, with a little left over for spending money.

As I backed out of T.J.'s driveway and drove to Mae's Gift Shop, I turned the radio on and was soon singing "You Ain't Seen Nothing Yet" with Bachman-Turner Overdrive. By the time the song ended, I was ready to take on the world. My growling stomach, however, had other ideas. *Shoot, I forgot to get some yogurt for lunch at the student union this afternoon.* No way could I handle working at Mae's on an empty stomach.

I stopped at Yancy's and ran inside to order a cheeseburger and a small diet drink with no ice—a trick I'd learned from my dad to make sure you got more soft drink than ice. Eating while driving was not ideal, but it was better than starving, and I was getting rather good at juggling the two.

After parking in the lot behind the gift shop, I finished my cheeseburger and then took a few minutes to unwind. I studied my reflection in the visor mirror and, despite my best efforts to be upbeat, the face staring back at me did little to mask the horror of my day. I rummaged through my purse and reapplied my eyeshadow, but no matter what I did, I couldn't hide my swollen eyes. Too much crying had taken its toll.

I slammed the lid down on the eyeshadow and dropped it back into my bag. I fluffed my hair, pinched my cheeks, and opened the car door, resolved to make the best of a bad situation.

As I walked into the store, I saw Mae standing in front of

the counter with her arms crossed, obscuring the front of her blue coral silk wrap dress—one of her designer acquisitions from her recent trip to the Big Apple. She was glaring at me. I checked my watch. I wasn't late, but she was obviously upset —not a good way to start the night. *Maybe I should have taken T.J.'s advice and called off.*

"Everything okay?" I asked as I walked toward her.

"No. How could it be?" She grimaced. "Someone murdered my sister this morning, and as awful as that is, it seems to be the only thing people want to talk about today."

"Mae, I'm so sorry. How did it happen?" But before she could answer, I put two and two together. "Wait, are you talking about Professor Anne Ladd?"

"We weren't close—not at all, and after what she did…it doesn't matter." She shook her head, obviously miffed. "She's been dead to me for years, but still."

"I…I didn't know," I stammered. "She was one of my journalism professors."

"Your professor? Oh, that's right. You're studying to be a reporter, aren't you? Terrible profession. Why in the world would you want to do that?"

Before I could respond, Mae continued. "Do the police have any leads?"

"I think it's still too early, but I'm hoping they'll solve it soon."

"I hope so too. Then we can put this terrible mess behind us, and everyone can quit talking about it." She paused. "They say a student discovered her body."

"That was me."

Mae's mouth dropped open, but she closed it without saying a word. I seized my opportunity to leave and started walking toward the back room to drop off my things.

I was halfway to the back when I heard Mae's voice behind me. "Was anything missing from her office? Was it ransacked?"

"I...I don't think so. I saw her. That's all I remember." *Weird...who worries about a murdered person's office?*

"I wonder..." Mae stopped mid-sentence. "Do you think she suffered?"

"I'm not sure. I hope not."

She was quiet for a moment, and then asked, "Do *you* have any idea who might have killed her?"

I shook my head. "No, I don't have a clue." I closed the door, relieved she didn't follow me.

After putting my stuff away and mustering my courage to face Mae again, I left the solitude of the back room and headed to the front of the store. But when I saw Mrs. Winterfield looking at the display of English china teacups, I went to talk to her instead. She had been in the store yesterday when Bob had his outburst. *I bet she got quite an earful yesterday. She was probably on the phone all night.* Mrs. Winterfield knew everything about the goings-on in Petersburg and loved nothing better than sharing her knowledge with whoever would listen.

Despite the white-haired woman being hunched over, she had a feisty soul. Close to ninety years old, Mrs. Winterfield was anything but feeble. I liked to imagine she had been a spy in her younger days, and I suspected the ornate walking stick she used housed a long, sharp blade to fight off the enemy.

"I'll take this, dear," Mrs. Winterfield said as she handed me a pink floral teacup and saucer. She linked her arm through mine as we walked toward the register. "My, my, but it's so sad about Anne. She was such a dear person. I do hope they catch who did it. And poor Mae. It's so hard to lose family."

"True—"

"I meant to buy this yesterday, but there was such a fuss with Bob and all, I forgot." The corners of her mouth turned up. As she placed her money on the glass counter, she whispered, "I believe Steve Goodright is in a bit of a financial mess. My niece, who works at the bank, says Barb's checks have been bouncing all over town." She leaned over the counter. "Barb needs to take Bob's threats seriously. He's not about to be pushed around by another Peterson family member."

"Another Peterson?" I asked, confused.

"Oh, yes, Bob worked as a chauffeur for Mae's father, Chauncey Peterson, many years ago. Bob and Mae had a thing for each other back in the day. But her father disapproved of the hired help courting his daughter. No way was he going to have a chauffeur for a son-in-law, so he made her break it off. I don't think Bob ever forgave Chauncey. But, back to my point, dear, something's not right with Steve. I feel it in my bones."

"What do you mean?"

"Now, mind you, I'm not one to spread rumors, but my granddaughter works at the post office, and she said Steve has had all his mail forwarded from his home address to his office at the lumber company. Don't you think that odd?"

I nodded, while trying to think of plausible explanations, but I couldn't come up with anything other than Steve having something to hide.

"Barb needs to get her head out of the clouds and figure out what's going on."

"What do you mean?"

Before Mrs. Winterfield could answer, Mae walked up to the counter and greeted her with a hug. "Mrs. Winterfield, how nice to see you. How are you?"

"I'm fine, dear, but how are you? I'm so sorry to hear about Anne. You must tell me if there is anything I can do."

I stood amazed as Mae responded, dripping with so much charm one never would have known someone had murdered her sister that morning.

"That is so sweet of you, but no need to worry about me. I'm doing fine. Do you have time for a spot of tea? I have some in the back room. It would be lovely to chat for a few minutes."

"Oh, that would be nice, but I'm afraid I can't do it today," Mrs. Winterfield replied. "I met my granddaughter for an early dinner, and I fear the time has gotten away from me. Maybe next time, dear."

"Surely a few minutes won't make that much of a difference. Besides, it might be a good idea for you to get you off your feet before driving home."

"As tempting as that sounds, dear, I must say no. I'm not particularly eager to drive home in the dark, and the sun will set soon." She smiled, grabbed her cane, and headed out the door with her package.

"How strange!" Mae peered at me. "Mrs. Winterfield always loves to stay and chat when she comes into the store. Did she say anything to you?"

"No, not really."

"Anything about Anne's murder?"

"Only that she was sorry it happened."

"How strange that she didn't want to talk more about it. Not that *I* want to talk about it, mind you, but when I was little…" She stopped.

"Did you know Mrs. Winterfield when you were growing up?"

She cocked her head as if trying to identify a sound. "Is that someone knocking at the back door? Another delivery? My goodness, this late? I better go see." And off she went.

Mae's sudden departure, which I knew was her way of ending our conversation, made me more curious about how Mae had known Mrs. Winterfield when she was growing up and how Mrs. Winterfield knew about the romance between Bob and Mae.

When Mae went home around 7:00, I wanted to jump for joy! It was the first good thing that had happened all day. The shop was quiet for the rest of the evening, allowing me to finish unpacking yesterday's shipment of boxed Christmas cards. I even had time to study for my photography midterm, but I found it difficult to concentrate. The image of Professor Ladd's dead body haunted me. *Who killed her? Why?*

After closing the store and making the bank deposit, I walked to my car. As I tossed my photography book onto the passenger's seat, I glimpsed a paper lying on the floor—Craig's paper! It had fallen out of my purse. *I know I need to return his paper to him, but surely it won't hurt to look it over when I get home.*

* * *

As I pulled into the driveway, I saw the living room lights on, which meant someone was probably watching TV. Sure enough, as I came through the front door, I spied my mother sitting on her corner of the couch watching *Columbo*.

She turned as I walked into the room. "Did you hear about that professor's murder on campus this morning? It's been all over the news."

"Yeah, Professor Ladd—she was my professor." I paused, holding back my words as I debated how much to tell her. If I said I found her, she would want more information, most likely more than I wanted to share. If I said nothing, I could go to my room, read Craig's paper, and do some writing. But, if my mom found out from someone else that I was the person who found Professor Ladd, she'd be furious because *I hadn't told her.* She'd wonder what else I was hiding from her. I reasoned it was better to err on the side of caution and tell her about my day.

"Where's Dad?" I figured if he was still up, I might as well tell them both at the same time.

"He's already gone to bed. He and the boys worked in the orchards all day." She sat up straight. "So, what happened? The news said that a student found her in her office."

"That was me." I settled in next to her.

"You! What in the world were you doing in Anne's office?"

"Anne? Did you know her?"

Mom's eyes lit up, happy to be the source of information. "Sure. Anne was a year ahead of me in school, but with her being a Peterson and all, she didn't hang around with people like me."

"Why? Was she a snob?"

"Back then I thought she was, but I've come to realize it was more a case of not having anything in common. Her family had money. Mine didn't. Her…I don't remember how many greats…but some grandfather founded this town, and her family owned most of it when I was growing up. She could always afford to do things I couldn't. Our worlds were different." She shrugged. "But why were you in her office this morning?"

She sat quietly while I explained why I had gone to Professor Ladd's office. But as soon as I finished, the barrage of questions began: "Did anybody see you in her office? Did you see anyone? How was she murdered? Could it have been suicide?" The questions went on and on.

I tried to answer each one, but no sooner had I answered one question than she had two more. It got to the point I could no longer handle talking about the murder. It was too hard to keep reliving it. My only recourse was to change the subject. "I found out today that Mae's maiden name was Peterson. But you already knew that?"

"Sure. She was a lot older than me—or at least it seemed that way back then—so our paths never crossed, but I knew of her."

"Why didn't I know that?"

Mom shrugged. "I don't know. I thought for sure I told you."

"Well, I don't remember ever hearing that." I slumped in my seat, crossing my arms.

"Oh, come on. It's not that big of a deal. A lot of people don't know about her connection to the Peterson family. Mae moved away shortly after her husband died—her first husband, that is. By the time she came back to Petersburg, the town had changed. A lot of the old faces had either died or moved away."

"I suppose."

Mom walked over to the recliner in the corner and grabbed the orange afghan and wrapped herself in it as she walked back to the couch. "I can't believe how chilly the nights are getting already." She sat down and pulled the blanket tighter around her. "Fall's definitely here."

I sighed in response but returned to the subject at hand. "So, what do you know about the Peterson family? Were Mae and her sister close? I never even knew she had a sister until yesterday."

"Well, supposedly, when Mae moved away, she cut off all ties with her family. It surprised me when she moved back here."

"Do you know how Steve and Mae are related? They're cousins, but are they, like, first cousins?"

"Let me think a minute. How did it go?" She paused for a moment before continuing. "His mother was Mae's father's sister. So, yes, that would make them first cousins."

"That's so funny." I shook my head. "I guess I always assumed they were distant cousins. They're so businesslike and formal when they're together. She's much closer to his wife, Barb. They do a lot of things together—fashion shows in NYC, charity fundraisers, that sort of stuff."

Mom's eyes darted toward the TV and zeroed in on Columbo while he made an arrest. "Wait a minute. This is almost over. The last few minutes are always the best." Mom stood up, fluffed the orange pillow she had been leaning on, and walked to the TV, where she turned up the volume.

Neither of us spoke until the show ended and the closing credits finished rolling on the screen. Mom popped up off the couch, still wrapped in her blanket. "Do you want something to eat? I'm a little hungry. How about some hot chocolate and cookies…oatmeal raisin?"

"Sounds good." I followed her into the kitchen and sat down at the rectangular oak table.

No sooner had Mom opened the refrigerator door than Gidget sashayed into the kitchen. She acted like she owned the place, and that I was there to serve her, which, in a manner of speaking, was true. She sat down by her saucer on the floor, staring at me with her tail swishing across the floor.

"How did you know we were getting milk? You must have very good ears." I chuckled as I filled her saucer. When I returned to the table, I found a cup of hot chocolate and a plate of cookies in front of my chair.

"Thanks. This looks good." I took a bite of a cookie. "And they taste good too!"

Mom took a sip of her hot chocolate. "Just what the doctor ordered."

"Is there anything else you can tell me about the Peterson family?" I asked as I swirled the hot milk around in my cup.

"Mae and Anne's father, Chauncey Peterson, started the family's lumber business."

"How did Steve get it? I didn't even realize he was related to the Petersons."

"Grandma said it was a well-known fact that Chauncey was disappointed he only had daughters. He desperately wanted to leave his lumber company to a son." She sighed. "He didn't think women should run a business—that was a man's job."

"Guess he wouldn't have been a big fan of the women's lib movement," I interjected.

She nodded. "Chauncey was determined to leave the business to a male descendant. He assumed one of his daughters would have a son at some point. He even tried to set both girls up with executives in his company, but nothing ever came of that. When Chauncey died, there was no grandson to inherit the business, so it went to Steve, the closet living male relative."

"Wow. I wonder if Mae ever resented Steve getting the lumber company? Maybe that's why they are always so reserved around each other."

"Could be," Mom said as she picked up our plates. She rinsed them off and put them in the dishwasher.

I placed the two empty cups on the top rack. "Guess I better go study." I kissed her cheek. "Thanks for the hot chocolate and the cookies." I walked toward the door and stopped. "Sweet dreams."

"You too. Try not to stay up too late."

I picked up my photography textbook and purse from the bottom of the stairs. Although I wanted to get to my room and write all my thoughts in my journal before I forgot them, I needed to study for tomorrow's midterm. But first, I wanted to read the paper that belonged to Craig. That couldn't wait any longer.

I flipped the switch to the overhead light in my bedroom, but nothing happened. *Shoot!* Once again, I forgot to get a light bulb from the pantry. Turning on the hallway light, I found the switch to my floor lamp, and after turning it on, tossed my book and purse onto the bed. I gazed out my window. Not a star in the sky. The light coming from T.J.'s room was the only thing breaking the darkness.

Gidget moved from the foot of my bed to where my textbook was lying and laid her head on it. I couldn't imagine that my book made a comfortable pillow, but the sound of her purr told me otherwise.

"At least I've got you, don't I?" I sat on the bed next to her and gently stroked her head. "You realize you're not helping, right? I have to read that *pillow* of yours sometime tonight, but first—" I pulled Craig's paper out of my bag and began reading it.

Why did Craig have this paper, and how in the world did he get it?

chapter six

Wednesday, October 16th

"Michelle!" My mom's voice floated up to my room from the bottom of the stairs. "T.J.'s here. Did you know he was coming early? You better hurry!"

"I'll be right down."

From my window, I saw T.J.'s car in the driveway. *Of all days for T.J. to show up early!* I was running late after losing ten minutes sitting at my vanity trying to rehash everything I had studied last night for today's midterm.

As I scurried around my room, gathering my books and purse, I heard the phone ring downstairs. *That's strange. No one calls this early around here.*

"Michelle, the phone!"

I closed my eyes and shook my head in disgust. A phone call was the last thing I needed this morning. I gave Gidget a quick pat on the head, flung my bedroom door open, and ran down the stairs.

"It's a Detective Douglas," Mom said as she handed me the receiver. "It's not my fault. Don't make faces at me."

"Sorry." I took a deep breath. "Hello, this is Michelle."

In a monotone voice, Detective Douglas told me he needed me to come to the station to answer more questions.

"I can come around 11:30 this morning. Would that be alright?"

As I hung up, Mom asked, "Is everything okay?"

I twisted the silver charm around my neck and tried to act like the call was no big deal. I didn't want her to worry; that would only add to my stress. "He needs me to stop by his office today. Nothing major."

She smiled. "I was afraid there was a problem."

"No. No problem."

She handed me my jacket and two warm cinnamon pastries wrapped in a paper towel. "I thought you might need to eat."

"Thanks. I'm running late, and he's early. What else can go wrong today? Forget I said that. I don't want to know." I smiled as I kissed her goodbye. "See you tonight."

"Do you have to work today after school?"

"No, I should be home after my last class. Love you."

T.J. leaned on his horn again as I closed the front door behind me.

Man, he's in a hurry today! He's probably as nervous as I am about the test. Poor guy. He signed up for this class because he thought it would be an easy four-credit A. Plus, he thought it would be fun to take a class together. I had a hunch, though, after studying for the midterm, he was having second thoughts about his idea of fun.

I ran to his car shouting, "I'm coming! I'm coming!" The sound of crunching leaves beneath my feet added a staccato-like beat to each step, accentuating how quickly I was moving.

"You're early," I said, trying to catch my breath. I hurriedly buckled my seat belt and looked out my window. "You ready for the midterm?"

"As ready as I'll ever be." He laughed. "I wanted to call you last night, but you know how my parents are about me using the phone after nine o'clock."

"I totally get it." I sighed. "First, they tell you they're going to treat you like an adult, and then, the next minute, they're laying down all these rules you have to follow. My favorite part is when my dad says, 'My house. My rules.'"

"Sometimes it's a bit much, isn't it?" T.J. looked in the rearview mirror as he backed out of the driveway.

"That's for sure. It makes me want to get my own place, even if I had to work more hours at Mae's." I paused. "What did you want to call about?"

"I wanted to make sure you were okay…after finding Professor Ladd and all."

"Yeah, I'm trying not to think about it too much. Working last night and then studying for today's test helped." I paused. "Hey, did you know Mae was Professor Ladd's sister?"

"You've got to be kidding me! How'd you find that out?"

"Mae told me last night. Can you believe it? After all this time working for her, I never even knew she had a sister until the other night. Anyway, when I got home last night, I asked my mom about it, and she told me what she knew about the Peterson family."

"The Peterson family?"

"Chauncey Peterson, the guy who started the Peterson Lumber Company, was Mae and Professor Ladd's father."

"Small world." He shrugged as he popped a cassette into the cassette player. "I picked this up last night at the record store near campus. It's Jethro Tull's new release, *War Child*. I haven't had time to listen to it yet."

"Play away, sir." I smiled, looking out the window.

While Ian Anderson sang in the background, we asked each other photography questions to prepare for the test. We kept score, being the competitive people that we were. T.J.

was ahead by one question when he flipped on his left blinker and then brought the car to a sudden stop. A group of school-aged kids was standing on the corner, so he motioned for them to cross. One of the smaller children put his hand out with his palm facing us until he reached the other side of the street.

"I don't think he trusted me to stay stopped." T.J. laughed as he finished turning onto the street leading to campus.

"One can never be too careful." I smiled as I looked at the porches decorated with their jack-o'-lanterns. When I was growing up, Halloween was only for the under-twelve group, but now, everyone, regardless of their age, celebrated it! *How fun!*

My happy thoughts of Halloween parties ended abruptly when T.J.'s voice broke the silence. "So, how was Mae holding up with her sister being murdered? I'm surprised she kept the store open yesterday."

"Me too. It was kinda weird. Sometimes she acted upset, and then, at other times, it was as if nothing had happened. Mae said she and Professor Ladd weren't close, and, boy, do I believe it. Can you imagine never mentioning she had a sister who taught at UP when she knew I went there?" I stopped for a moment, realizing the pitch of my voice was going higher the more upset I got. I took a deep breath and focused on talking slower. "She went home early last night, which was nice. Oh, and I almost forgot to tell you, but you remember I told you about Craig and me colliding in the hallway? And how he dropped a bunch of papers, and I accidentally kept one that I needed to return to him later?"

T.J. nodded.

"Well, I forgot about the paper until last night, and when I finally read it, you'll never believe what it was about."

"What?"

"It was a letter from Professor Ladd to the board of the

Peterson Lumber Company. She wanted them to have an audit done of the company's financial records. She told them she suspected someone was embezzling funds."

T.J. turned onto campus, and the row of fraternity houses decked out with bats and spiders on their doors greeted us.

I sighed. "I've been thinking…"

"Oh, trying something new?" T.J. grinned.

"Cute." I pretended to glare at him. "Seriously, I've been thinking this whole murder thing has all the makings of a good story for the school paper, or maybe even the *Toledo Blade*. You know, Petersburg is practically a suburb of Toledo. But think about it—there's a murder, the prestigious Peterson family, two sisters who were not on speaking terms, and someone embezzling at the family business. And then there's something Mrs. Winterfield—she's one of our customers—said last night. She told me she thought something fishy was going on with Steve Goodright." I stopped and took another deep breath so I could slow down. "What if he is involved with the missing money? I thought I'd talk to Keith—he's the editor of the *Wildcats' Daily News*—and see what he thinks about my idea for a story."

"And if he doesn't like the idea?"

I bit my bottom lip and raised my eyebrows. "I'll do it anyway."

T.J. started to tell me that if Keith didn't like the idea, I should drop it, but before he could finish his lecture, I said, "Detective Douglas called me this morning. He wants me to meet him at the police station after class this morning."

"What does he want?"

"He said he had a few more questions." I smiled mischievously. "But this time, I've got some questions of my own." I paused. "I can see it now. Michelle Kilpatrick, renowned investigative reporter, gets tight-lipped detective to spill the beans."

* * *

After ninety minutes of labeling the parts of a camera, discussing exposure and metering modes, writing an essay on the history of photography, and describing the rule of thirds, I emerged from the classroom exhausted, rubbing my tired eyes. T.J. was waiting for me by the wall opposite the classroom door, rolling his neck from side to side.

"You okay?" I asked as we headed down the hall to the stairs.

"Yeah, I think I did okay, but that was brutal."

"He asked about every single thing he talked about in class! Was there anything he left out?" I rubbed the back of my aching neck.

"You remember the morning he talked about his new dog, right? At least he didn't ask us what his name was." T.J. laughed. He pulled the glass door open, letting me escape into the outside world first. "You off to see Detective Douglas?"

"Yeah. Hopefully, I can get enough info from the dear detective to sell my idea of an investigative piece to Keith. At least, that's Plan A."

"And Plan B?"

"I don't have one." I grinned.

"You sure this meeting is no big deal? I mean, he doesn't suspect you of anything, does he?" T.J. stopped. I could hear the concern in his voice.

"Oh, don't be silly. I did nothing wrong. He probably just wants to know if I remember seeing anything unusual while I was in the building."

"Do you plan on telling him about the letter?"

"Yeah, and maybe use it to get some information from him."

T.J. patted my shoulder. "Just be careful. There may be a killer out there."

"I think I should be pretty safe at the police station." I smiled.

"I meant while you're walking there, Miss Smarty Pants." He gave me a gentle shove. "See you later at the Commuter Lounge?"

"You got it."

"Cool, see you then."

I'd made it to the street corner when I realized I should make a couple of copies of Craig's letter. I went back into Sheffield Hall and up to the journalism office. Betsy was busy typing at her desk.

"Could I use the copy machine and make two copies of this paper?"

She looked up from her typewriter, her eyes narrowed. "Is it for a class?"

"It's for a piece I'm writing for the school paper." I crossed my fingers, despite reasoning that I wasn't telling a little white lie because I was sure Keith would like the idea.

After making copies of Craig's letter, I started my fifteen-minute walk to downtown Petersburg. With the warm mid-morning sun beating down, I removed my jacket and threw it over my arm as I walked along South Boundary Street. I envied my fellow students as they lounged around, carefree, on their blankets spread under the almost-bare trees. I gave a little shrug when I saw many of them wearing shorts. Would the day really stay that warm? October temperatures in the Midwest were all over the place. Days could start off warm and stay that way, or they could get so cold you would think winter had come early. Not brave enough to rely on the morning temperature as my guide for the day, I tried to outsmart fall's ever-changing thermometer by layering. My bell-bottomed jeans, white tank top, navy-blue cardigan, and jacket were perfect for a day like today. Like the mailman, I liked to think that I was ready for whatever the weather threw my way.

While walking, I rehearsed the questions I wanted to ask Detective Douglas. *Did he have any leads? Did he know about the letter from the professor? Could her death have anything to do with it? Did he have any idea how Craig Miller got the letter?*

When it became apparent I had more questions than brain space to store them, I stopped, sat on a bench at the bus stop, and jotted my questions down in my notebook. Looking around, I was amazed at how life in Petersburg continued as usual. Yesterday, someone had murdered a professor not far from where I sat, yet life continued unchanged. People were going about their daily lives, the birds were singing, and the sun was shining. Except for the headline in the school newspaper that morning about the murder, it was a day like any other. I guess the administration was making sure of that. Still, I knew life would be different until I discovered why someone murdered Professor Ladd. Her death had connected us more than her life ever had.

After I entered the police station, Lawrence was standing behind the reception desk, sorting papers.

"Hi, Lawrence. I didn't know you were working today."

"You caught me! This is where I live on Wednesdays, before I go to class."

"How many hours a week do you work?"

"About twenty. A little less during finals week and a little more over the holiday break." He shrugged. "It all evens out." He pushed his glasses back up his nose. "What brings you here?"

"Detective Douglas called me this morning and asked me to stop by. I guess he's got a few questions for me."

"Do you know where his office is?" He laid the papers on the counter.

"Nope. Which way is it?" I looked at the hallways on either side of the reception desk, not sure which one to take.

"I can show you where it's at." He came out from behind the counter, walked in front of me, and led me down the hall.

He walked so quickly that I had difficulty keeping up with him. I've never had a good sense of direction and, without his help, I would have gotten lost in the maze of hallways. Everything looked the same: endless glossy white walls with fluorescent lights shining onto the black speckled floor.

Lawrence glanced over his shoulder and immediately slowed his pace so I could catch up to him. "Detective Douglas is the lead detective in the Ladd case."

"I figured as much."

Lawrence narrowed his eyes. "Just a piece of advice—be careful how you answer his questions. You might even want to tell him you'll come back with your lawyer."

"Why would I need a lawyer?" I gasped.

He shrugged nonchalantly. "Just to be on the safe side. I was talking to a couple officers in the break room this morning, and, no surprise, they said the mayor and the university president want this case solved *now*. They're putting a lot of pressure on Douglas to arrest somebody. The problem is, when people are under that kind of pressure, they sometimes rush and jump to the wrong conclusion. I don't want you to get hurt because they are in a hurry to do their job."

"I'm sure I'll be fine."

Since Lawrence wasn't known for being sympathetic, I was unnerved by the look on his face. Still, my resolve to find answers for my story about Professor Ladd's death took precedence over my fears. I had to face Douglas. I needed as many answers from him as he needed from me.

Lawrence stopped at room #156 and tapped on the open door. "Detective Douglas, Michelle Kilpatrick is here to see you."

The detective looked up from his desk. "Sit down, Ms. Kilpatrick." He moved some papers to the side of his desk, clearing the space in front of him. He grabbed a pen from the wooden pen and pencil cup and wrote something down.

Following his lead, I retrieved my pen and notebook from my purse and readied myself to take notes.

Detective Douglas lifted his eyes from the paper on which he had been writing and directed his attention toward me. "Were you angry with Professor Ladd?"

"I was upset, but I wouldn't say angry." I tightened my grip on my pen.

"It says here that witnesses said you were upset with the professor." He paused as he thumbed through a stack of papers on his desk. "And that you thought she was a real pain and destroying your GPA and your future...your words, I assume?"

I sat up in my chair. "Who are these witnesses you keep talking about?"

"Who they are doesn't matter, Ms. Kilpatrick. What matters is whether or not you said those things. Did you?"

"I might have said something like that. I was upset, but not enough to kill her."

"But you were upset with her?" He paused. "Would you please tell me again what happened yesterday morning? What time did you get to Sheffield Hall?"

"8:35 a.m."

"And what did you do between your arrival at Sheffield Hall and when you found Professor Ladd's body?"

I recounted the previous day's events, but this time I made sure I told him about Betsy's skirt and my run-in with Craig Miller. "You know, Betsy and Craig both had the opportunity to kill Professor Ladd too. Do you think either of them had a motive?"

"Ms. Kilpatrick, may I remind you I am the one asking questions?"

"Yes. I understand that, but were you aware that Professor Ladd wrote a letter to the Peterson Lumber Company board requesting an audit because she suspected someone was stealing money from the company?"

"And how do you know that?"

I handed him a copy of the letter.

"How did you get this? Did Professor Ladd give it to you, or did you take it from her office? We found your fingerprints on her desk. Is that where you found it?"

"What? No!" I leaned forward in my chair, shocked, as I tried to visualize everything I did in the professor's office yesterday morning. "Wait, I think I know how my finger-prints got there. When I tried to wake her, I started feeling faint and leaned on her desk. That must be what happened."

He held the paper I had given him in the air. "And this paper? How'd you get it?"

I collected my thoughts. "Yesterday, when Craig ran into me, he dropped some papers. I helped him pick them up. After he was gone, I realized I still had one of them. I forgot about it until last night. Why do you think he had it?"

Detective Douglas threw the paper down on the desk and leaned back in his office chair.

With arms crossed, he barked, "Why didn't you tell me about this yesterday morning?"

"I told you, I forgot. I wasn't thinking clearly."

"Obviously," Detective Douglas snarled. "Is there anything else you have *suddenly* remembered?"

"No, I don't think so, although I was wondering if you have any idea what time Professor Ladd died?"

He frowned. "Why do you need to know that?"

"I'm writing an article about Professor Ladd for the student newspaper. I'm one of their reporters, and I want to write about her ties to the community and, of course, the murder. The time of death would be an important fact to include, don't you think?"

"Ms. Kilpatrick, may I give you some advice?"

I nodded and sank back into my seat.

"Find something else to write about. I think you have more important things to worry about than this story for the school paper." He opened a drawer on his desk. "Do you recognize these?" He held up a plastic bag with a pair of white cloth gloves inside.

"No." I shook my head.

"We found them in the bushes below Professor Ladd's office with traces of the professor's blood on them."

He stood up, walked to the front of the desk, and then leaned against it while holding the blood-stained gloves closer to my face.

I closed my eyes and grimaced.

"Did you or did you not shoot Professor Ladd and then take off the gloves and throw them out the window?"

I jumped up from my seat. "I told you I didn't shoot her. I did not kill Professor Ladd!" He stared at me as I shouted. "I don't know who killed Professor Ladd, but it wasn't me."

Silence enveloped the room as he returned to his chair behind the desk and scribbled some notes. After what felt like several minutes, he looked up. "I understand you live with your parents."

"Yes, that's correct."

"You said yesterday that there are guns in your house."

I hesitated to answer, yet knew I had no choice. "Yes, my father owns a few hunting rifles."

"Any revolvers?"

"I don't know. He keeps everything locked in a gun safe."

He ran his fingers through his short brown hair. "You may go now, but remember what I said yesterday. Don't leave town, and…you might want to think about getting a lawyer."

My heart started racing. "A lawyer? Why would I need a lawyer?"

He moved the pile of papers back in front of him, pushed up his shirt sleeves, and muttered, "Standard procedure. Nothing to worry about unless—" he looked straight at me, "—you've got something to hide. Do you know your way out?"

"Yes. Thank you." I got up, grabbed my things, and went into the hallway.

Rattled by Detective Douglas's questions, I wanted to get away—far away—from his office as soon as possible. Although I had no idea which way to go, I just started walking down the hall. If I was going the wrong way, hopefully, I would find someone to help me.

After several turns led me further into the maze, I panicked, but I knew I had to keep walking. Finally, I turned and saw the reception desk.

Lawrence looked up. "Everything go okay?"

I threw my hands up in the air. "Can you believe the audacity of that man? I bring him information. I tell him about two people near Professor Ladd's office yesterday morning—two *suspicious* people, I might add—and he practically insinuates I'm the one who killed her."

Lawrence leaned on the counter and whispered, "He's only doing his job."

"Perhaps, but—"

"Let's go outside where we can talk." He turned to the officer standing next to him. "Can you watch the desk for a few minutes? I'll be right outside."

As soon as we stepped beyond the door, I asked, "How could Detective Douglas even *think* I was the one who killed Professor Ladd?"

"Let's look at the facts: they found a disgruntled student in the room with Professor Ladd's dead body. What would you think?"

"Just because someone finds a dead body doesn't mean they're the killer!" I shook my head. "I mean, where's the murder weapon? How in the world did I get rid of the gun?" My voice was shaking.

"That's one thing in your favor at the moment. Once the police find the murderer or the gun, you'll be in the clear." He took a breath before continuing. "But until then, there's the issue of the police finding gunpowder residue on your hands."

"What?" I stumbled and then leaned against a lamppost to steady myself. "That's why he asked me about my father's guns. But it doesn't matter. I didn't shoot her!"

"I believe you. They did find gunpowder residue on both the desk and the chair and on the blinds. You could have picked up the residue from the desk and the chair when you touched them, if that's what happened."

I stepped back. My heart was beating faster. "What do you mean, *if* that's what happened? Of course, that's what happened. I didn't make it up!"

"I didn't say you did. I'm just looking at the evidence the way Detective Douglas would. He doesn't know you like I do."

I cocked my head. "How do you know about the gunpowder residue?"

"The advantage of working with the case files and having a few good friends on the force." He smiled. "And in Detective Douglas's defense, I don't think he's convinced you did it. If he was, he would've slapped the cuffs on you by now. I'm sure he'll look into the names you gave him, but for the time being, you are a person of interest."

I stood silently as I mulled over what Lawrence had said.

"Are you okay?" Lawrence asked. As I nodded, he continued. "What's next on your schedule? Do you have class?"

I glanced at my watch. "Not until later this afternoon. I'm going back to the Commuter Lounge for a while."

"I'll see if I can go with you. Wait here while I run inside and see if it's okay for me to take my lunch break now. If it is, I'll drive us back to campus."

I waited for Lawrence on the bench outside the police station and watched the cars drive down the street. It was becoming clear to me that I could be in a great deal of trouble.

I knew I was innocent, but I needed to convince Detective Douglas.

Tears welled up in my eyes. Had it not been for Lawrence bounding out of the building with his army green jacket and camo backpack, I would have stayed under the lamppost and had a good cry.

* * *

The Commuter Lounge went strangely quiet as Lawrence and I walked to our table. It was weird experiencing the sensation of a hundred eyes burning a hole through me. As we reached our table, T.J. pulled out the chair next to him while Lawrence sat down across from me. Soon, the quiet murmuring of voices returned, so I glanced around the room, hoping people were no longer looking at me, but found the sea of eyes still focused in my direction.

Turning to T.J., I asked, "Is it just me, or is everyone staring at me?"

"You haven't seen the paper?" He slid today's *Daily News* in front of me, pointing to the paragraph in the article about Professor Ladd. It included the name of the student who found her body—Michelle Kilpatrick.

Lawrence looked straight at me. "Ignore them. They're gawkers. They're not worth your time." He tapped his fingers on the table. "I sure wish this place had a coffee machine. I should have stopped by the student union on our way here."

Amy, sitting at the end of the table, looked up, smiling. "Want me to go get you some?"

"Yeah, if you don't mind." The corners of his mouth curved up ever so slightly as he reached into his pocket and pulled out some change.

"T.J.? Michelle? Either of you want anything?" Amy asked as she slipped Lawrence's change into her trench coat pocket.

"Yeah, I guess I'll take one too. Thanks," T.J. uttered. He

pulled thirty-five cents from his pocket and slid it across the table.

Amy beamed as she added it to her collection of coins.

"I'll be right back." She tied the belt on her coat and slung her purse over her shoulder.

As Amy disappeared up the stairs, T.J. leaned over. "How'd it go with that detective?"

"Okay, but..." I started choking up.

"But what?"

"They found my fingerprints on Professor Ladd's desk." I took a deep breath before continuing. "Which makes perfect sense because I touched it." I sighed. "But they also found gunpowder residue on my hands."

"When Michelle touched the desk and the chair, she probably picked up the residue that was on them," Lawrence explained. "Unfortunately, when you add that to the witnesses saying Michelle was upset with Ladd, it paints a pretty clear picture of Michelle being a person of interest."

T.J. gasped. "What are you going to do?" His eyes grew wide.

"I don't know." I shook my head and thought of my options. *I can do nothing and see what happens, or I can talk to a lawyer and see what he says or...*"I'm gonna clear my name by either finding the murder weapon or the killer or...both."

"And how are you going to do that?" T.J. looked puzzled.

"If I think like an investigative journalist, I should be able to solve this." I opened my notebook and began writing. "We know the police found a pair of gloves with Professor Ladd's blood on them. That means the murderer wore them the day they shot her, so we can deduce the police won't find their fingerprints on the weapon or anything else."

"The blood on the gloves is probably from the blood spray when the bullet hit the professor," Lawrence added. "So... chances are, other pieces of clothing will have blood on them too."

"Right." I nodded. "That also means the murder was premeditated. Somebody brought a gun and wore gloves when they went to see her. They must have had a pretty intense grudge against Professor Ladd. If I were a betting person, I would say it had to do with the missing money at the lumber company, so that's where I'm starting."

chapter seven

I rubbed the charm dangling around my neck as I tried to visualize the bullet points on the handout Professor Ladd had given us on how to write an investigative journalism piece.

"You look worried. What's wrong?" T.J. asked.

I stared at the words I had written in my notebook. "I feel like I'm missing an important piece to this puzzle. The money from the lumber company is key, no doubt about that, but what if someone had a reason to kill her that was not connected to the lumber company? We've got to look at her murder from all angles."

Lawrence rocked his chair back, clasping his hands behind his head. "So, where do you want to start?"

"As the song says, 'let's start at the very beginning.' I went to Professor Ladd's office and found her dead at 9:00 a.m.—"

"And you were in the hallway before that, right?" T.J. interjected.

Lawrence bent over and pulled a chicken salad sandwich out of his backpack, along with a notebook and pen. He began fervently writing with one hand while he bit into the sandwich he held in the other.

"I remember sitting outside her office and looking at the

clock. It was 8:35, and I debated whether to study or go get some pop from the vending machine."

I recounted my activities that morning, and when I finished, Lawrence turned his notebook around so I could read his notes. "Did I miss anything?"

He had written Professor Ladd's name in the center of the page and surrounded it by four circles. Each circle had one name in it—Michelle, Betsy, Craig, and lumber company. The circle with my name included my timeline that morning. Betsy's circle included notes about the water spot on her skirt and the approximate time our paths crossed. Under Craig's name was the time of our run-in, that he was coming from the direction of the professor's office, and that he had the letter Professor Ladd had written to the board. The words *missing money* were in the last circle.

"It looks like you got everything." Until that moment, I had done my best to ignore the facts, but seeing them in black and white made it clear why I was a person of interest. As I copied Lawrence's diagram into my notebook, I consoled myself that at least I wasn't the only suspect.

I slid the notebook back to Lawrence, and he wasted no time scribbling more notes on it. He looked up, tapping the pen on the table. "We need to get the medical examiner's report. We know someone shot her, but there's an off chance the wound wasn't fatal. She could have been strangled, suffocated, or even poisoned before the shooting. We can get the exact cause of death from the report."

"I never even thought of that. Can you actually get a copy of the report, or is that confidential?" I asked.

"I'll have to run it by Douglas, but I'll see what I can do." He winked with a slight grin. "I'm sure I can find a way."

"Anything you can find out will help, but don't risk your job."

"Trust me, I won't. Jobs are too scarce right now with this recession."

"Okay, as long as you're sure." I looked down at my notes and twirled my pen between my fingers as if it was a miniature baton. "Next, we should focus on motives. Why would Betsy or Craig want to kill Professor Ladd?"

"What's Betsy's last name?" Amy asked, as she put Lawrence and T.J.'s coffee cups on the table. She pulled out the chair on the other side of T.J.

"Braxton."

"Long blond hair? Real pretty?"

"Yeah, that's her. Why?" I asked.

"I might know why she would want Professor Ladd dead." Amy slipped off her trench coat, and a whiff of cigarette smoke passed over the table. Her brown eyes were wide with excitement as she sat down. "While I was on the way to get the coffee, I thought of something." She had our undivided attention. "I work at a diner in Watertown—"

"Isn't that kind of a long drive from here?" asked T.J. as he took the lid off his coffee cup, letting the steam escape.

"Yeah, it's about forty minutes from here, but," she quickly added, "it's only about twenty minutes from where I live in Pickney." She took a deep breath and regained her thoughts. "For several weeks, Betsy and Professor Ladd's husband, Burt, have been coming in for dinner. They always sit at the same table in my section, the one back in the corner. They look pretty cozy, like a couple, if you catch my drift, always huddled together over the table."

"How do you know Betsy and Professor Ladd's husband?" I asked. I had never heard of Amy having anything to do with the journalism department.

"Betsy and I went to high school together in Pickney. She was a few years older than me—cheerleader, homecoming queen." She shrugged. "Betsy ran around with the cool kids, not people like me. I heard she was working at the university, but I didn't know she was in the journalism department."

"And how did you meet Professor Ladd's husband?"

"Oh, that's easy. He's the one who helped me open a checking account at the bank here in town. He's the bank's district manager and told me he almost never did that kind of stuff anymore, but the branch was short-handed that day, and he was helping to keep the line moving. When I mentioned I went to school here, he asked if I had ever met his wife, a journalism professor."

A hundred questions rushed through my mind. I didn't know where to focus first. I remembered the argument I'd heard the day before the murder between Professor Ladd and her husband. *What if Burt and Betsy were having an affair? Maybe Professor Ladd wouldn't give her husband a divorce, and he and Betsy wanted to get her out of the way? Perhaps they worked together, or maybe Betsy acted alone? What if it had been blood and not coffee on Betsy's skirt yesterday morning?*

So many questions, but before pursuing any more possibilities, I looked at Amy. "If you see Betsy again, do you think you could try to find out how serious it is between her and Burt?"

"Sure, if she pops in, I'll see what I can do." Amy smiled and gave T.J. a quick wink.

I couldn't see T.J.'s face, but from the broad smile on Amy's face, he must have smiled back. Amy and I had always been cordial but certainly not the best of friends. There was no reason for her to help me. However, if she thought helping me with the murder investigation would get her in T.J.'s good graces, I knew she would be more than willing to help.

"Okay, we've got Betsy covered. Who's going to investigate Craig?" I stopped. "That should be me; we're in a class together." I sighed, dreading the thought of having to see him. "I probably should stop by his office today and give him back his paper. At least maybe I can ask him some questions."

"The dude's got an office?" T.J. asked, his eyes narrowed.

I nodded. "He's a grad assistant, remember? One of the perks of the job."

Lawrence jumped up from his chair, startling me.

"What's wrong?"

"Nothing." He laughed. "I just realized I have to get back to work." He tilted his coffee cup up, drinking the last few drops, and then crunched it before tossing it into the garbage can. "Do you think it's a good idea to see this Craig guy alone? What if he's the killer and thinks you're on to him?"

"I'll go with her," T.J. volunteered.

"Thanks, but I'm sure I'll be okay."

"Yeah, you will 'cause I'm going to be right outside his office door if you need any help. What time are you going?"

I smiled. It was nice to know I wasn't the *only one* who worried too much. "When's your next class?"

"At two."

"Mine too. How 'bout we go see Craig in a few minutes? But first, I was wondering..." I pulled the letter from my notebook and slowly read the words aloud. "Peterson Lumber Company. Do we know anyone who works there?"

Amy answered matter-of-factly. "Yash is doing an internship there this quarter."

Yash was another member of our Commuter Lounge group. Born in India, he and his family moved to Petersburg when his father started teaching at the university about six years ago.

"Great," I said, feeling optimistic. "Will he be here this afternoon?"

"I don't think he has classes in the afternoon on Wednesdays," T.J. said, "but I can call him tonight."

"That'd be great. We need to find out if money is missing from the lumber company and, if it is, who might be taking it. I don't know if he has access to that information, but see if he's heard any rumors about Steve Goodright or the lumber company having money problems."

I closed my notebook and put my pen away. "Okay, I'm ready to go, but I'd like to stop by the *Daily News* office and see if Keith is in. It might be nice to be officially working on this story. It should only take a few minutes."

* * *

Sally, a freshman and newbie to the *Wildcats' Daily News* staff, sat at the front desk, typing away.

"Hi, Sally! Is Keith in?" The door closed behind me.

Keith and I met last year at the freshman orientation for commuters. He was from southern Ohio and already had a lot of newspaper experience, having worked for his community paper and as editor of his high school's newspaper. Over the past year, our paths crossed in the newsroom, and we had written a couple of articles together. Last month, the editor had promoted him to assistant editor. He lived and breathed newspaper reporting and reminded me of Lou Grant on *The Mary Tyler Moore Show*—a real softie underneath that gruff exterior.

Keith's office door opened, and there he stood with his blue oxford shirt sleeves rolled up and his tousled shaggy brown hair. He looked every inch a busy newspaperman. "Sally, get me Detective Douglas on the phone. I want the latest info on Ladd's murder. The administration is not going to shut this story down if I have anything to say about it." He started to close his door and then stopped. "Michelle! Come on in. I've got something I want to talk to you about."

I followed him into his office and took a seat.

"Have I got an assignment for you, and it's right up your alley," he said as he closed the door.

"I'm intrigued. So, what have you heard about the Ladd case? I gather you're working on it?" I put my books and purse on the floor and leaned back into the chair.

"Crazy, right? A professor was killed right here on campus, and the man wants us to pretend like it never happened. Hey, sorry about you being the one to find her, but I wanted to ask you about that."

"Actually, I was wondering—"

Keith started talking before I could finish. "Between you and me, any number of students could have offed her. She made a lot of people angry. She was one tough teacher."

"That's for sure. Do the police have any leads?" I pulled out my notebook and pen.

"Well…there is the rumor that she and Craig Miller—you know, that author slash grad student—were having an affair."

"Interesting." I jotted down *Craig and Ladd affair*.

"I don't suppose your path has crossed with Miller's?"

"We're in, or *were in*, Professor Ladd's class together. In fact, I'm on my way to see him now. I don't know about any affair, but I'll see what I can find out. There are some other things regarding the professor I want to ask him about."

Keith leaned back in his chair and twisted it from side to side several times. "I like your initiative. How would you like to work on the Ladd story? Your choice as to the direction you want to take. I trust your instincts."

I nodded and smiled. This was perfect. I got the story assignment I wanted, and he thought it was all his idea. Things were looking up.

He opened a desk drawer and retrieved a manila envelope. "Here, look through these. Maybe something will pique your interest."

I pulled the papers out of the envelope and glanced through them. "Where did you get these?"

"I have my sources." He grinned.

"No, seriously, where did you get them?"

"Off the record, a friend of mine works here as a janitor. When the police searched Ladd's office yesterday, they found one of her desk drawers locked. Since the university issued the desk, they called my friend because he had the master key. As luck would have it, it was his day off, and he was out of town. Since the police had to leave before he could get to the office, they asked him to meet them there this morning."

"The police let him make copies of what they found?"

"Not exactly." He scratched the back of his head. "He went to Ladd's office last night after he got back into town and looked in the drawer out of curiosity. When he saw what was in it, he thought there might be something I could use for the paper. He made copies of everything."

"Isn't that called tampering with evidence?"

"Maybe…but I'm not going to tell." He smiled and winked.

"Have you read them?"

"Haven't had time. Let me know what you find out."

"Will do." I gathered my things off the floor and stood up to leave.

"Are you going to Ladd's memorial service on Friday?" Keith asked.

"What time is it?"

"Don't tell me you didn't see the announcement in the *Daily News*?"

I could feel my face turning red as I opened the door.

"Don't answer that." He laughed. "It's at noon at First Baptist. It's the church right across from the university on South Boundary."

"I'll be there."

Keith smiled and then hollered to Sally, "Did you ever get through to Detective Douglas?"

She looked up from her typing. "No, he was out of the office, but I left a message for him to call you."

"Then get me Coach Ryan on the phone. I've got a few questions about that hockey player on his team who's eyeing the '76 Winter Olympics!"

I found T.J. halfway down the hall, sitting on the floor, almost asleep. "Sorry, that took longer than I had planned, but…the good news is, he gave me the assignment."

"Well, that's a relief." He feigned a sigh. "I mean, we all knew you were going to write your article—with or without his blessing."

I gently elbowed him. "You got that right."

We headed upstairs to the journalism office so I could ask Betsy where I could find Craig's office.

"I'll wait for you out here," T.J. said as I opened the glass office door.

Betsy looked up from her typing. "May I help you?"

Overcome with the realization I might be face-to-face with a murderer, I froze—unable to speak for a few moments.

"Are you okay?" Betsy asked as she studied my face.

I shook my head to regain my bearings. "I'm...I'm looking for Craig Miller's office."

She pulled a piece of paper from her desk drawer and brought it to the counter—her black pumps made a clunking sound with each step. She pulled a pencil from a nearby black ceramic pencil holder and, using the pencil's eraser as a pointer, put it next to Craig's name and dragged it across to his room assignment.

"Room #52. If you go down to the basement, take a left at the first hallway, and go almost to the end, you'll find his office."

While telling Betsy "Thank you," I regretted not asking Keith if he knew where Craig's office was. I could have saved time and energy by not running up to the journalism office, but since I was here, I decided not to waste the opportunity to question Betsy.

"How is Professor Ladd's husband doing...with his wife's death and all?"

Betsy raised her eyebrows and took a step back from the counter. "How would I know? I'm sure he's devastated."

She spun around and returned to her desk, where she resumed typing. The steady beat of the typewriter played in the background as I closed the door behind me.

I tugged T.J.'s arm and pulled him toward the stairway. "The strangest thing just happened. I asked Betsy about Professor Ladd's husband, and she got really defensive. She acted like she barely knew him."

"That doesn't jive with what Amy said at all."

I bit my bottom lip. "Betsy's hiding something."

T.J. and I retraced our steps to the basement and found our way to Craig's office. With T.J. close by my side, I timidly knocked on the closed door. Nothing. I knocked harder and held my breath as I relived what happened the last time someone didn't respond to my knock. *Not again. Please, not another dead body!*

"Come in."

As much as I didn't relish meeting with Craig, I was glad he was alive. I opened the door. He was sitting behind his desk, and to my surprise, Detective Douglas was sitting across from him in a gray metal fold-up chair.

"I…I can come back later," I stammered while two of my least favorite people stared at me.

The detective rose from his seat. "No, I'm finished here." He turned to Craig and repeated the words all too familiar to me. "Don't leave town. I'll be in touch." He walked past me without saying a word, closing the door behind him.

Well, that didn't go like I had planned. I was going to leave that door cracked open so T.J. could listen. Now what do I do?. "If now is a bad time—"

"Sit down," Craig ordered.

I walked over to the metal chair and hesitantly took my seat.

With clenched jaw and furrowed brows, he said, "We need to talk. Did you tell Detective Douglas I had a letter from Anne about the Peterson Lumber Company?"

I wanted to deny it and say, "No," but I'd be lying, and I knew the truth would come out at some point, so I sat there and said nothing.

"It *was* you, wasn't it?" His ears began turning red. "So... when you helped me pick up the papers yesterday, you kept one of them for yourself. *Really?* And then you go to the police and accuse me of murder? Why didn't you come to talk to me first?" He rose from his chair. His six-foot frame hovered over his desk. "You have no idea what you've done!"

"What *I've* done? You're the one who killed her!" There, I said it. I had no proof—I wasn't even sure it was true—but the words were out, and there was no going back.

"You honestly think I killed her?"

I nodded. "You had the opportunity and—"

"—and what? Motive? Tell me, Sherlock, what was my motive?"

"I don't know, but it's a little suspicious that you had this letter." I pulled my copy of the letter out of my purse and laid it on his desk. "And you can't deny you were in a mighty big hurry coming from the direction of Professor Ladd's office." I paused, trying to put my thoughts together while thinking about the tactic Perry Mason would use to get the guilty party to confess.

I grabbed my purse and books and jumped to my feet, ready to defend myself in case he attacked me. "You shot her in cold blood, and you were running away from the scene of the crime. And...and don't even think about shooting me. I've got help right outside that door, and plenty of people know I came here to talk to you."

"Sit down, Michelle. Honestly, have you ever thought about writing fiction? You've got a real gift of imagination... misguided, but..." He rubbed the side of his head and sat down.

"Relax. I didn't kill Anne. I'll tell you what I told Detective Douglas," he said calmly, with an undeniable look of sincerity.

Why does he keep calling her Anne? Is it a grad student thing, or is it because they had something going on?

"Michelle?"

"Yes, go on, I'm listening. How did you get that letter?" I sat down with my purse and books in hand, ready to make a quick getaway or throw something at him, whichever I needed to do. T.J. would come to my rescue if I made enough noise.

"Anne had me make a copy of the letter she sent to the lumber company. Pure and simple."

"Why would she want you to have it?"

Craig leaned back in his office chair and took a deep breath. "Anne was investigating the Peterson Lumber Company. She suspected there were some things not quite on the up-and-up with the finances. She didn't want me involved with the investigation, but wanted me to be aware of the letter."

As he talked, I became so distracted by his intense green eyes I had to look away so I could concentrate on what he was saying. I studied his office, trying to gain insight into the man who sat behind the desk. A row of plants neatly arranged in groups of three sat on a shelf by the window. A bookcase, featuring stacks of books piled as high as the shelf would accommodate, was to the left of his desk. I couldn't make out all the titles, but two of them were plain enough to read—*The History of Petersburg, Ohio* and *The Petersons and Other Notable Families of Petersburg, Ohio*. More books were behind him, but my roaming eyes stopped when they locked with his.

"Why is it again she wanted you involved?"

"In case something happened to her. She had a funny feeling, and considering what happened, I should have asked more questions." He looked down at his desk. "I wish we had had more time together."

More time together? Is he talking about their affair?

Craig continued. "In the beginning, Anne and I were working on a mysterious death that occurred in this area several years ago. She thought my expertise in researching crimes for my novels would prove beneficial. But when she found the discrepancies with the lumber company's finances, she felt she needed to put all her energy into that for the time being."

He stood up and walked to the front of his desk, where he sat down. "The plan was for me to work on the mystery alone and to meet with her to discuss what I had found. She didn't tell me much about the lumber company. I'm actually surprised she even showed me this letter." He held it in the air.

"The whole thing sounds complicated." I shrugged, sensing there was more to the story.

Craig crossed his arms. "Anne and I didn't want anyone to know we were working together. But, thanks to you, I had to fill the detective in on our work."

"Sorry I jumped the gun. I should have talked to you first."

An awkward silence followed. I shifted in my seat as I tried to think about how to change the subject. "Are you still going to be in class tomorrow? I mean, now that Professor Ladd is..." I couldn't bring myself to say the word *dead*.

He looked puzzled. "Of course, I will. I still have my research to do for my book; that hasn't changed. Why?" He paused. "Oh, the pairing for the class project. Guess that would mess things up if I quit now. I assume whoever they find to teach the class will keep the final project as assigned. Don't worry. I won't leave you stranded."

That wasn't exactly the answer I was hoping to hear. If Craig dropped the class, that would solve one of my problems. I could get a new partner or do the project by myself. Either way was better than having to work with him.

Craig continued. "Since we're a team, I guess we better figure out a time to get started on our project, but—" he glanced at his watch, "—I've got a class to teach in ten minutes, so I need to get going." He thought for a moment. "Would you have time to meet after our class tomorrow? Maybe we can grab a bite to eat and figure out our game plan."

Meeting with Craig again was the last thing I wanted to do, but before I could think of an excuse, I replied, "Sure, tomorrow will be fine."

As I closed the door behind me, my heart sank. *Did I just agree to work with Craig Miller? What was I thinking?*

T.J. jumped up off the floor when I came out of Craig's office. "How'd it go? Did you find out anything?"

"Not much. I couldn't believe Detective Douglas was sitting there when I walked into the room."

"Talk about bad timing. I couldn't hear anything when he closed that door. Do you know what he wanted with Craig?"

"I think to find out why he had the letter and how he got it. Craig was pretty miffed with me for going to the police before talking to him."

"Did Detective Douglas tell him you were the one who gave him the paper?"

I shrugged. "Either Douglas told him, or he gave Craig enough info to put two and two together and figure it out. Anyway, he asked me if it was me, and I told him it was."

"That's a bummer."

Neither of us said a word until we reached the landing at the top of the stairs. T.J. held the door open. "Did you find out why he had the letter from the professor?"

"He said he and Professor Ladd were working on some project together and that he explained everything to Detective Douglas."

"Anything else?" T.J. prodded.

"Yeah, we're meeting tomorrow after class to work on our class project."

"That'll be the perfect cover for finding out more about this guy, but you've got to be careful!"

"Don't worry, I will." I pulled my sleeve up and glanced at my watch. "Guess it's time for class already. One more, and we're done for the day. See you in a little bit!" I smiled, but secretly wondered what I had gotten myself into and if I could find my way out.

chapter eight

"You're awfully quiet tonight."

I looked up from my plate and met my mother's eyes, staring at me. She cocked her head, waiting for my answer.

"Guess I've got a lot on my mind, that's all." I took a bite of macaroni and cheese.

"Did you see that detective today? How did it go?"

My father interrupted. "What detective? Are you in trouble?" From the tone of his voice, I knew he assumed I was in the wrong, even before hearing my answer.

My mother placed her hand on his and calmly explained, "You remember, I told you last night Michelle found that professor dead in her office. No need to get so upset."

He frowned and then yelled, "Are you going to answer your mother? What did he say?"

"N-Nothing," I stammered. "He wanted to go over what happened yesterday, that's all."

I put my fork down. I wasn't hungry anymore.

Mom placed another serving of broccoli on her plate. "Well, I'm glad your meeting went okay. Hopefully, that will be the end of that." She sounded relieved. "Do you want any more broccoli?"

I shook my head.

She sipped her coffee and glanced at the clock on the wall. "Your father and I are going to your sister's house tonight. I guess I better hurry and get this kitchen cleaned up, so we're not late."

I got up from my chair and helped her clear the table. As she took the last dish to the sink, she turned back toward my father. "It won't take me but a minute, and I'll be ready."

Although I always helped her with the dishes when I was home, tonight I had an ulterior motive. The sooner they were gone, the sooner I would have some peace and quiet.

"If you want to get going, I can do the dishes," I volunteered.

"Thank you. That would really help."

Within a few minutes, my mom and dad were out the door and on their way to my sister's house to watch *The Waltons* on her new color TV. I smiled, remembering the night Dad brought our color TV home about seven years ago, and I watched *The Monkees* in color for the very first time. Man, did I think I had arrived!

According to my calculations, Mom and Dad would be gone until at least 10:00. Dad wouldn't want to miss one minute of *The Nights of San Francisco*, which came on at 9:00, so he'd most likely watch it there.

With the house to myself, I turned on the radio—louder than I dared when my parents were home, and glided across the floor with some pretty smooth dance moves mixed in with a bit of air guitar to Aerosmith's "Dream On." For the first time since the horrible nightmare of finding Professor Ladd's body began, I felt free, and by the time I finished my air guitar duet with Three Dog Night's "Shambala," I was ready to get to work.

I sat at the kitchen table and brainstormed ideas for my news story that would, hopefully, lead to catching Professor Ladd's murderer. After several minutes, I remembered there was a piece of poster board in the basement. I found it buried under a pile of fabric my mom had set aside for making a quilt with her ladies' group at church. Once upstairs, I laid the poster board on the kitchen table, and with a black marker from the junk drawer, wrote the names of everyone I thought might have a motive for killing Professor Ladd in bold black letters—Craig, Betsy, Burt Ladd, Steve Goodright, the lumber company's bookkeeper and/or accountant. Who else might it be? Another professor? What about Mae? The sisters didn't get along, but were their differences enough to result in murder? I added the headings of Another Professor and Mae to my board. What about a student who was upset with their grades?

When I finished writing Disgruntled Student, I cringed, realizing my name would be listed under that heading if Detective Douglas had such a list. However, I had one advantage over him—I knew I wasn't the killer.

Even though the medical examiner's official cause and time of death would be helpful, I didn't need his findings to get started. I knew Professor Ladd was alive when I went by her office Monday afternoon around 1:30 p.m. and that she was dead when I found her at 9:00 a.m. the following day. I made a notation to find out where all my suspects were during that time frame.

Next, I emptied the contents of the envelope Keith had given me onto the kitchen table. There was a copy of a loan application Steve had submitted recently, and several photos of Steve, Barb, Bob, and Mae taken by a private detective Professor Ladd had hired. His report included a timeline for their activities during August and September. I spread the pictures out and studied each one. An old black-and-white photo caught my attention. The woman looked like a young Professor Ladd in the arms of a man who looked nothing like Burt Ladd.

* * *

Thursday, October 17th

I slowly opened my eyes and wondered why I had set my alarm to go off earlier than usual. It was only 6:45. I didn't recognize the song playing on the radio, but then again, I'm not sure I could recognize anything playing that early in the morning. Gidget raised her head in disgust, glared at the clock radio, and then glared at me. I rolled over and turned the radio off; I wasn't feeling the Thursday love. The only thing I felt was the need for more sleep. Gidget concurred and, refusing to take the wake-up call seriously, lowered her head onto her front paws, and went back to sleep at the foot of my bed.

My gaze fell on my vanity, and I suddenly remembered why I'd wanted that extra thirty minutes this morning. Before my parents got home last night, I had gone to my room and worked undisturbed late into the night. By 1:00 a.m., I knew my list of questions would probably not make sense in the morning, so I decided to get up early and revise them before I started my interviews that day.

Sitting up in bed, I reached for the radio and turned it back on just as "Takin' Care of Business" by Bachman-Turner Overdrive started playing. *How à propos!* I chuckled. As I maneuvered out of bed so as not to disturb Gidget, I slid my feet into my pink fuzzy slippers and walked over to my vanity.

I tugged the dainty gold handle on the vanity drawer. At first, it wouldn't open, so I jiggled it a few times. The change of seasons always made the drawers act quirky. Frustrating, but manageable. One more firm tug, and it slid open. After pulling out three pens, I gingerly closed the drawer, not pushing it in all the way, hoping it would be easier to open the next time. I read through my notes, added a few thoughts, and fought the urge to lay my head down and go back to sleep.

With my task completed, I chose an outfit that would have made Professor Ladd proud—black slacks and a white shirt topped with a black cardigan. *Perfect!* With enough pens in my purse to make even Craig Miller smile, I turned my thoughts to breakfast.

When I walked into the kitchen, my mom was finishing washing the breakfast dishes. "You just missed your father. He wanted to get an early start in the orchard."

Mike, not as eager as my father to get to work, had stayed behind to finish his breakfast at a leisurely pace. "Hope you're not too hungry," he said. "Dad ate almost everything in the kitchen."

"Oh, he did not." Mom laughed.

"Really? He had three fried eggs, four pieces of bacon, and two buttermilk biscuits just since I got here. And he was already eating when I walked through the door." Mike smiled. He took a long sip of his coffee and turned back to *The Today Show* on the small black-and-white TV perched on the bookcase in the corner.

My brother and sister lived on either side of my parents' house. Dad gave each of them a five-acre plot when they got married. The family joke was, if I ever got married, the only land left for Dad to give me would be five acres in the back forty, far away from everybody.

When a commercial came on, Mike peered at me over the rim of his cup. "So, how is my favorite kid sister?"

"You know, living the life," I answered, laughing.

With narrowed eyes, he put his cup down on the table. "What's the lowdown on you finding your dead professor? I hear the police are asking you all sorts of questions?"

Mom stopped putting the dishes away and turned her head so she could hear my answer.

"It's all cool. He just had a few questions." I took a biscuit off the platter on the table, sliced it, and drizzled some honey on the two halves.

Mom put her dishtowel down and crossed her arms across her chest. "I can't believe anyone would think you had something to do with Anne's murder."

"I know. I only hope Detective Douglas can find the killer soon. It makes me nervous knowing there's a murderer out there running free. Oh, don't forget I have to work tonight, so I won't be home until late."

"You be careful when you walk to your car after work tonight. Make sure you park under a light and—" she paused, "—check that no one is following you."

"I'll be careful, Mom. Don't worry."

I gave Mike a hug. "I wish I could stay and talk. I never get to see you anymore, but it's my morning to drive, and T.J.'s probably already outside his house waiting for me." I stopped in the doorway. "I hope you guys can finish with the orchard today. I heard you still have a lot to do."

Mike nodded and smiled. "Fingers crossed."

Mom picked up Mike's empty plate and turned toward me. "I will be so glad when you're done with school, and you have time for your family again."

"Mom, give her a break." Mike winked and waved. "Bye, sis, have a good one!"

T.J., always dependable, was waiting for me when I pulled into his driveway. After he buckled up, I put the car in reverse and backed up toward the street.

He looked over his shoulder for oncoming traffic and asked, "So, what's the plan for today?"

"Don't trust me to check for cars?" I laughed before answering his question. "First, I'm gonna ask around and see if there was anyone on campus who had a beef with Professor Ladd—a student, another professor, or even a janitor, who knows?"

"That could be a mighty long list." He grinned. "How are you going to get all those people to talk?"

"Trrrrust me, I have my *vays*." I squinted my eyes, trying to look sinister.

T.J. rolled his eyes while shaking his head. "Why do I have a bad feeling you're going to get in over your head?"

"I don't know what you mean." I laughed. "Just because I'm meeting with a probable murderer and planning on extracting valuable information from him, all the while not letting him know what I'm up to—I don't know what you're worried about."

"That's exactly what I am worried about."

"I'll be fine." I looked at T.J. and smiled, but I knew he didn't believe me. "Honestly, it'll be okay. Hey, were you able to get a hold of Yash last night?

"Sure did. He's going to ask around today and see what he can find out about the finances at the lumber company. He said he's pretty good friends with the bookkeeper. Word is she's been trying to match him up with her daughter."

"Typical Yash. He knows how to turn on the charm, especially with older women, right?"

T.J. shook his head. "Yeah, I don't get it."

"I think when he looks at them with those big brown eyes and flashes that smile of his, he looks so innocent. They'd do anything to help him. I mean, you've seen him with Alice. He can get away with things like no one else can."

"He definitely has a way about him."

We laughed. The Yash we knew was anything but innocent. His parents had arranged a marriage for him after he graduated. But for now, he was a free man, dating two girls at the same time—both of whom thought they were in an exclusive relationship with him. He could drink most people under the table, which he often did. Despite all his rather wild tendencies, he was a good friend and a hard worker. If there was dirt to be found at the Peterson Lumber Company, I knew Yash would find it.

I turned into the commuter lot, and a parking spot was right in front of me. What an unexpectantly nice way to start the day! I crossed my fingers that the rest of the day would go as smoothly.

T.J. released his seat belt and grabbed the door handle. "If you're right that Steve Goodright is having financial problems, I think he's your man. He's probably been embezzling money from the lumber company and was angry with Professor Ladd for looking into it."

"I've thought about that, but I'm just not sure Steve had the opportunity." I opened my car door and looked back at T.J. "But I need to consider him, and let's not forget Professor Ladd's husband. If he thought she and Craig were having an affair, it could have been a crime of passion."

T.J.'s eyes twinkled with the possibilities. "We've got two solid suspects with motives. Not bad! And, if either one was with her that morning, we might have our killer and—" he did a drum roll on the top of my car, "—case solved." He beamed at the prospect of quickly bringing the mystery to an end.

I nodded. "I need to find out whether Betsy or Craig saw Professor Ladd that morning. Maybe one of them saw someone lurking around her office."

"You mean, besides you?" he teased.

"Definitely besides me," I replied.

* * *

As I walked into my investigative journalism class for the first time since the murder, Professor Ladd's absence eerily filled the room and reinforced my desire not to be there. Apparently, I wasn't the only one. Most of the seats were empty.

I sat at my desk in the back and watched as a few dedicated students straggled into the room. Professor Martin, the head of the photojournalism department, paced back and forth behind what had been Professor Ladd's desk. He waited ten minutes before starting class and spent the time alternating between running his fingers through his silver-gray handlebar mustache and checking his watch.

Once he began class, he asked the ten of us scattered about the room to move to the first two rows. Craig quickly took the seat closest to the window in the front row. I went to the opposite side of the room and sat in the second row so I could keep an eye on him. He must have felt me staring at him because he turned and we locked eyes for a moment before I turned away.

Homewrecker! I thought about Keith mentioning the rumor that Professor Ladd and Craig were romantically involved. *Was he responsible for the fight between the professor and her husband?* I wanted him to feel my disgust, but I fought the urge to stare at him. He wasn't worth my time or energy at the moment.

Professor Martin told us he didn't know who would be teaching our class for the rest of the quarter, but we would have a permanent professor starting next week. "There may be some changes to the assignments and readings listed on your syllabus, but no new books will be required. Dean Brown has decided the final project will remain the same, allowing you to get started on it without delay."

The professor pulled out the chair where Professor Ladd once sat and looked like he was going to sit down. Instead, he pushed it back under the desk.

After an awkward silence, he walked to the front of the desk. "Professor Ladd's death has been a shock to all of us. But the police are using all their resources to find the killer. The *Wildcats' Daily News* will post all updates."

For the next sixty minutes, Professor Martin shared his expertise in photojournalism. He argued it was the most essential branch of journalism, because it reflected reality and was unbiased.

I'd recently read an article about using creative darkroom techniques to manipulate images. My hand shot up. "Professor Martin, what about the ability to alter photos in the darkroom?"

He gave his mustache a few turns. "Manipulating photography has no place in the world of journalism. That is for art and art alone."

Maybe, but that didn't change the fact that photography was changing. So much could be done with a negative in the darkroom. Even with my limited darkroom experience, I could create an alternate reality. A few other contradictions to Professor Martin's premise that photojournalism was without bias crossed my mind, but I decided one confrontation per class was enough, just in case he ended up teaching our class longer than expected.

After our class ended, I waited in the hallway for Craig. I counted eight students as they left the room, but Craig was not among them. *Where is he?*

I headed back toward the classroom, but as I grew closer to the door, an arm stretched out, grabbed the handle, and pulled the door closed. More curious than ever, I positioned myself against the wall in the hallway so I could look through the window into the room.

Craig and Professor Martin appeared to be having a rather intense conversation. The professor stood with his arms crossed, jaw clenched, and brows furrowed. Although I could only see Craig's back, I watched as his posture grew more rigid the longer they talked.

Suddenly, Craig threw his hands up and turned to leave. With catlike reflexes, I moved further down the hallway, sat down, pulled out my notes from the class, and pretended to be reading.

chapter nine

Craig looked down the hallway both directions until he spotted me. "Are you ready to go?" He sounded agitated.

I took a deep breath and nodded, not knowing what to expect.

"Where do you want to eat?" he asked.

"Wherever you want is fine with me." I gathered my belongings as he scowled at my answer. "I mean, if today is a bad day, we can do it some other time."

"No, today is as good as any." He shrugged. Craig set his briefcase on the floor, took his glasses off, and put them in his inner blazer pocket. "How 'bout Giovanni's for pizza?" He attempted a smile as he picked up the briefcase.

"Yeah, sure, sounds good," I said, but I wondered if agreeing to have lunch with a murder suspect was a wise decision. Then again, I was also a suspect, so I supposed we were both in the same situation. At least we were eating in a busy restaurant. No harm should come to me there, I reasoned. Besides, sometimes, a reporter has to take risks to get a story, and I had a lot of questions I needed him to answer.

As the chilly autumn air blew against my face, my black cardigan added a layer of warmth under my jacket. Craig, however, did not fare so well with his oxford shirt and tweed blazer. He shivered and rubbed his hands together. *I would have thought a New Yorker would be used to the wind.* Mae often complained about the wind tunnels she'd encountered in NYC. Of course, she also complained about the rats running back and forth down the sidewalk. Although she loved shopping in New York, she claimed she would never want to live there. Things like people yelling at anyone they thought was walking too slowly on the sidewalk got on her nerves. She said people in the city were always in such a hurry that it made her appreciate Petersburg, where life was slow, and a traffic jam was sitting through two lights.

From the look on Craig's face as we walked into town, I doubted he would agree with Mae. I imagined he missed life in the Big Apple. He looked in the store windows, but nothing caught his attention. *I wonder what he thinks of small-town living.*

As if he read my mind, he asked, "So, what do people do around here for fun?"

"Go to the movies or to the mall," I said, struggling to think of what it was we did for fun. As ideas popped into my head, I blurted them out. "Going out to eat and watching the Toledo Mud Hens play baseball. Of course, that's in Maumee. Does that still count?" I laughed. "Then there's Ann Arbor, it's not too far away, and they've got Big 10 Football. And in Toledo in the fall, there are festivals like the German-American Festival and the Greek Festival. Oh, and the county fair, which is practically in our own backyard."

"Uh-huh." He shrugged.

"Of course, Toledo has a nice art museum, and there is always the zoo." I wanted to tell him about more things to do, but he didn't seem to be listening anymore. "What do you like to do in New York?"

His eyes lit up. "I enjoy going to plays."

"Broadway?"

"Yeah, and Off-Broadway."

"When you say Off-Broadway, does that mean the play hasn't made it to Broadway yet, or does it mean something different?"

For the first time since class ended, he relaxed and laughed. "Off-Broadway refers to the size of the theater in the city. It has nothing to do with the location." He had my undivided attention. I had never been to NYC, but I hoped to go there someday. "Off-Broadway is any theater that seats between 99 and 499 people. If it seats more, it's Broadway. And yes—" he smiled, anticipating my next question, "—every so often, an Off-Broadway play will get produced on Broadway."

When I heard footsteps behind us growing louder, I turned and saw a guy wearing a sweatshirt with the University of Petersburg on the front. He was quickly gaining on us. As he passed by, his backpack bumped into Craig, knocking him off balance.

Instead of being annoyed, Craig smiled. "Now I feel like I'm home."

"You have a pleasant smile. You should use it more often." I blushed, realizing what I'd said and how it must have sounded. "I mean, with everything that's happened, it's good to…uh…"

"To enjoy life?" He finished my thought. "Yeah, life is too short to waste by dwelling on all the bad stuff."

The waitress at Giovanni's Pizza led us to a booth in the back. Everyone in town knew their Supreme Pizza was the best around, so we didn't even need to look at the menu. Soon after taking our drink order, she returned with a diet soft drink for me and an iced tea for Craig. Our conversation turned to the business at hand while waiting for our pizza.

He began. "When I talked to Professor Martin after class today, he said we have to keep our partner assignments for the final project. It's not ideal, but that's how it is."

Taken aback, I asked, "Did you ask him if you could change partners?" It was one thing if *I* wanted to change partners, but how insulting to think he didn't want to work with me.

"There is the small matter of you thinking I killed Anne. That doesn't bode well for a productive working relationship, does it? I don't mean to be blunt, but it's not fair to either of us to be teamed together to work on the project. Let's face it, I have more experience than you, so it would only seem natural for you to defer much of the work to me." He leaned back on the red plastic bench. "You wouldn't get the experience you need, and I would have to spend time double-checking everything you did."

"Well, excuse me if I'm such a burden to you." Crossing my arms, I sank into my seat.

"Don't take it so personally."

I sat straight up. "So, why did you invite me to lunch today if you didn't want to work with me on the project?"

He shrugged. "Since you don't trust me, I thought the news about getting a new partner would make you happy, and then we could celebrate."

I started to answer, but our waitress appeared with fresh drinks, despite our glasses being only half empty, so I held my words. She placed the red plastic glasses on the table and then left to take the order from the table across from us.

I pulled the paper off my straw. "I told you I was sorry I didn't talk to you first. But you gotta admit it did look a little suspicious that you had a copy of the letter Professor Ladd was sending to the Peterson Lumber Company board."

"On the surface, yes, but, as I explained to you and the police, Anne and I were doing research. Nothing more and nothing less."

I blurted out, "Well, that's not what I heard."

He set his drink down with a thud and leaned on the table. "And what exactly have you heard?"

"That you and Professor Ladd were having an affair. How could you? She was married."

He looked into my eyes. "Are you finished? First, you thought I killed her, and now you think I was having an affair with her? Anything else in that creative mind of yours?"

"Actually, there's a lot more—" I stopped as the waitress placed our plates in front of us.

"Here's your pizza. Watch the pan. It's hot." She flashed a mandatory smile before pivoting around. I sensed she knew she had walked into a heated discussion and was eager to get away from our table.

As soon as she was out of earshot, I continued. "Well, were you? *Were* you having an affair with Professor Ladd? Not only was she married, but, man, she was old enough to be your—"

"Mother?" He calmly picked up his pizza and took a bite.

"Yes." I nodded my head in disgust. How could he sit there and eat his pizza as if nothing wrong had happened? *Disgusting!*

"Do you think I'm Dustin Hoffman in *The Graduate?*" He set his pizza back on his plate. "But to answer your question, no, I was most certainly not having an affair with Anne. She contacted me last spring to see if I would be interested in helping her work on that mysterious death I told you about, and it intrigued me. Anne knew I wanted to get my MFA, so she pulled a few strings and got me into the program at UP in the fall. It was a win-win. I could work on my MFA and my book, while being close to the sources I needed for doing the research for our project."

"No offense, but why you?"

"Now that's a weird story." He took a bite of his pizza and then leaned back in his seat. "It seems Anne took her car into Bob's Auto Repair shop one day. He used to be the chauffeur for her father. Anyway, he had *The Today Show* on in his office, and it was the day I was being interviewed by Barbara

Walters. The amount of research I do for my books impressed Anne, so she took a chance and contacted me."

"And that's all it took?"

"I guess she got me on a good day." He smiled.

"So, nothing was going on between you two, just a working relationship?"

He stared at his pizza for a few moments. "That's all it was, simply one writer helping another writer. I only wish there had been more time to become better acquainted with her. She was a fascinating person."

I cupped my chin in my hand as I leaned on the table. "Did her husband know nothing was going on between the two of you?"

"Anne told him, but I'm not sure he believed her." He paused. "She didn't want to tell him too much about the case we were working on. She didn't want to put his life in danger."

"What about yours? Wasn't she worried about your life being in danger?" I picked up my glass of diet pop to take a sip, only to discover it was empty.

"She was, but it was a risk I was willing to take," he answered without hesitating.

"Why?" None of this was making any sense to me.

"Let's just say I had my reasons."

I shook my head as I picked up my pizza. "You're not going to tell me, are you?"

He smiled. "You catch on quickly. There might be hope for you after all."

I put my slice of pizza down and stared at him. "I'll let it drop for now, but you're not off the hook."

"Understood."

I took a deep breath. "Do you think someone killed Professor Ladd because she was looking into this case?"

"I don't know." He shook his head and looked down at the remaining slice of pizza on his plate.

"What about the missing money at the lumber company? Do you think that connects to her murder?"

Craig said nothing.

"You do, don't you?" I asked again, convinced I was onto something.

"I'm not sure."

"How did Professor Ladd find out about the missing money?"

"Anne's father started the Peterson Lumber Company. He assumed he had no male heir, so when he died, he left it to his sister's son, Steve Goodright. Anne received a sizable share of the company in his will, but he left nothing to his other daughter, Mae."

"You know Mae is my boss, right?"

"Yes, Anne told me."

I shook my head in disbelief. "How'd she know that? What did she do? Have me investigated?"

"No, Anne said you mentioned it in the bio you turned in at the beginning of class. Remember?"

I sighed. "I guess so…vaguely."

He looked at me. "Can I go on now?"

I nodded. "Sure."

Our waitress placed a fresh glass of pop in front of me and refilled Craig's iced tea. She left quickly, without saying a word. I smiled, surmising she didn't want to risk interrupting our argument again.

Craig took a sip of his tea and continued. "While investigating Anthony Romano's death—that's the guy who mysteriously died—Anne came across information about the lumber company that led her to believe someone was embezzling funds. She hired an independent accountant to go over the books and discovered her hunch was correct."

"That's why the letter to the board of the lumber company," I said, thankful that at least that much was making sense.

"Yes. The morning you bumped into me—"

"I believe it was the other way around," I corrected him.

"Okay, maybe it was me who bumped into you. The thing was, I had met with Anne earlier that morning. She gave me a stack of papers to go through—copies of old newspaper articles, police reports, and a copy of the letter she was sending the board."

"That explains why you had the papers, but why were you in such a hurry? You were practically running when we collided." I leaned closer to him over the table.

"I'd been in the office, making copies of Anne's papers. Actually, I made two copies of everything."

"Two copies?" I asked, puzzled.

"Yes, I…I have a nasty habit of eating or drinking coffee while writing, which can make for some messy papers." He smiled. "Anne made me promise to make two copies of everything, so at least one would be clean."

I nodded, holding back a grin as I pulled out my pen and notebook from my purse. Mr. Perfect had a flaw.

"After making the copies, Anne and I walked back to her office and talked for a few minutes. I was at the gym by 7:30, worked out, and was back in my office by 8:40. Are you taking notes? Make sure you get my alibi right." He grinned.

"I just don't want to forget anything, okay?"

"Sure, Sherlock. Anyway, where were we?"

"Back in your office around 8:40 a.m.," I said, reading my notes.

"Yes…I realized I'd left my copies in the journalism office, so I ran up to get them before a meeting I had with a student at 9:00."

"Was Betsy in the office both times you were there?"

"Yes and no. When Anne and I went into the office the first time, she wasn't at her desk, but after we started the copy machine, she came out of Dean Brown's office. She said she had been getting things ready for him before he came in that afternoon." He thought for a moment. "The second time, I met her in the hallway. I had just come up the front stairs, and she was coming from the direction of the restroom. She said she had spilled coffee on her skirt and had been trying to wash it out. We didn't talk very long. She was upset, and I was in a hurry." He shrugged. "I went into the office, got my papers, and left. That's when I ran into you."

Our conversation stopped as our waitress refilled our water glasses.

As soon as she left, Craig looked sternly at me. "Now, let me ask you a question. Why were you outside Anne's office that morning?"

I bit my bottom lip. "I wanted to talk to her about my grades, because I thought they should have been higher."

"You and a half dozen other people. When did you get to her office?"

"Like I told the police, around 8:35."

"That matches what Betsy said. See, I already checked you out." He raised his eyebrows. "Word is that you were quite upset with Anne."

"Sure I was, but I didn't kill her."

"It's not fun being a suspect, is it?"

"No, it's horrible."

"I agree. But since we have to work together, maybe we can clear our names in the process. It could be a coincidence, but what if there is a connection between the missing money, Romano's death, and Anne's murder? I don't think we can rule any of it out. I owe it to her to get to the truth in both matters. If you're up to it, we can use our final project to investigate the Romano death." He paused a moment and looked pensive. "That was Anne's plan and why she paired us together. I told her I didn't think it was a good idea, but she insisted you would be trustworthy and that you would be an excellent researcher. I'm still not convinced it'll work, but if Anne thought you were up to it, and considering I have no choice in the matter, I'm willing to at least give our partnership a try."

"Wait, Professor Ladd thought I could do something *well*?" I leaned back in my seat, and crossed my arms, bearing down on the cushion. "You'd never know it from the way she graded me."

"That's because she wanted to challenge you, that's all. Regardless, I still think it's too risky for you to get involved. But since Professor Martin won't change his mind, if you still want to do it, I guess I'm stuck with you."

"For a successful author, you sure have a way with words," I said, disgusted with his arrogance. "And for your information, I can take care of myself, and I most definitely will *not* slow you down."

He took a sip of water and set the glass on the table. "Good, because my agent is hounding me for the first draft of my next book, and there is still research that needs to be done for the Romano case. I could get it done by myself, but if you're willing to help—"

"I said I was."

"Okay." He gazed into the distance, but his eyes returned to mine after a few moments. "The problem is, with Anne's murder, I don't know how much time we have to get our answers. Every day her killer roams free is a day someone else could get hurt or worse. Plus...until the police catch them, we are at the top of the suspects' list." He frowned. "We've got two cases to solve. More help would be nice, but I'm not sure who I can trust."

"If it's more help you need, that's easy. I have some friends who would be more than happy to help."

He looked at me with narrowed eyes.

"And yes, they are trustworthy." I almost added that I already had a few of them gathering information but decided he didn't need to know everything.

He raised his glass, stopping before taking a sip. "If your friends want to help, that might work."

As I studied Craig's face, my gut feeling told me he had a few secrets of his own he hadn't shared that might be important to our research.

"Are there any other secrets I should know about?" I asked.

He smiled and picked up the last piece of pizza from the platter.

chapter ten

As I approached Mae's Gift Shop, I was shocked to see two police cars pulling away. I quickly parked my car in the back lot, gathered my purse and books, and dashed to the front entrance. Mae stood by the counter, staring at the floor and wringing her hands.

"Are you okay?"

"I don't understand," she muttered. "I don't understand what just happened."

"What? Were you robbed?"

She shook her head. "No, I wish I had been. It'd be better than this."

I took her by the arm and led her to a stool behind the counter. "Here, why don't you sit down? Can I get you something?"

"I think I need to call my lawyer."

"What in the world happened?"

Mae looked at me, and at first said nothing. Finally, she took a deep breath. "The police had a search warrant. They took the gun I kept in the safe in the back room."

"You had a gun in the safe?"

"A small revolver. I keep it for when I'm here alone after closing."

"Did anyone know you had a gun in the back room?"

Mae looked dazed. "I don't think I ever told anybody… but I must have told someone. The police had a warrant to search the back room and the safe. Nothing else." She paused and shook her head. "What am I going to do?"

"Did you shoot Professor Ladd?"

"No, of course not. Just because I wanted nothing to do with her doesn't mean I wanted her dead. She was still my sister."

"I'm sorry, but I had to ask." I took her hand. "If you didn't shoot her, you have nothing to worry about."

"No, you don't understand. Somebody knew about my gun and told the police about it. What if someone's trying to frame me for Anne's murder?"

She had a point. "I guess you should call a lawyer, just to be on the safe side. You said you have one?"

"Yes, he's the son of a friend of mine."

I looked at the phone sitting on the counter. It was the only one in the store and, I surmised, not the best place from which to call her lawyer. A quick look around the store revealed there weren't any customers at the moment, but Mae didn't need to risk anyone coming in and overhearing her conversation.

"Is there someone I can call who can take you home? Then you can give your lawyer a call."

She suggested Barb Goodright, and within thirty minutes, she was there to take Mae home. Barb assured me she would help Mae get in touch with her lawyer and stay with her as long as Mae needed her.

After they left, I felt emotionally drained and collapsed on the stool. The adrenaline rush I had while helping Mae was gone, but I knew I needed to pull myself together and keep the store running. Between customers, I kept my mind occupied by restocking the greeting card racks and dusting the front displays, but I couldn't help wondering if Mae could be the killer...or had someone set her up?

I looked out the storefront window, and my spirits lifted when I saw Yash walking across the street toward the store. Mae disapproved of her staff talking to friends while on the clock, but Mae wasn't here, and the store was empty. Perfect!

As Yash pulled open the glass door, his wavy dark hair fell across his brow. He brushed it off to one side, revealing his large, dark eyes. With eyes like that and a huge smile, it was no wonder women swooned over him.

"Hi, Yash! How you doin'?"

"Doing good, sexy lady." Yash flashed a flirtatious smile. "How about you?"

There's nothing like a good-looking guy flirting with you to make you forget all your troubles. He looked like he'd stepped off the cover of a fashion magazine in his mono-chrome ensemble—a brown-toned multicolored sweater vest over a brown oxford shirt and tie, all topped with a brown tweed overcoat.

"What are you doing here? It's Thursday night...party time."

"It's always time to party." He grinned. "But tonight, I thought seeing you was more important. Besides, I can hit one or two after I leave here. The night's still young." His mischievous eyes twinkled. "I got some information from my friend in bookkeeping today, and—" he glanced around, "—is it okay if we talk?"

"Yeah, actually, it's a great time. Mae's gone, and—" as I looked at the round security mirrors mounted in the corners of the store, they confirmed what I already knew, "—the store's empty. What's up?"

He moved closer, and a whiff of his cologne teased my nostrils.

"The bookkeeper told me Steve has been buying supplies

for the lumber company at Mae's Gift Shop for the past three years."

"That's strange." I wrinkled my forehead. "What supplies would he get here?"

"Exactly. That's what she thought too. Steve gives her a bill from Mae's every month, but nothing is itemized. She didn't want to rock the boat and risk losing her job, so she didn't press the issue with him and just wrote the checks and mailed them to Mae."

"Do you know how much the checks were for?"

"She said they're always for the same amount, $1000. Except for one check. About four months ago, it was for $4000."

"That's a lot of supplies," I said in disbelief. I mulled the timeline around in my head. In June, Mae always went to the Chicago Gift Mart to place her Christmas and holiday order—that was four months ago.

"Here's the strange part, as if it can get any stranger." He looked around the store again, even though no one had come in after him. "The checks to Mae stopped two months ago."

"And now Mae is getting those notices about unpaid bills," I said, thinking out loud.

"What?"

"Earlier this week, I found a bill in the back room stamped Past Due. I thought it was strange, but business has been slow."

"And if another source of income dried up…" Yash added. "Can you think of anything the Peterson Lumber Company would buy from here?"

I shook my head. "No, I can't. What could we possibly have that the lumber company would need? Maybe birthday and Christmas presents?" I said, trying to rack my brain for ideas.

"I suppose that could be some of it."

Yash looked around the store. "Steve might give his

employees birthday presents. I know they sometimes get Christmas bonuses, but who knows, maybe Santa brings them something for their stockings? Quite the mystery, isn't it?" He sighed. "I'll keep asking around and see what else I can find out."

"Thanks." I smiled, but I was confused. Instead of getting answers, I now had more questions. By no stretch of the imagination was Mae perfect, but I didn't want to believe she could be involved in an embezzling scheme or a murder. In her defense, I uttered, "Maybe the invoices are fake, and Steve is just taking the money?"

"But that doesn't explain why the checks are made to Mae's Gift Shop," Yash corrected me. "Hang in there. We'll sort this thing out." He sounded optimistic, but as he bit his lower lip, I wasn't so sure he was convinced.

I glanced at my watch. It was 9:00 and time to close the store. I pulled a set of keys from the drawer under the register and fumbled through them, looking for the key to the front door.

"Guess I better get going so you can lock up."

"At least it won't take long tonight. No last-minute shop-pers." I smiled. "Thanks for your help and for stopping by to let me know what you found out. It means a lot."

"Anytime."

"See you tomorrow?" I asked.

"Nope," he said with a huge grin. "Classes got canceled, so I can party all night and sleep 'til noon."

"Lucky you! I'm so jealous." I laughed.

As I let Yash out the door, I saw Mae walking toward the store.

I held the door open. "I didn't know you were coming back tonight. Is Barb with you?"

"No, I had her drop me off down the street and sent her home. I needed some fresh air." Mae's blond hair shimmered as she tossed her head like someone who didn't have a care in the world. "My lawyer said there was nothing to worry about and that he'd go with me if the police want to question me. I feel much better now about the whole thing."

The complete change in Mae's outlook was remarkable. When she left the store earlier, she was a total wreck, but now she was in complete control of her emotions. Her transformation flabbergasted me.

Mae continued. "I couldn't get my mind off Anne and… everything, so I thought I would come here and pay bills and take care of some odds and ends. In fact, why don't you go on home? I'll take care of the banking tonight, and you can get home early."

"Are you sure?"

"Of course I am."

After locking the front door, I followed her into the back room. Mae, being uncharacteristically attentive, picked my coat up off the chair and held it for me to slip my arms through. *Wow, she's in a hurry for me to get out of here tonight!*

As I buttoned my coat, I heard what sounded like a knock at the back door. "Did you hear something?"

"Probably the wind. It's too late for any deliveries. Here, let's get you home a little early." Mae ushered me out of the back room and led the way to the front door. She smiled as she held the door open and said, "Have a good night."

"You too."

I walked around the block to the parking lot behind Mae's Gift Shop and climbed into my car. As I sat behind the steering wheel, I noticed the large gray industrial door to Mae's back room was open. Perhaps she did get a delivery, but I didn't see a truck. Instead, I saw two figures standing in the doorway. The bright lights on a car leaving the parking lot blinded me momentarily, and when I regained my vision, the door was closed almost all the way, letting only a sliver of light escape into the darkness. *Perhaps Mae took out the trash and forgot to close the door, but that makes no sense. Mae always double-checks the door to make sure it's deadbolted.*

Maybe Mae was in trouble? She was acting weird when she came back to the shop. *What if Anne's killer is in there with her right now? What should I do? The gas station isn't too far away. I could use their phone to call the police, but what if they take too long to get here?* I had to act fast.

After grabbing a flashlight from the glove compartment for protection, I walked toward the tow truck parked in front of the dumpster and read "Bob's Auto Repair" in big white letters. *Bob must be with her, but why?*

Bob was so upset the other day when he came into the shop, I worried about Mae meeting with him alone. When I got close enough, I could hear them talking, but I couldn't make out what they were saying, so I moved closer to the door.

"I'm telling you, Mae, don't trust him. He's not the person you think he is," said Bob.

"What are you talking about? Steve has always been good to me. You remember when my husband died, and I had all those medical expenses?"

"Yes, but—"

"No, you listen to me. When I was worried about the money, Steve found a way for the lumber company to reimburse me for the shares in the company that should have been mine."

"Have it your way. You'll be sorry." And with that, heavy footsteps moved in my direction.

My instinct told me to hide before anyone came out of the back room, but when I looked at my car, I knew I better get out of the parking lot and fast. Mae and Bob knew what kind of car I drove. If they spotted it, they would know I was nearby. Of all nights to park the Orange Bomb under a bright light.

I ran to my car, opened the door, and closed it as quietly as possible while keeping my eyes on the back door. Someone appeared in the doorway. I just needed one more minute, and I'd be out of here. Bob made his way to the driver's side of his truck and looked in my direction as my car's engine started. I turned on my bright lights, hoping to blind him long enough to get away, and threw the car into reverse. After a quick shift into drive, I peeled out of the parking lot and saw Bob's tow truck pulling away from the store in my rearview mirror.

As I drove home, I kept checking to see if I was being followed, and sure enough, a vehicle had been behind me for a couple of miles. Although I couldn't see what kind it was, the lights were higher than if they were on a car, so I guessed it was probably a truck.

With hands clenching the steering wheel, I turned on the street before mine and breathed a sigh of relief when it didn't follow me. After finding a driveway to turn around in, I made it home and parked underneath the basketball hoop Dad had put up for Mike when he was in junior high.

I fumbled for my keys and opened the front door, only to find my mother standing in front of me.

"Thank goodness you're home! The police were here this evening with a search warrant." She was talking so fast I thought she might hyperventilate. "They took your father's handguns."

She looked at my father, who was talking on the phone in the living room. "He's talking to Crystal's brother-in-law right now. He's a lawyer, and he's going to help us. Michelle, why didn't you tell us you were in so much trouble?"

I threw my purse and books on the stairs. "I didn't think it was that serious. The police searched Mae's back room, too, and found a revolver in her safe. I don't know what's going on."

My father looked at my mom and me and mouthed, "Be quiet!"

A few minutes later, he hung up the phone. "From now

119

on, young lady, when you go to the police station, you are going to take a lawyer with you. Understand?"

He handed me a piece of paper with the lawyer's name and phone number written on it. "This is not a game. This is your problem, and I expect you to clear it up." And with that, he returned to his seat on the couch. It would take more than a police search to stand between him and his Thursday night TV show.

Mom headed for the kitchen, while I hung up my jacket in the closet. As I picked up my books and purse from the stairs, she returned and handed me a scrap of paper with Craig's name and phone number on it.

"Who is this Craig guy? He said he wanted you to call him, no matter what time you got home." She paused and looked at me severely. "What could be so important that he needs you to call him this time of night?" She stopped and took a deep breath. "It's just not proper for a young lady to call a gentleman when it's so late."

"I think it'll be okay, Mom. It's not the Dark Ages. Women actually call men these days. They even ask them out for dates."

She stepped back, and with wide eyes, said, "Well, that may be, but I'll not be having my daughter—"

I looked at my watch. "It's not even ten o'clock yet. I'm sure Craig is still up, and it must be important if he wants me to call him tonight. Besides, I need to tell him about the search warrants. He might be able to help."

Thankfully, she didn't ask me *how* he might help, because I didn't know if there really was anything he could do.

"Can you two be quiet? I'm trying to watch TV," my dad yelled from the couch. *The Rockford Files* was on, and he had no tolerance for people talking while he was watching his show. I smiled, thinking how lucky the police were that they did not come by and interrupt his TV watching. Who knows what would have happened?

Mom whispered, "Going to this school has put some strange ideas in your head. It's not proper. Crystal never acted this way. She didn't need some fancy education. She found herself a nice boy and—"

"Enough already," my father grunted. "I'll tell you one thing. Crystal knew better than to talk during my show. And *she* and your brother never had a run-in with the law." He got out of his chair and turned the volume up several notches on the TV.

I shook my head and, without saying another word, went straight to my room. Exhausted, but determined to forge ahead, I plopped on my bed, spread open my notebook, and began reading through the notes I had taken during my lunch with Craig. Gidget, who had been sleeping at the foot of the bed, walked over to the notebook and gave it a thorough sniffing.

"I know. It's not supposed to be here." I rubbed her head as she pawed at the notebook, knocking the small book next to it onto the floor. As I reached down to pick it up, I thought about my parents. With everything else going on in my life, I didn't need them to be upset with me. I remembered a saying about not throwing pearls before swine. Although my dad would not appreciate being likened to swine, I better understood what that meant—it would be a waste of time talking to him right now. He was in no mood to listen.

My mother, however, was a different story. If I wanted life to be tolerable at home, I was going to have to make the first move, even if I had done nothing wrong. I went downstairs and, undetected by my snoring father, went to the kitchen and found my mom putting away the last of the dried dishes.

"Forgot to tell you goodnight," I said as I walked over and kissed her cheek. "It's been a long day. Guess my nerves are a little frayed with everything that has happened. I think I'm getting paranoid. I thought someone was following me home from work."

She hung her damp, yellow-checkered dishtowel on the small hook below the sink. "I'll be glad when you don't have to work so late at night. I do worry about you. This whole murder thing is getting out of hand."

"I know, Mom, but don't worry. As Grandma used to say, 'It'll all come out in the wash.'"

"Your father's mother did have a way with words." Mom laughed.

"That she did." I paused and gingerly asked, "Is it okay if I take the phone to my room?"

"Just make sure you don't wake your father."

"I'll be quiet."

Mom reached into the cupboard and pulled out the plates for the morning. "I still don't think it's a good idea to call anyone this late, but if he can help straighten out this mess—"

"It'll be fine." I smiled reassuringly.

After quietly disconnecting the black rotary phone on the end table next to my sleeping father, I returned to my room and scooted my desk so I could reach the phone jack. I eased a sleeping Gidget off the pile of notes on my bed. "I'm sorry. I know you were sleeping, but I need these." She stood up, stretched, jumped off the bed, and went underneath it in a huff—unimpressed with my apology.

As much as I disliked making phone calls, I knew I had to call Craig. It mattered little that he was hiding something. I needed his help. I sat straight in the desk chair, took a deep breath, and dialed his number.

"Hello, Craig speaking."

"Hi, this is Michelle. My mom said you called tonight. I just got home from work. What's up?"

"I forgot to ask you this afternoon if you're going to Anne's memorial service?"

What is it with everyone wanting to know if I'm going tomorrow? I shrugged. "Yes, I'm planning on it. Why?"

"Would you have time to go with me after the service to the library to do some research?"

"Sure, that would work. I don't have any classes tomorrow afternoon."

"Great. I'll see you tomorrow."

I sighed. *Just what I needed—another afternoon with Craig Miller.*

chapter eleven

Friday, October 18th

True to form, T.J. was ready and waiting for me as I pulled into his driveway. He ran down the porch steps and flung the passenger door wide open, dropping his books on the floorboard as he hurriedly climbed into the car.

"Are you going to the memorial service for Ladd today?" He stopped and studied what I was wearing—a black skirt, black shirt, black cardigan, black nylons, and black shoes. "Oh, I guess so."

"I don't look too morbid, do I?"

He shook his head. "No, you look…very professional."

"That's a nice way to put it." I smiled.

"You know it's supposed to snow today, right?"

"Yeah, my coat's in the back seat. Gotta love the weather around here—65 degrees this morning and snow this afternoon!" I laughed and then noticed he had his black wool pea coat in his lap. "Aren't you going to be hot carrying your coat with you all day?" I paused. "I wish I had a spare key to give you, and then you could keep it in the back too."

"That's okay. I'll leave it in the Commuter Lounge and get

it this afternoon. I'm sure somebody can watch it while I'm in class."

"Good idea." I put the car into reverse and started backing up. Several cars whizzed by before I could pull into the street. While waiting, I turned to T.J. "You wanna go with me to the memorial service?"

"I would if I could, but I have a group project I'm working on, and we're meeting after our photography class."

"That's a bummer," I said.

T.J. looked at me over the rim of his sunglasses. "You gonna be okay?"

"Sure, I'll be fine," I straightened up in my seat. "You know me." I smiled out of habit and added, "I'll probably sit near the back and slip out early."

"Not a bad idea!"

"Hey, I've been meaning to ask, how are things going with you and that girl in your class? Meg?"

T.J. turned and looked out the window. "Uh, well, we're going out tonight."

"You're kidding? I didn't know you asked her out," I said, trying to sound happy, although I didn't feel that way at all.

"Yeah, no big deal. We're going to see the new *Airport* movie."

"That'll be fun." I twisted the knob on the radio and turned the volume up. I no longer felt like talking.

Copies of today's *Wildcats' Daily News* lined our walk to class, making it impossible to avoid seeing Professor Ladd's photo on the front page. I picked up a newspaper from the pile lying on the floor outside our classroom and when I took my seat, I started reading the article underneath Ladd's large black-and-white photo. The writer documented the professor's professional accomplishments and included several quotes from her colleagues.

Before I could finish reading the teaser in the sidebar about an upcoming article about Professor Ladd that *you won't want to miss*, someone tapped my shoulder. I jumped and then realized it was T.J.

"Are you sure you want to be reading all that stuff? You don't look so good."

"You're probably right." I folded the paper and placed it in the back of my photography book, but the professor's image was engraved on my mind, and I began reliving the horror of finding her lifeless body slumped in her office chair. Despite going through the motions of taking three pages of notes, the class was nothing more than a blur—my mind was on finding Professor Ladd's killer.

The temperature had dropped enough during class that I decided to go to the car and get my coat before heading to the church for the memorial service. Afterward, I stopped at the student union and bought a container of cherry vanilla yogurt. I certainly didn't want my stomach growling during the service. Luckily, the line wasn't long, and I got in and out within a few minutes. I made it to the church by 11:30. The service didn't start until noon, but the sanctuary was almost full.

I maneuvered down a pew in the last row, doing my best not to step on anyone's foot, and slid into an empty seat halfway down. It wasn't the best location for a quick getaway, but at least it was in the back.

Although I had never seen him before, I assumed the man sitting in the front row next to Steve Goodright and his wife, Barb, was Burt Ladd. Seated behind him were Betsy Braxton and Dean Brown from the journalism department. A few rows further back was Bob from the auto repair shop, who I almost didn't recognize in his suit and tie. He actually looked quite dashing all cleaned up—at least for an older guy.

As I looked around the church to see if I knew anyone else, I saw Craig sitting in an aisle seat in the center of the room. From what I could see, he was reading the program for the service. A group of five college students, dressed in jeans and carrying backpacks, walked down the aisle, looking for a place to sit. They couldn't find seats altogether, so they split up. One guy chose the pew in front of me. I had to stop myself from laughing out loud as I watched the heads bop back and forth like dancers in a chorus line as they tried to avoid being hit by his backpack as he moved down the pew to the empty seat.

After everyone in front of me got situated, I resumed surveying the crowd. I thought I saw Mrs. Winterfield with her daughter, but a woman with a large-brimmed hat and her companion sat down behind them, blocking my view. Professor Martin came in with a redheaded woman— perhaps his wife? They were holding hands as they walked to the row marked "Reserved" behind Dean Brown. Other than the few faces I recognized, a sea of strangers filled the church.

I turned to look out the windows on the left side of the building and caught sight of Keith coming through the door and walking past Detective Douglas. The detective nodded in my direction. Seeing him at the church made me more uncomfortable than I already was, although it made perfect sense he would be there. He, like me, probably thought the murderer might show up, and from what I could see, the entire cast of suspects was assembled except for one—Mae Emerson.

I knew Detective Douglas would be watching me, which only made me self-conscious of all my looking around. Would he think I was nervous? Why, I wondered, had I told Keith and Craig I would be at the service? But, perhaps, if I had not shown up, Detective Douglas would have found that *more* suspicious. If only I knew what he was thinking.

Consumed by second-guessing whether I should have come to the memorial service or not, I failed to hear the minister tell everyone to stand. Suddenly, I realized I was the only one seated and popped up and stood at attention while scouring my program, trying to find the words to "Blessed Assurance."

As we sang, a woman dressed from head to toe in black—including the veil over her face—slowly made her way down the aisle to the front. When she came to the row where Craig was standing, she turned and looked at him, and he at her. It was only for a second, but it was as if they knew each other. He turned away, and she continued walking to the front row. Barb hugged her and motioned for her to take the vacant seat next to her. She then helped the woman take off her black wool coat and situated it on the chair.

The latecomer, a picture of poise and elegance with her slim-fitting black dress and veil, brought to mind pictures of Coretta Scott King, Ethel Kennedy, and Jackie Kennedy at their husbands' funerals. *Only one person I know carries herself like that—Mae Emerson.*

I glanced behind me and saw Detective Douglas looking at Mae. Did he think she could be the murderer? I reached for the charm on my necklace. As much as I wanted the murderer to be found, I didn't want it to be Mae.

After Reverend Lasky asked the congregation to be seated, I reached down and got my notebook and pen from my purse so I could observe the congregants and jot down any quotes I could use for my newspaper article. Reverend Lasky, a soft-spoken man nearing retirement age, addressed his opening comments to the family, and then had the congregation read John 14:1-3 in unison. "Do not let your hearts be troubled. You believe in God; believe also in me..."

As the minister talked about Anne's life and the many charities she had been involved with in the community, Bob became fidgety—constantly looking around the sanctuary. I reminded myself not to read too much into it, as I was behaving the same way. But when Steve went to the podium and began talking about growing up with Anne, Bob started coughing, got up, and left. By the time Steve wrapped up his remarks, Burt was sobbing, and Betsy leaned forward and gave him a long hug. The woman in black sitting next to Barb never moved a muscle throughout the service, seemingly unfazed. It had been an emotional morning for me, and I was glad the service was ending.

When I opened my eyes after the closing prayer, the woman I assumed to be Mae and the detective were gone. My hunch was that Detective Douglas had either stopped her outside the church or was following her. I wanted to know which one. However, the people next to me thwarted my grand scheme to exit quickly, as they were having difficulty getting the woman's walker situated. The couple to my left stopped to talk to the people in front of them, leaving me no way out.

By the time I got outside, the only face I recognized belonged to Craig, leaning against a nearby tree. I turned in the opposite direction, hoping he didn't see me. I bounded down the stairs, determined to find Mae or the detective, but stopped when a familiar voice boomed in my direction as I reached the sidewalk.

"Michelle," Craig called, motioning for me to come over to where he was standing.

I nodded and begrudgingly walked over.

"Nice service. I think Anne would have liked it," he said as he looked off into the distance.

"Yeah, it was," I said as I looked across the street for any signs of Mae or Detective Douglas. "Was that Mae in the black dress and veil? The one who sat in the front row?"

He reared back. "Why would I know?"

"I figured you two knew each other by the way she stopped and looked at you when she was walking down the aisle."

He shrugged. "I must have looked like somebody she knew." After a brief pause, he continued. "Did you notice how antsy Bob was? I thought he was going to crawl out of his skin."

"Yeah, I noticed that too. And did you see Betsy comforting Burt Ladd during the service? There's a rumor they were having an affair. Do you think that could be true?"

"I suppose stranger things have happened." He shrugged. "You ready to go to the library?"

"Sure."

"Let's hurry, though. It's cold."

I shivered as snowflakes fell from the sky. On the way to the library, I filled him in on the previous night's events. "My friend Yash—he's interning at the Peterson Lumber Company —came by while I was working last night, and he told me that Steve has been *buying supplies* for the lumber company from Mae's Gift Shop for the past few years. All the checks have been for $1000, except one four months ago for $4000. Then the checks stopped two months ago. What do you make of all that?"

"Do you think he *was* buying supplies?" He brushed flakes of snow out of his hair.

"I can't imagine what. Maybe a few presents, but nothing that would warrant a $1000 a month."

"Perhaps Mae is in on a money-for-supplies scheme."

"Surely not. I may not know a lot about Mae, but I can't see her getting involved in anything shady."

He squinted his eyes. I knew he wasn't buying my defense of Mae. "Sometimes you think you know someone, and then you find out you didn't know them at all," he said, looking pensive.

"Did I tell you I'm writing a piece on Professor Ladd for the *Wildcats' Daily News*? Hopefully, I can use some of our research for it."

He cocked his head and replied, "Interesting idea…"

"The assistant editor gave me copies of some papers that had been in Professor Ladd's desk."

"And how did he get those?"

"That's privileged information at this point."

He furrowed his brow.

"Do you want to know what they are or not?"

"Of course, I do. What did you find?"

"A loan application with Steve's name on it, and…get this…a bunch of pictures of Steve and Barb Goodright, Bob the auto repair guy, and Mae. Professor Ladd had hired a private detective to follow them. Any idea why?"

"I'm guessing it had something to do with the missing money." He stopped walking and put his hand on my shoulder. "Be careful. I worry you're getting in over your head."

"I'm not doing anything you wouldn't do," I said.

"No," he corrected me, "I've been investigating the Romano death. Anne was the one looking into the missing money…and now she's dead."

I took a deep breath. "True enough, but we can't solve the puzzle if we don't have all the pieces. Which reminds me, there was also a picture of Professor Ladd taken a long time ago. She and some guy were in quite the embrace. He doesn't look like Burt. Any idea who that could be?"

He abruptly answered, "No idea. I'd have to see it."

I was going to tell him about the search warrants for Mae's safe and my house but decided against it. He seemed agitated, and I didn't want to give him any additional reasons to suspect Mae of killing Professor Ladd.

However, the more I thought about Mae, the more curious I was about his connection with her, especially after observing their encounter at the memorial service. I was more convinced than ever that Craig was hiding something.

chapter twelve

Despite the library on campus being closer, Craig said he preferred using the public library for his research. A fifteen-minute walk from campus, the downtown library allowed him to work without the prying eyes of the faculty and students. Although he wouldn't tell me why, he said he didn't want people on campus to know what he was working on. He did, however, fill me in on a few details about Anthony Romano's death in a car accident during our walk.

Craig held the heavy wooden door open as I entered the library and stepped onto the marble floors. I stopped and studied the massive room with its intricate crown molding.

Craig stood next to me and turned his head from side to side. "What are you looking at?"

"Whenever I walk in here, I feel like I'm stepping back in time. Just look at that ceiling and—" I pointed, "—and that staircase. Can you believe how ornate it is?"

"Reminds me of some of the old buildings in New York." He smiled.

We walked up to the circulation desk, and after Craig picked up several request forms for newspapers, we stepped down to the end of the counter to make room for the people behind us. Craig put on his glasses and pulled a note from inside his black tweed blazer pocket, which he often referred to as he filled out the forms. After some intense scribbling, he raised his hand and got the attention of the elderly woman behind the counter.

"Ma'am…could you get these for me?"

Without looking at him directly, she took the slips from his hand and disappeared into the room behind her desk. She looked the stereotypical part of a librarian with her gray hair in a tight bun, her white blouse tied in a small bow at the neck, and a black cardigan sweater. Her black checked A-line skirt gently swayed as she returned with Craig's newspapers. "Here are your papers, sir. Make sure you return them to me before you leave." Her pursed lips barely moved as she spoke, never once cracking a smile.

I followed Craig into the reading room and pulled out a chair across from him as he promptly laid out his collection of newspapers on the table and said, "Tony Romano's accident occurred on July 2, 1951."

I looked at the dates on the newspapers on the table. "This one is from the day before the accident." I pointed to another one. "And this is from the morning *of* the accident. You don't think they wrote about the accident *before* it happened, do you? What exactly are we looking for?"

"Something doesn't feel right. Here." Craig divided the stack of papers and pushed them in front of me as he sat down. "But before we dig in, let's go over everything I know."

I pulled out a spiral notebook and began taking notes as he went through his list of facts.

Anthony Romano

- found in a shallow part of the river
- died July 2, 1951
- car accident

- drinking/drunk
- rainy night
- curvy road by the river
- lost control
- car rolled over
- body thrown out of car
- Mae Peterson Romano's husband

I looked up from my notes. "Did you say Mae Peterson Romano?"

"Yeah."

"As in Mae Emerson, my boss?"

Craig nodded.

"You mean Anthony Romano was Mae's first husband, and you didn't think it was important to tell me that?"

"I'm telling you now, and that's what's important. What's the big deal? It changes nothing."

I shook my head, disgusted that he could not understand that this was another example of him not being forthcoming with what he knew about the case.

Craig, oblivious to my frustration, read over my list. "Looks like everything I know so far, but I'm curious about the rainy night. Look through the papers printed right after the accident. Double-check, but I don't think there is a reference about that night being rainy until a few days later. Also —" he rolled his white shirt sleeves up, "—let's check the papers published before the accident to see if the weather forecast ever mentioned rain for the day of the crash. I want you to look for *any* mention of rain that day and, if you find one, did it rain in the morning? The afternoon? The evening?"

I nodded. "Okay, easy enough."

After looking through my stack of papers, I moved one of them closer to Craig. "Look at this." I pointed to the accident report in the *Petersburg News* one week after the Romano accident. "It listed heavy rain as a contributing factor in three accidents in the morning. Then there's Anthony's accident, also attributed to heavy rain." I slid another paper over. "This article, written two days *after* the accident, talks about the heavy rain in the morning, but never mentions rain in the evening." I paused, gathering my thoughts, then hypothesized, "Do you think it could have rained hard all day? But then, why not say so?"

Craig looked at the paper in his hands. "This one is from the day after the accident: 'Yesterday morning's heavy rain contributed to several automobile accidents in the city of Petersburg.' Okay, we've confirmed it rained that morning, but that still leaves two unanswered questions. Was it still wet enough from the morning rain to contribute to an accident that night or did it rain later in the day?"

Craig put his paper down. "I have a friend who works at the National Weather Center. I'll call him and see what he can find out. I should have done that first, but I didn't want to call in a favor if we could find what we needed without his help."

"It might be a stretch, but my friend Rick is an urban planning major. Maybe he would know how long roads stay wet after a heavy rain. Might be worth a try." I shrugged.

Craig reached over and pulled some papers out of his briefcase. "Here's a copy of the police report that was filed. Recognize the name of the person who reported the accident?"

My jaw dropped. "Robert Lane? As in Bob, the auto repair guy?"

"Yeah. I'm thinking we need to go talk to him. What do you think?"

"Definitely. When do you want to go?" I glanced at my watch and saw it was 3:30. "I'd like to go today, but I didn't know it was so late. I need to get back to campus so I can give T.J. a ride home."

"Is it that late already?" Craig looked at his watch in disbelief. "Do you think this friend of yours would mind going with us to the garage so we can talk to Bob? I don't think it will take us very long."

"I can ask him. He might not mind."

As Craig gathered the newspapers into a neat pile, I remembered something. "Do you know who the mayor of Petersburg was at the time of the accident?"

"Why? Was it in one of the papers?"

"Yeah, it was in a couple of pieces unrelated to the accident. It was Mae and Professor Ladd's father, Chauncey Peterson."

"Interesting," he said. However, he looked neither surprised nor intrigued by the revelation as he finished stacking his newspapers before taking them to the circulation desk.

Well, that's not the response I was expecting. While I waited for him by the front door and mulled over his reaction, Betsy came into the library. She walked straight to the circulation desk and must not have realized she was standing behind Craig, because when he turned around to head for the exit, she jumped. *Glad I'm not the only one he scares!*

They chatted until the librarian returned from the back room and then parted ways. Craig joined me at the door, and we ventured out into the snow.

"How well do you know Betsy?" I casually asked.

He smiled, flashing his brilliantly white teeth. "Not well. Why do you ask?"

"Just curious," I answered nonchalantly. "I didn't know you were such good friends with one of our prime suspects, that's all."

He looked taken aback.

"I was kidding." I laughed.

"Funny." He grinned. "Betsy and I are acquaintances, not friends. As you very well know—" he gave me a playfully stern look, "—she's the secretary for the journalism department. Since my office is in the building, I go to the journalism office to make copies. I see her there, and we talk a little. Satisfied?"

"Sure, but I've been wondering, why do *you* have an office in the journalism building? I mean, you're an English grad student, right? I thought grad assistants had offices in the department associated with their degree program?"

"Ideally, that's how it works. But by the time I applied to the program, there were no empty offices in Williams Hall. Anne pulled a few strings and got me one in her building, which worked out better because it made it easier for us to work."

We walked about a block before I finally got the courage to say, "Speaking of seeing Anne—"

He interrupted me before I finished. "Were we?" He smiled.

"A minute ago, we were," I said, flabbergasted.

He laughed. "What's on your mind?"

"The morning you went to see Anne and made copies of her papers, did you see anyone around her office?"

"Haven't we been through this before, Sherlock?" He stopped walking. "Betsy was in the office. I ran into you in the hallway, and that was it."

His answer was not the one I wanted to hear. I had hoped he'd seen something or someone.

"But…" he teased as he started walking again.

"But, what?"

He said nothing but flashed that I-know-something-you-don't-know grin, which infuriated me.

"Come on, do you know something? My life could depend on it."

"Cool your jets. I'll tell you." He took a few steps, saying nothing, and I suspected he was enjoying keeping me in suspense. "I saw Bob working on Anne's car in the parking lot. She told me she had locked her keys in the car that morning, and he was getting them for her."

"And you told the police that?"

"Yes, I told them. Feel better?"

I sighed. "Guess that's another good reason to go talk to Bob." This time I stopped as a sense of dread came over me. "Do you think Bob could have killed Professor Ladd?"

"Over keys locked in her car?" He smirked.

"No. Think about it. He was at Mae's the other day, yelling that Steve owed him money, and then he said something about Anne. I can't remember exactly what he said, but he implied she was going to cause trouble for Steve. What if he was protecting Steve from Anne?"

"That makes little sense. If Bob was mad at Steve, why would he want to protect him?"

"Yeah, you're right. We need more info." I sighed as I shook my head. "Something bothers me—"

"You're kidding. Something bothers you?" He smiled.

I squinted my eyes and glared at him. "Seriously?"

"Okay, what bothers you?"

"How did someone shoot Professor Ladd, and yet no one heard the gunshot? I've gone over the timeline again and again, and the closest I can figure she was killed—that is, providing you and Betsy are telling the truth—was between 7:15 a.m. and 8:35 a.m."

"How did you arrive at that time?"

"Because you saw her around 7:15 a.m., and I was in the building by 8:35, and, except for going to the vending machine, I was outside her office the entire time." I shook my head. "But that time frame doesn't really make sense."

"Why not?" he asked.

"Because Betsy was in the journalism office during that time, and she would have heard the gunshot, as well as anyone else who was in the building that morning. Why didn't anyone hear—"

National Guard jets flew overhead and drowned out the rest of my thought.

After the sound of the jets faded, Craig grinned broadly. "The jets. I remember hearing them when I was in the parking lot by the gym. If a gun went off when the jets were flying overhead, someone might have confused the sound of a gun with the sound coming from the jets. And remember, they flew over the campus several times that morning."

"You might be right. That could explain why no one heard the gun go off."

As we entered the commuter lot, I didn't see T.J. by my car. But when I looked behind me, I saw him ambling along with slumped shoulders, looking exhausted. Fridays were long days for him—two classes and a lab. He was usually too tired to do much talking on the way home on Fridays, but I was hoping he would be up to going to Bob's auto shop with Craig and me.

I waved, trying to get his attention. When he saw me, he smiled, but cocked his head when he saw Craig standing by the car. He picked up his pace, and I brushed the snow off the windows while waiting for him.

"How was your day?" I asked as he approached.

"Rough. My classes went okay, but my lab at the end was brutal." He rubbed his forehead. "I got a headache from working on that small screen for two hours. But enough about me. How was your day?" Before I could respond, he cast an awkward glance toward Craig.

"Oh…T.J., this is Craig. Craig, this is T.J."

"Craig Miller?" T.J. asked.

Craig stretched out his hand. "Yes, glad to meet you, T.J."

Things became very tense as Craig and T.J. appeared to size each other up. They reminded me of two roosters getting ready to fight.

"T.J.?" I asked, getting his attention.

"Yeah?"

"Craig and I need to run by Bob's Auto Repair to ask him

a few questions. Would you have time to go with us? If you don't, that's okay. We can go another time."

"Sure, I'm game. Let's go."

I climbed inside the car and reached over to unlock the two passenger doors. With no hesitation, T.J. stepped in front of Craig and got into the front seat, leaving Craig to get in the back.

As I pulled out of the parking lot, I filled T.J. in on Bob's association with the Romano accident that Craig and I were working on. "Bob was the one who reported the accident, and we want to find out what he remembers about that night."

* * *

"Looks like a busy place," Craig commented as I parked next to Bob's tow truck. The lot had more than a dozen cars and pickup trucks in it. "Do you think he works on all these in one day?"

"I'm guessing some of them are long-term projects," I said, feeling proud that I knew more about something than Craig. "My father's friend, Syd, bought an old Hudson that needed a lot of work, so he brought it here and had Bob work on it a little bit at a time. It took several months, but Bob likes to work on old cars in his spare time, and Syd liked not having to pay for all the repairs at once.

"I'll have to keep that in mind if I ever collect old automobiles." Craig smiled. "Assuming, of course, Bob doesn't turn out to be our murderer. That would put a damper on things."

I shook my head. "Sometimes, you are so warped. It's a nice garage, though. T.J. just had them put a cassette player in his car, and I bring my car here for oil changes. I usually work with a guy named Randy."

The three of us walked into the garage, but neither Randy nor Bob greeted us. No one was there. Craig and I stepped inside the office, but it was empty too. Through the large window in the office, we saw T.J. walking around the garage in search of either man.

"That's weird." I shook my head.

I saw Craig's mouth moving, but I could barely hear him as Grand Funk Railroad's "We're an American Band" blared through the speakers in the office.

"What? What did you say?"

Craig cupped his right ear with his hand. "Think they like their music loud?"

We both laughed, and then I pointed to the garage and shouted, "There are two cars on lifts, and there is one still on the floor. They've been working, but where are they?"

"Do only two people work here?" Craig asked while he casually started shuffling papers on the desk.

"Once in a while I've seen another guy, but most times, it's just Bob and Randy."

We joined T.J. in the empty garage, and after looking around and finding no trace of Bob or Randy, I shrugged my shoulders. "Must be break time, I guess."

Without warning, the music in the garage became softer, and I heard a familiar voice behind me.

"Guess Bob wanted to rock the place out," Randy said, flashing a big smile and holding a cardboard drink carrier with a large paper bag squeezed between two tall drinks.

"How's my favorite coed?"

I laughed, wondering why anyone would want an ice-cold drink on a day like today. Hot chocolate would have been my drink of choice.

"Hi, Randy. How are you? Here, let me help you." I took the carrier from his hands and placed it on the counter along the wall. As he hung his coat on the coat rack and brushed the snow off, I continued. "These are my friends, Craig and T.J."

Looking at T.J., he said, "Yeah, I remember you. I put a cassette player in your car the other day, right?"

T.J. nodded.

"We need to talk to Bob," I said. "Do you have any idea where he is?"

Randy looked around the garage and shook his head. "No. We were so busy today that we didn't get lunch, so when we finally slowed down, I went to get us something to eat. When I left, he was in here working on that Mercedes. He might be around back. Did you look there?"

"No, that's a good idea. We'll go look." I breathed in deeply, trying to take as much of the warmth from inside the garage with me as I could before venturing back into the cold and trudging through an inch of fluffy snow covering the parking lot.

Craig, T.J., and I walked around the back lot and then to the adjoining lot on the side.

"I don't see anyone. Bob must not be here," Craig said. His breath lingered in the air.

"Me neither." I shook my head. "I wonder where he is. Let's go back inside. Maybe he went in the front while we've been back here."

Just as we got to the front door, the sound of crunching metal made me jump. I looked over my shoulder but couldn't see anything except the row of evergreens between the parking lot and the street. Despite the lack of visual evidence, I assumed two cars had collided. "Somebody's having a bad day."

As I turned back, two legs sticking out from under a car parked in the lot caught my attention. "Oh, there he is." I recognized the coveralls as the same kind Randy was wearing. "How did I not see him when we walked by?"

"Bob?" I gingerly called his name, wanting to get his attention without startling him. My father always warned me about sneaking up on people while they were working. "Accidents happen that way," he would say.

"Bob?"

He still didn't move.

Craig crouched down on the ground and touched Bob's leg. "Bob, it's Craig Miller. Do you have a minute?"

Still no movement. Craig looked at me. "Something's wrong." He pulled Bob's body out from under the car. "Go inside and call 911."

"Is he…?"

"I don't know."

I looked around. The only footprints in the snow belonged to the three of us.

chapter thirteen

Without saying a word, Craig, T.J., and I watched as the paramedics lifted Bob's motionless body into the ambulance. He was alive, but barely.

Cold and upset, I shivered as the snow continued to fall. Craig put his arm around me in a comforting sort of way, and T.J. crossed his arms, glaring at him.

Craig, either unaware of T.J.'s stance or ignoring him, leaned closer to me and whispered in my ear, "Are you okay?"

"No, it's not right."

"Life isn't fair, is it? But, hopefully, he's going to be alright," Craig said.

"It's not just that...the accident doesn't make sense. The paramedics said he probably hit his head on the underside of the car he was working on. But did you see all the blood on his head? Do you seriously think a trained mechanic would hit his head on the car so hard that he not only put a huge gash in his head, but knocked himself out?"

"You've got a point," Craig agreed.

"Besides, did you notice he didn't have a coat on? I mean, wouldn't Bob have put on a coat if he was going to work outside?" I paused, still processing the situation. "Even if he didn't grab a coat, he would have grabbed some tools." I walked over to the car and squatted down to look underneath it. "There are no tools under here. I think someone hit him someplace else and then put his body under the car. They might have thought he was dead, or that he would be soon."

A voice behind me concurred. "Exactly the conclusion I would come to, Ms. Kilpatrick."

It was Detective Douglas. Lieutenant Grogan stood next to him.

I jumped to my feet. "Detective, I didn't know you were here."

"I hope you didn't touch anything," he said, annoyed.

"No, of course not. I was just curious—"

"About the tools?"

"Yes."

"And who is this?" he asked, looking at T.J.

"That's T.J. We ride to school together, so he came with us."

"And why were the three of you here?" Douglas pulled out his pen and notepad, ready to take down my statement, as Lieutenant Grogan gestured for Craig and T.J. to follow him. I watched as they walked to the lot behind the building.

"Ms. Kilpatrick?"

I turned my attention back to the detective, who was impatiently waiting for my answer. "Craig and I are investigating a car accident that happened in 1951 for a class project. Bob was the one who phoned the police about the accident. We were hoping he would remember the details of that night."

"Is that the only reason you wanted to talk to Mr. Lane? It wouldn't have anything to do with Professor Ladd's murder, would it?"

I took a step back. "Do you think whoever attacked Bob killed Professor Ladd?"

"I don't know, but what I do know is I have a murder and

now, at the very least, an attempted murder to solve. I don't want anyone else to get hurt, and you, Ms. Kilpatrick, always seem to be in the middle of everything that's happening. Perhaps you and Mr. Miller should leave Mr. Lane alone and find a different project for your class."

"Well, that's not going to happen," I said, looking at him squarely in his eyes.

"I'm telling you to back off. Do you understand?"

I nodded but said nothing as he stared at me for a few moments. I stood confident, knowing I had every right to talk to Bob, and there was nothing Detective Douglas could say that would convince me otherwise. Bob knew something, and I was going to find out what it was.

Finally, the detective turned his gaze away from me and looked at his notepad. "I need you to tell me everything that happened once you got here." As he scribbled my version of the events leading up to the discovery of Bob's body, he never once looked up from his notepad.

I grew tired of the inquisition and twisted my wrist to read the time on my watch. It was 5:30 p.m.

"Do you have someplace you need to be?" Detective Douglas asked.

"Yes, and if I don't get home soon, my parents are going to think something happened to me. I really need to get home."

He looked at me for a moment and then closed his notepad. "Okay. You're free to go for now. I'm sure Lieutenant Grogan is finished with Mr. Miller and your friend. I'll be in touch if I have any more questions. Just remember—"

"I know. I know. Don't leave town." I rolled my eyes.

* * *

After dropping Craig off at his car, T.J. and I headed home. Overwhelmed by the events of the past week, I tried my best to fight back my tears, but it was a losing battle. A steady stream of tears ran down my cheeks.

"Michelle," T.J. said, almost whispering. "It's okay. You've been through a lot. Why don't you pull off, and I'll drive us home?"

I nodded and pulled into the nearest parking lot, where we exchanged seats. Poor T.J.! I never realized how much shorter my legs were than his until I saw him sitting behind the steering wheel with his knees practically in his chest.

As he adjusted the driver's seat, he breathed a deep sigh, signaling he could breathe once again, and then fiddled with the rearview mirror until he was happy with its position.

Between sobs, I stammered, "I think Detective Douglas knows more than what he's letting on."

T.J. cocked his head and smiled. "I'm sure he does. He *is* a detective."

I dabbed my eyes with a tissue. "It's more than that. He told me to stay away from Bob. Why would he say that?"

"Maybe because somebody just tried to kill him?" T.J. looked at me sternly.

"Maybe…but I think there's more to it. Bob was a chauffeur for the Peterson family at the time of the Romano accident, and he was the one who alerted the police to the accident. Then the other night, when I was at work, Bob came in and yelled at Barb about Steve owing him money. Did you know he was in the parking lot the morning Professor Ladd was murdered?"

T.J. shook his head. "Who saw him there?"

"Craig. He told me this afternoon that Professor Ladd called Bob because she locked her keys in her car."

"What do you think it means?" T.J. shrugged.

"That's the problem. I don't know, and I don't know how to find out." I looked out the window.

"Do you think the guy who works for Bob knows anything?"

147

"About Professor Ladd's keys?" I asked.

"No, not that, but maybe he knows something that would be helpful. What if Bob talked to him about the accident or his life when he was younger?"

"You're right. Talking to Randy is a great idea. Maybe I can do that tomorrow."

"Better yet, why not today? Do you want to go back and see if he's still at the shop?"

"You bet I do!" I thought for a moment. "And while we're there, let's look and see if we can find any clues about who tried to kill Bob."

T.J. made a U-turn. The hunt was on, and nothing and no one was going to hold us back.

When we got to Bob's Auto Repair, yellow caution tape surrounded the parking lot. We parked around the corner and hurried to the garage, hoping Randy hadn't left. We were in luck. From the sidewalk, I could see him sitting in one of the folding chairs in the reception area. He had propped the front door open with a brick, despite the chilly temperature, and the wind had blown snow onto the floor. Perhaps he was in shock, and who could blame him?

I kicked the brick out of the way and closed the door. "Hi, Randy. You okay?"

He nodded and formed a slight smile.

"I hate to bother you, but..." I crossed my fingers, as if that would cover for the lie I was about to tell. "I lost my gloves and thought maybe I left them here during all the commotion. Is it okay if we look around?"

With a blank look on his face, I wasn't sure he was going to respond, but finally he said, "Sure, I think that would be okay." He turned and ran his fingers through his hair. "The police told me to go home, but I've got some work to do..." His voice drifted off.

"Can we help you with anything? It'd be good to get you

out of here and get you home. It's terrible what happened. Any idea who would want to hurt Bob?"

Randy stared into the distance.

I knelt next to him and put my hand on his arm. "Randy, what can I do to help?"

He thought for a few moments. "You help Mae with the bank deposits, don't you? Could you do ours tonight? Bob always takes care of the money stuff. I don't know how to do it."

"I'd be happy to. Just show me where everything is, and I'll take care of it."

"Guess you better put these on." He handed T.J. and me each a pair of gloves. "The police left these so I wouldn't mess anything up."

As I put on the gloves, he pulled out another pair for himself. "They wear these all the time on *Police Woman* when they're handling evidence, so it must work, right?" he said with the smallest of grins.

I followed him into the office, while T.J. made his way into the garage.

"I put the money from the cash register in this bag." Randy handed me the burlap bag printed on one side with the words "Petersburg Savings and Loan." He opened the top desk drawer and pulled out a deposit slip and the checkbook register.

To buy T.J. enough time to look around the garage for "my gloves," which was code for anything that might look suspicious, I barraged Randy with questions.

I knew Bob was not presently married, but I knew nothing about his family. The best way to find out was to ask Randy. "Has Bob ever been married? Does he have children? Are his parents alive? Does he have any siblings?"

All to which Randy replied, "No."

"Is there anyone from Bob's family we need to call?" Finally, I got a reaction.

"I remember him talking about a cousin he's close to. I should try to find his number and let him know. Thanks. That's a good idea."

Next, I tried to get Randy to recall any stories Bob might have told him about being a chauffeur for the Peterson family.

"Can't think of any." He stopped at the door as he was leaving the office. "He doesn't much like talking about his life back then. He once said he wished he had never worked for those Peterson folks, even if it would have meant not getting his own garage. Said the price had been too great." He shook his head and disappeared into the garage, where I heard him ask T.J., "Any luck finding her gloves?"

Alone, I got straight to work and looked at the check register for the checking account. It didn't take long to notice several deposits in the account from the Peterson Lumber Company. I flipped back through the pages until I got to the first of the year. Every month, a check for $2000 was deposited, until two months ago, when the deposits increased to $6000.

Why would Steve pay Bob for car repairs when Steve had his own mechanic, Jimmy's dad, on the payroll?

Randy peeked his head through the office door. "How's it going? Everything all right?"

"Just about done. Do you want me to drop it off at the bank for you?"

Randy nodded and smiled as he put on his coat and hat.

I zipped the deposit bag and waited in the lobby for Randy and T.J. After we vacated the building, Randy pulled a key from his pocket and locked the door, but before we reached the sidewalk, Detective Douglas pulled up in his squad car and motioned for us to stop. He pulled to the curb and walked over to our group.

"Everything okay, Randy?"

"Yes, Michelle was helping me with the bank deposit."

Detective Douglas raised his eyebrow and took a deep breath. "I thought you left earlier, Ms. Kilpatrick. Something about getting home so your parents wouldn't worry?" His sarcasm did not fall on deaf ears.

"Yes," I piped up and pointed to T.J. "But I lost my gloves, so we came back to look for them."

"Your gloves? And did you have any luck?"

T.J. spoke up. "No, sir, we couldn't find them." He laughed nervously. "Michelle is always losing her gloves."

"I see." He looked me in the eye. "And did you find anything else?"

"Randy needed help with the deposit," I said, holding up the bank bag.

"I see." He looked like he wanted to say something.

"Yes?" I asked.

"Next time you lose your gloves, you might want to try looking in your coat pocket first."

I looked down and saw a glove dangling out of each pocket.

"I can't believe I didn't see them there."

"Weird, huh?" Detective Douglas flashed me a look that said he knew what I was up to.

"Well, if there's nothing else, we gotta run and get this deposit made!" I grabbed T.J.'s arm and quickly led him toward my car.

After closing my car door, I exclaimed, "Wow, that was close! I didn't expect Detective Douglas to show up. And my stupid gloves. I thought for sure I left them in the car."

"At least you were already out of the office by the time he got there. It would have been disastrous if he had walked in on you."

"Isn't that the truth? He would have had a fit. How 'bout you? Did you find anything?"

"I'm not sure. I didn't have time to sift through it—"

"Sift through what?"

"Sawdust. I know garages use it to soak up the oil on the floor, but there was a trail of sawdust leading from one of the bays to the parking lot. Randy came in before I could see where the trail went or what it was covering." He stopped. "Do you think I should have told that detective?"

"I don't think so. At least not yet. He'd just get mad because we were snooping around."

"Yeah, probably." He looked upward as he sighed. After a moment, he turned his gaze toward me. "What did you find? Anything?"

After I told him about the deposits from the lumber company, T.J. became adamant that we should tell Detective Douglas.

"You know, if we tell him what we found, he's going to be mad, right?" I argued.

"Yeah, but we have no choice."

The look of determination on his face let me know there was no way I was going to talk him out of doing what he thought was the right thing to do. Besides, it didn't matter what I thought. He was in the driver's seat, and without a moment's delay, he headed toward the police station.

* * *

We found Detective Douglas in his office, and I told him about the checks. T.J. described the sawdust trail to him, and it turned out he already knew about it.

He turned his attention back to me. "Is there anything you can tell me about Bob Lane?" His tone was calmer than I had expected.

"No, not really." I shrugged. "I mean, you know about him being in the parking lot the morning Professor Ladd was murdered, right?"

He nodded.

"Oh, and he sort of threatened Steve Goodright's wife

over some money that Steve owes him. I think he knew about that letter Professor Ladd was sending to the Peterson Lumber Company's board."

He cocked his head. "Why do you say that?"

I told him about the day Bob came into Mae's Gift Shop and his ranting and raving at Barb. "Then he said something about Steve needing a lawyer because of Anne. I'm sure that was about the embezzling charge. Were you aware that Steve's strapped for money?"

"And you know that *how*?" He looked interested and annoyed at the same time as he grabbed a pen and wrote something on the yellow legal-sized pad of paper on his desk.

"Mrs. Winterfield—"

"And *who* is Mrs. Winterfield?" He tapped his pencil on the desk. The light coming from his desk lamp illuminated a few faint lines across his forehead.

"She's a customer at Mae's, and she said, according to her niece, Barb's been writing bad checks to businesses around town."

He shook his head and sighed before asking, "And how would her niece know all this?"

I felt like the town gossip as I filled him in on all the *whos* and *whats* I had heard from Mrs. Winterfield.

Detective Douglas closed his eyes and rubbed his fore-head, pushing his brown hair to the side. "Okay." He jotted down a few more notes. "Now, back to Bob and Barb."

I continued, although I was concerned I was giving him too much information to process at one time, but I didn't want to leave anything out that might be important. "That was it, as far as Bob and Barb were concerned, but the other night Bob was at Mae's store after closing. I hid around the back, so I could listen—"

"You did what?"

"My car was in the parking lot behind the store, so when I saw Bob's truck by the back door, I went to see if everything was alright. I heard Bob tell Mae not to trust Steve. Why would he say that?"

Detective Douglas put down his pen. "I appreciate you wanting to help, but *please* let the police do their job. It's one thing if information comes your way, but don't go looking for it. You could get hurt if the murderer is still out there."

"What do you mean, *if* the murderer is still out there? Of course, he—or she—is out there. It's not me." I rose to my feet defiantly.

"Sit down, Ms. Kilpatrick. I should have said 'until the murderer is found.' Listen, all I'm saying is that, until this investigation is over, I will do the detective work, understand?"

I sat back down, and T.J. put his hand on my shoulder.

"Yeah, I understand. I just want to help."

He smiled. "I got that, but for now, the best way you can help is—"

"I know. Stay out of it."

He cast a stern look toward T.J. "And that goes for you too."

* * *

By the time T.J. pulled into his driveway, he was late for his date with Meg, but, to my relief, he didn't seem too worried. "I'll call her and tell her what happened. I'm sure she'll understand. She's like that."

"I didn't mean for everything to take so long."

"That's okay. It was my idea to go back to the garage and to the police station, but what we did was important. Meg and I can catch a later showing of the movie tonight. It's all good. The main thing is we accomplished something."

"You think?"

"No doubt about it. You discovered the checks from the lumber company to Bob. And even though the police already knew about the blood inside the garage, it was nice having someone else agree I was on to something. If my life as a computer genius doesn't pan out, maybe I'll become a private detective." He grinned.

"You're a good friend, T.J."

He smiled as we both opened the car doors and got out. "I know. One of the best."

As we passed in front of the car, he gave me a quick hug and then continued on his way to the front door while I climbed into the driver's seat.

Any hope that my parents would be as understanding as T.J. thought Meg would be vanished as I turned into my driveway and saw my father, with arms crossed, standing in the doorway.

No sooner had I stepped into the house than he started yelling. "Where have you been, young lady? You should have been home hours ago. Your mother's been worried sick."

I moved in front of him and placed my books on the stairs. "I'm sorry. It's been a crazy day." I recounted the afternoon's events, but my explanation did nothing to ease the tension in the room.

My mother came down the stairs and stood behind my father, letting him take the lead in reprimanding me.

"You didn't think to use the phone at the garage? At the police station? And what did I tell you about having a lawyer with you the next time you talked to the police?"

"I didn't think it would hurt to tell Detective Douglas about what we found out."

"That's the problem with you, Michelle. You don't think."

He raged on. "Your mother and I could use your help running this farm. Your brother and sister understand that. They are here almost every day helping, and so are Mel and Suzie. But, oh, no, not you. You have to chase those fancy dreams of yours, thinking you're better than the rest of us..."

Something inside of me snapped. I couldn't be quiet any

longer. "I am thrilled to death that Mike and Crystal are so happy working on the farm. Great for them, but it's not what I want to do. Is that so hard to understand?"

I turned around and ran upstairs as my father's words, "We're not finished with this, young lady," trailed behind me.

I closed my bedroom door, threw myself onto my bed, and held Gidget close. My parents were wrong. I didn't think I was better than them or anyone else. I only wanted different things. Not better. Not worse. Just different.

With the Eiffel Tower charm pressing against my chest, I cried myself to sleep.

chapter fourteen

Saturday, October 19th

In the middle of the night, I woke up with a start. *The checks of the higher amounts to Bob started at the same time Mae's checks stopped. And if my calculations were right, Craig probably moved to the area in August to start his MFA program and his research into the Romano accident, which was also two months ago. Was it coincidence, or were the increased amounts on the checks related to Craig and Professor Ladd looking into the case?*

I hopped out of bed and grabbed the poster board with the suspects' names written on it. I added a circle for Bob and included that he had been a chauffeur for the Peterson family and the one who reported the Romano accident. *Think, think, think.* I added that he inherited enough money from Chauncey Peterson to start his own business and had regularly received checks from the lumber company. *I wonder when Bob started receiving checks? And for what? Blackmail?* I was convinced the missing money from the Peterson Lumber Company and the checks Mae and Bob had been receiving were connected.

I crawled back into bed, but I may as well have stayed up. I tossed and turned all night.

In the morning I dragged myself out of bed and got ready for work and, considering my parents' moods last night, put off going downstairs until the last minute.

I fastened my chain with the Eiffel Tower charm around my neck, gave Gidget a quick pat on her head, and told her goodbye. Once downstairs, I grabbed my coat hanging by the front door. From the sound of clanging dishes in the kitchen, I knew Mom was cleaning up, so I took a deep breath and decided, once again, to be the bigger person in this disagreement. However, my attempt at peacemaking was in vain. She refused to even look at me when I told her goodbye. I turned around and left with a heavy heart.

For once, I was glad I had to go to work. It was better than staying home with all this tension. As I pulled out of the driveway, I turned on the radio and halfheartedly sang along with Chicago's "(I've Been) Searchin' So Long." After the song finished, I flipped through the stations, hoping to find something I liked, but I gave up and turned it off. I drove the rest of the way in silence.

When I walked into Mae's Gift Shop, I was surprised to see Stacy behind the counter.

"Mae called me last night and asked me to come in this morning. Something about having a meeting and not being able to get here until noon or so. She let me in and said to wait for you, that you knew how to open up," Stacy said.

I put my purse and a textbook I had brought with me in the back room and turned on the lights after I told Stacy how to set up the cash register drawer. At 10:00, I unlocked the front door, and a group of five men hurriedly stepped inside and headed for the greeting cards under the Sweetest Day banner.

"Somebody waited until the last minute," giggled a woman as she walked in behind them.

Another woman, holding onto a small child's hand, nodded in agreement. She pulled the little girl, who was clutching her plastic baby doll, toward the candles at the back of the store.

Stacy and I chuckled when we saw her slowly make her way to the Sweetest Day cards. She, too, had apparently waited until the last minute.

Saturday was typically the busiest day of the week at Mae's Gift Shop, but today it was even busier than usual. *How strange that Mae would schedule a meeting today, of all days— Sweetest Day!*

I worked the floor, helping customers find gifts to go with their Sweetest Day cards. More often than not, a box of chocolates wrapped in pink floral watercolor paper fit the bill. Stacy worked at the cash register and rang the bell when she needed me to get a box from the back room.

We restocked the Sweetest Day card display and the boxed chocolates during the brief lulls between customers and chatted about everything happening in our lives.

After talking about the murder and school—she was a junior at Weston, a small private college about fifteen miles from Petersburg—I asked her, "Was the store busy yesterday?"

"Yeah." She paused. "Mae went to her sister's memorial service, and, of course, it got hectic while she was gone."

"I bet you were glad when she got back."

"Yeah, but she left again after about an hour. I was getting worried, because I was supposed to leave at 4:30 for my 5:00 class, and she wasn't back yet."

"That had to be nerve-racking!"

"It was. But luckily, Mae came in a few minutes later, so it all worked out."

"Thank goodness. It's not like Mae to be late. How strange!" *Attending the memorial service would explain where she was the first time she left the store, but where was she the second time?*

I looked out the window and saw Mae on the sidewalk. She rarely wore slacks, but today was an exception. Her golden blond hair provided a dramatic contrast to her navy blue ensemble—a turtleneck sweater, wide-legged slacks, an unbuttoned wool coat, and matching flats and purse. As chic as she looked, the scowl on her face negated her beauty.

I glanced at my watch. Only half an hour more to work. Since Mae was back earlier than expected, maybe she would let me leave, since I had a busy afternoon in front of me. However, all thoughts of a shorter workday ended as Mae walked past Stacy and me without uttering a word on her way to the back room. We stood behind the counter and looked at each other, shocked.

"That's weird," Stacy said.

"Glad I get to leave soon," I said without thinking.

"Oh, sure, brag about it...I have to work with her until 6:00...yuck." Stacy looked despondent, and I couldn't blame her.

Mae emerged from the back room promptly at 1:00 and told me I could leave but added that she'd appreciate it if I could do a small favor for her. "Mrs. Winterfield's daughter was in last night and reminded me it was her mother's birthday today. I was going to drop off a present at her house this morning, but I forgot to take it home with me last night. Would you mind dropping it off? The family is having a small party at her house this afternoon."

"Sure. I'd be happy to do that. What's her address?"

"I'll meet you in the back and get it for you."

As I walked toward the back room, I overheard Mae tell Stacy she would be working in the back room and to ring the bell if she needed her. Our quiet time at the store had ended, and several customers were milling about. Yet that didn't change Mae's plans to work in the back room. I felt bad for

Stacy. She would have her hands full with customers and no help, but I also told myself she would have a much better afternoon not having Mae around.

* * *

I rang the doorbell, and Mrs. Winterfield opened the door. "Mae wanted you to have this. Happy birthday!"

"Oh, how sweet! Please tell her thank you." She smiled as she reached for the wrapped box. "Won't you come in, dear? My great-grandkids made cupcakes, and I have more than enough for this afternoon."

"Okay, but only for a few minutes." I followed her into the living room and sat in a gold velvet chair while she went into the kitchen. The ivory sheers and heavy green drapes hanging over the picture window obscured the sunlight coming into the room. A white doily underneath a crystal candy dish on the coffee table caught my attention, and I wondered if she had crocheted it. My grandmother had tried to teach me to crochet once, but I couldn't get the hang of it—not enough eye-hand coordination, I guess.

Lost in my memories, I failed to notice Mrs. Winterfield return to the living room until she handed me a cupcake on a floral china plate.

"Thank you, Mrs. Winterfield. This looks so good." I took a bite of the chocolate cupcake and savored its sweet taste. Had I not been in someone else's home, I would have devoured it…I was so hungry. However, behaving in a way that would have made my mother proud, I refrained myself and ate it slowly. "These are delicious!

"I'm glad you like them, dear. Now tell me, how is Mae doing?" Mrs. Winterfield settled into her chair, leaning her cane next to the Queen Anne end table that looked just like the one my grandmother used to have in her living room.

"She's doing fine. Actually, a lot better than I would have

expected. It's got to be hard losing a sister, especially to murder."

Mrs. Winterfield leaned back in her chair. "It's sad, really. Those two girls were so close growing up."

"Do you mind if I ask, how do you know them?" I took another bite of my cupcake.

"Oh, heavens no. I worked for years as Chauncey Peterson's housekeeper. In the beginning, he was a wonderful man to work for, but after his wife died, he changed. Money and his reputation became more important to him than anything else."

"Why?"

She sighed. "When he couldn't save his wife, he put all his energy into elevating his social standing and his bank account. Somehow, I think he thought those things would take away his grief, but they didn't. So sad."

"You said Mae and her sister were close at one time. What happened?"

"After their mother's death, Mae became her father's favorite. I think it was because she looked so much like her mother." She shook her head. "No matter how hard Anne tried, she could never measure up. She so wanted her father to love her as much as he loved Mae." She sighed deeply and then continued. "But since she couldn't win his love, she took it out on Mae."

"That explains a lot."

"Yes, it does, dear. Anne always had a lot to offer, but she really didn't come into her own until Mae moved away. Of course, I always wondered what would have happened if Anthony had not come into their lives. Perhaps they would have mended their fences, but we'll never know."

"Anthony?" I asked, hoping to encourage her to keep talking.

"Mae's first husband. Anne was smitten with him. I dare-

162

THE PECULIAR CASE OF THE PETERSBURG PROFESSOR

say, had Anne met him first, I believe she would have won his heart."

"Did Mae know?"

"Of course, she did, dear. Anne did nothing to hide her feelings. When Anthony died, it devastated both Anne and Mae. Anne went back to school and married Burt." She leaned forward. "I always suspected it was a rebound marriage for her, although I believe Burt always adored her."

"What happened to Mae?" I scooted to the edge of my seat.

"Mae moved away too. Had her baby and remarried—"

"A baby? Mae has never mentioned having a child."

Mrs. Winterfield straightened up in her chair. I sensed I had struck a nerve. "That, my dear, is another story for another day. I've kept you far too long. Thank you for letting an old lady ramble on about the past, but you have things to do, and I have a party to get ready for." She reached over and grabbed her cane to steady herself as she got out of her chair.

"Thank you, Mrs. Winterfield, for the cupcake. I hope you have a very happy birthday!"

After I left Mrs. Winterfield's house, I pulled into the nearest parking lot and jotted down everything I had learned from Mrs. Winterfield about Professor Ladd and Mae. *Baby? Never saw that one coming!*

* * *

After stopping at Yancy's for lunch, I headed to the police station with a hamburger in one hand and the steering wheel in the other. Within minutes, I pulled into the station's parking lot. I crumbled the hamburger wrapper, threw it into the paper bag, and headed to the brick building.

Seeing my reflection on the glass doors, I immediately wiped the few remnants of my fast-food lunch off my face. The last thing I needed was to have catsup all over my chin. If

Detective Douglas saw me, he would probably accuse me of being a vampire.

As the door swung shut behind me, I saw Lawrence standing behind the counter. He was alone. Perfect!

"Hi, how's your day going?" I asked, doing my best to partake in some idle chitchat before getting to my real purpose.

"Good. It's been quiet here today." He stamped the last few papers in front of him and moved them to a nearby pile.

"That's because everyone is at Mae's buying stuff for Sweetest Day." I laughed.

"Sweetest Day?" He looked up, confused.

"It's today, you know, the day you remember your sweetest and dearest…"

"I thought that was Valentine's Day." He shook his head.

"That's in February, and Sweetest Day is in October." I paused for a moment. "Lawrence, are you telling me you've never heard about Sweetest Day?"

"Not a thing." He shook his head. "Do you suppose my wife knows about this?"

"Oh, yeah, and you better get on it. You don't want to go home empty-handed tonight," I teased.

"But yesterday was her birthday. I already got her some-thing," he protested.

"That doesn't count. This is totally different."

After giving him a few ideas—a card with some flowers or a box of chocolates—he relaxed.

"Good thing you came here today, or I would have been in the doghouse for sure," he said, relieved.

"Glad I could be of help."

For all his gruffness, Lawrence still surprised me with his tenderness from time to time.

"Nice look," I said, smiling while pointing to his attire. He looked quite dapper today in his blue button-down shirt and paisley tie.

"Uh, thanks. What I do for the man." He laughed, slightly embarrassed by my compliment. He grabbed a stack of papers from the counter behind him. "Paperwork. It never ends." Lawrence walked over to the edge of the counter and dragged a stool to where he was working. "Hey, did Rick get a hold of you?"

"No, why?"

"We're all getting together tonight at his house. Kind of came about yesterday afternoon. We didn't see you or T.J. around, so Rick said he would call you. Can you let T.J. know? Rick said he didn't have his number. About 8:00 p.m. or so." He sat down on his newly acquired stool and started sorting the papers into three piles.

"Sure, I'll call him. Are you going?"

He looked up from his work. "Well, I was, but since somebody informed me it's Sweetest Day, I guess I better come up with something more romantic than taking my wife to a party with a bunch of college kids."

"That'd probably be a good idea." I grinned. "Hey, have you, by any chance, seen the medical examiner's report on Professor Ladd?"

He looked around and then leaned closer to me. "Detective Douglas has it now, but I heard the time of death was most likely between six and eight o'clock that morning, from a gunshot wound. There were no signs of a struggle."

"Okay, that fits what we know…except for the struggle part. I would think that means she knew her killer."

"Possibly, or at least was someone she didn't think posed a threat."

"What about a ballistics report? Did you know the police seized my dad's and Mae's guns?"

He nodded.

"Do you know if they found a match with Mae's gun?"

"I haven't heard, but if they *had,* she would be behind bars now."

I breathed a sigh of relief. "Yeah, that's a good sign. I mean, I know I didn't shoot Professor Ladd, but I was worried that Mae had."

We stopped talking as two officers passed through the lobby and greeted Lawrence.

After they were gone, I asked, "Can you find out if there is a file on Mae Emerson?"

"There probably is one, since they had a search warrant to look for her gun."

"I don't suppose there would be any way you could get a look at it?"

Lawrence turned his head and thought for a moment. "I might know someone who could help with that."

"That would be great. I want to know when she moved away from Petersburg. I heard a rumor that she had a child, and I'd like to verify that, if possible. If you have a piece of paper, I'll give you my phone number, and you can call me if you find out something. Oh, and one more thing…on July 2, 1951, an accident occurred in which an Anthony Romano died. Can you also check and see if the accident report lists anything about weather or alcohol playing a role?"

"Let me write all that down or else I'll forget. I'll see what I can find out."

"Thanks."

As I jotted my number down and handed it to Lawrence, Detective Douglas walked into the lobby. "Ms. Kilpatrick. What a surprise to see you here. Are you working on your story?"

"Yeah…yeah…that's right. Got a deadline, you know," I stammered.

"Let me know if you find any new information for *your story*." He smiled slightly.

* * *

Whenever our Commuter Lounge group got together at someone's house, everyone brought something to eat or drink —our version of a potluck, I suppose. The guys usually brought beer or soft drinks and chips, and the female component of the group brought desserts. My specialty was brownies or cookies, but tonight I had a craving for something different. I wasn't sure what that *something different* would be, but I needed to decide quickly. It was already 4:00, and I still had homework to do before leaving for Rick's house.

As I walked through the front door, the aroma of Mom's pot roast greeted me. I went into the kitchen to tell her I was home, but it was empty, so I went to my room. There was a note taped to my door, which read, "We are at Mike's house. Turn off the oven if we are not home by seven." *Thank goodness they're gone!* I wasn't in the mood for another confrontation. However, reading the note reminded me I was supposed to call T.J., so I dashed down to the living room to use the phone. His mom answered and said he wasn't home, but she would tell him about the party.

"I'll be leaving around 7:30 p.m., so if he wants to ride with me, tell him to call me."

After checking "call T.J." off my list, I ran back to my room and pulled my recipe box from the top shelf in my closet. I thumbed through the recipe cards in search of the perfect dessert for tonight while sitting on the edge of my bed. Gidget sauntered in and jumped by my side to investigate what I was doing.

"Gidget." I rubbed her head while easing it away from the box. "I can't see the recipe cards if you keep putting your head on top of them. You've got to move." I picked her up and placed her on top of the pillow behind me.

While going through the recipe cards, I looked over my shoulder and saw Gidget's eyes focused on the recipe box, slowly moving toward it.

"Fine. You win…again." I picked up my recipe box and moved it to my desk. Gidget shot me a disapproving look and sat on the bed glaring at me. Sometimes, I wondered which of us was the boss—Gidget or me?

As soon as I picked up the card with "Pumpkin Cake" written across the top, I knew what I was going to bake. Pumpkin was perfect for a cold autumn evening. I would bake it in a Bundt pan and slice it when I got to Rick's house.

I ran down to the kitchen and gathered all the ingredients. With the house to myself, I turned on the radio and got busy baking. Gidget wandered into the kitchen and rubbed against my legs, purring loudly.

"I'll get you some in just a minute." I patted her head. "Great. Now I have to wash my hands before putting the puréed pumpkin in the bowl. As cute as you are, nobody wants one of your hairs in their piece of cake."

Gidget, ignoring my mini rant, walked over to her empty saucer, sat down, and stared at me. *Such a sweet face, even when she's angry.* I went to the refrigerator, pulled out the milk container, and filled her saucer.

While she was busy enjoying her milk, I finished the pumpkin cake batter and put it in the oven. Mom's double-wall oven came in handy for times like this. It was a lifesaver around Thanksgiving. With the turkey in one oven, there was room in the other for browning the marshmallows on the sweet potato casserole and warming up the stuffing and dinner rolls. Today, Mom's roast could cook in the upper oven, and I could get my cake baked in the lower one.

When I sat down in my room to do some homework, I realized I had left my photography textbook at the gift shop. *I'll stop by and pick it up tomorrow. Goodness knows, I've got plenty of homework to keep me busy.* I opened the book for my journalism law class to the first page of our reading assignment.

As I skimmed the page, my suspects' poster board, which

was standing in the corner, caught my attention. I put the book down and grabbed my black marker and began adding the day's new info to the board: the cause and the time of death for Anne, Mae's mysterious absence from the store yesterday afternoon, the attack on Bob, and the biggest surprise of the day, Mae had a child.

As I stared at her name, I hoped she was not the murderer. Yet, one thing remained quite certain—I really didn't know her at all.

The phone rang downstairs, interrupting my thoughts.

It was Lawrence, and he had some information. "The accident report doesn't mention weather or alcohol as contributing factors to the Romano accident, and regarding Mae Emerson—she married Anthony Romano in 1949. In 1951, he died in a car accident. Soon after that, she moved to Boston and gave birth to a son on March 15, 1952, and married a Jonathan Miller later that year. Within days of their marriage, Jonathan started adoption proceedings for her son.

Curious about the son's name?" he asked.

I said nothing.

"Michelle, are you still there?"

"Yes, I'm here." I sighed deeply as I clenched the charm around my neck.

"It was Craig—Craig Miller."

chapter fifteen

I yelled and screamed with each step as I went upstairs to my room. *How could he keep something like that from me? The jerk! I knew he was hiding something! But why? Why didn't he tell me?*

I glanced at my clock. It was 7:00 p.m. already. I turned around and ran downstairs, where I turned off the oven just as my parents were coming through the kitchen door, laughing.

"Sounds like you guys had a nice time."

"Yes, we did. Mike had us laughing so hard with his stories that we almost lost track of the time." Mom was grinning from ear to ear.

My father walked past me and went into the living room, where I heard him turn on the TV. Mom followed him but stopped and gave me a quick kiss. Apparently, all was forgiven, at least on her part.

"I see you remembered to turn off the oven. Thank you. I'm making roast beef sandwiches for tomorrow. Your father and I are going to Grandma's house after church, and we're going to eat them on the way. You wanna come with us?"

"Thanks, but no. I've got a lot of schoolwork to do."

"Well, if you change your mind..." She stopped. "Something sure smells good, and it's not my roast."

"That's not a nice way to talk about your roast." We both laughed. "I'm making a pumpkin cake. In fact, I better pull it out so it can cool." I put on a pair of orange oven mitts and placed the Bundt pan on the cooling rack. "Rick is having a bunch of us over at his house tonight, and I needed something to take. I should be home around midnight or one."

"Well, it smells delicious. I'm sure they'll love it. Is T.J. going with you?"

"No, I called him, but I never heard back," I said, trying to hide my disappointment.

Her eyes narrowed as she slipped off her coat. "Isn't midnight a little late for you to be out by yourself?"

"No, I'll be fine, but I better hurry and get ready, or I'm going to be late." I left before she could voice any more objections. My father's loud snores told me he had conked out on the couch, so I tiptoed up the stairs.

As I got ready, I tensed up, and my heart started beating faster as I thought of Craig—the master of deception. Thankfully, he wouldn't be at the party tonight since he was not part of the Commuter Lounge group. That was a relief!

I pushed all thoughts of him out of my mind so I could focus on getting ready for the party. I could deal with him tomorrow. With the latest issue of *Glamour Magazine* opened to an article on applying eyeshadow, I removed my glasses and did my best to follow the instructions by smudging the green eyeshadow on my eyelids. After adding a swish of white highlighter under the brow bone, some black eyeliner, and a couple of coats of mascara, I compared the image I saw in my mirror with the picture in the magazine. I smiled as I put my glasses back on and straightened the Eiffel Tower necklace around my neck. *Not bad!*

According to my watch, it was 7:20, and still no word from T.J. As I grabbed my purse hanging on the desk chair, I peeked out the window to see if his car was in his driveway.

No. He wasn't home yet. I started to close the drapes when Gidget jumped on the desk to look out the window.

"My, aren't we demanding tonight?" I patted her head, smiling. There was no way I was going to close the drapes now and deprive her of some serious evening bird watching or whatever it was she was hoping to keep an eye on.

Back in the kitchen, I tipped the cake out of the pan onto a plate. *Now I need something to carry it in.* Inside the pantry, I pulled the step stool out. Even with the added height, I still could not reach the harvest gold plastic cake carrier. Since I had been in this situation before, I knew what needed to be done. I grabbed the yardstick in the corner and used it to slide the carrier off the top shelf, catching it on its way down. *Mission accomplished!* I spied a light bulb on a lower shelf and grabbed it too.

With the pumpkin cake safely in its carrier, I opened the kitchen door and, once again, the sound of my father snoring on the sofa greeted me. *Gotta be careful not to wake him.* I had two options. I could forego wearing a coat and go out the back door, which would avoid disturbing my father. However, since there were no lights in the back or at the side of the house, my chances of running into a skunk or a raccoon were pretty good. The second option was the front door—the squeaky front door. If I opened it slowly, perhaps I could get out without waking him.

I took a chance on option two. First, I put the light bulb on the table by the front door. Then I opened the door only wide enough for me to slip through, and in one swift motion, grabbed my coat hanging on the nearby hook and slowly closed the door. *Success!* Things were looking up.

The temperature had dropped since this afternoon. Thank goodness I had added a navy pullover sweater over my shirt. I was still cold, even with my winter coat, but I would survive.

The aroma from the pumpkin cake riding shotgun in the

passenger seat permeated my car's small space. If smells could be a blanket, the pumpkin cake guaranteed I would soon be warm on this crisp autumn night. And if the aroma wasn't enough to warm my blood, my rage against Craig would surely do the trick.

Cars parked bumper-to-bumper lined Rick's street, so I drove to the next block before parking. I looked for T.J.'s car along the way, but didn't see it. Luckily, I found a spot at the end of the block. Parallel parking was something I avoided at all costs, even if it meant walking a little further, but I rationalized I could use the exercise anyway.

I reached over to the passenger seat to pick up the cake carrier. As I walked down the street, I decided not to tell anyone about Craig being Mae's son. I wanted to talk to him first—to hear his side of the story—not that he could say anything that would ever make me trust him again.

I remembered Rick mentioned last week that his mother would be gone for the weekend, which had probably led to the impromptu party at his house. She and a friend had gone to Columbus, Ohio, to look at several fitness centers in the area. With twenty years of experience as a nutritionist, she was exploring the idea of creating a place where she could provide people with a place to exercise and get guidance in making healthy food choices. I wondered if her former husband's new girlfriend had kick-started her desire to make a change in her life and open a health and fitness center in the Petersburg area. The idea of paying to exercise someplace sounded foreign to me. However, Rick, one of her biggest supporters, assured me it was the wave of the future, just like those new video rental stores that were opening in the area.

As I walked up the driveway, I could hear "Bungle in the Jungle" by Jethro Tull, Rick's favorite group, playing loud and clear. There was no need to knock. The front door was wide open, despite the evening chill.

On my way to the kitchen to drop off my cake, I saw that

almost everyone from our Commuter Lounge group was at the party. Tasha, wearing a maxi peasant dress, was in the living room, sitting in the corner talking politics with Jimmy, dressed in jeans and a neatly pressed white button-down. His tweed jacket was lying on the floor next to him. Not to be outdone in the fashion department, Yash, the *GQ* star in our small band of commuters, was dressed to the nines. It was hard not to miss his green plaid pants, green-on-green patterned knit sweater vest, and solid green shirt. I felt incredibly underdressed until I saw Amy walk up to Yash—she, like me, was in jeans. A navy sweater set for her and a navy crewneck sweater for me. To quote *Anne of Green Gables*, we were "kindred spirits," at least for the moment.

"You want something to drink?"

I turned around, and Rick beamed as he pointed to the three coolers along the kitchen wall, filled with ice and canned drinks. "We've got some beer, soft drinks, and some diet stuff…see, I remembered, and, oh, yeah, some special beer my brother brought back from his trip to Colorado."

"A diet drink would be great, thanks. Gotta drive tonight, you know." I laughed.

"Did T.J. come with you? I haven't seen him around yet."

"No, I left a message with his mom, but I never heard from him." I acted as uninterested as I could. "Is that Billy's guitar in the corner?"

"Yeah, I asked him to bring it and play some tonight, but he brought Bethany, and you know how much she dislikes him playing the guitar."

Too bad. Billy was so talented. I was sure he could quit school, take his band to LA, and become one of those overnight sensations. But I guess it was true what they say, "opposites attract."

Rick handed me a diet pop. "Haven't seen you in the Commuter Lounge the last couple of days. Anything new on Professor Ladd's murder?"

"No, sad to say." I paused, thinking of a way to segue into my questions, but there didn't seem to be one. "This probably sounds like a random question, but do you know anything about how asphalt reacts to rainwater?"

"Uh, not sure what you mean,." He cocked his head, puzzled by my question.

"Let's say it rained in the morning or early afternoon. Would an asphalt road still be wet at night?" I took a sip of my drink and watched the wheels turning in his head as he thought about my question.

"Not knowing the particular road, I couldn't be sure. As a general rule, asphalt roads are built with a slope, so the water runs off and, because they're black, they absorb the heat from the sun, causing the water to evaporate."

Amy sashayed up to Rick and whispered something in his ear.

"Excuse me," he said. "I'll be back in a sec."

She smiled and gave me a quick wink.

I knew what she was up to, and it annoyed me she could get any guy's attention whenever she wanted. *Maybe she'll get bored with Rick and ditch him so she can find another guy with whom to occupy her time. Then Rick and I can pick up where we left off.*

As she led Rick out the back door, I looked over my shoulder and saw T.J. coming through the front door. Todd was behind him, his head towering above T.J.'s. They were both nodding and laughing as they entered the living room. The third person in the group had her arm linked with T.J.'s. *That's got to be Meg. I bet they've been together all day. That's why he didn't call.*

She was pretty. Actually, *stunning* was more accurate. She could have passed as a model, with her perfect olive-colored complexion and long wavy dark hair.

I pushed my glasses back up my nose. My heart sank.

175

T.J. and Meg made their way to where I was standing. "Hey, Michelle, I'd like you to meet Meg."

The three of us exchanged a few pleasantries, but our conversation felt forced. Instead of carrying on like we were the best of friends, T.J. and I were like strangers struggling to find something to talk about. In the past, when T.J. and I went to a commuter party, I always had him to talk to when I needed a break from talking to everyone else, but tonight, I needed a break from him.

After a few painful minutes, T.J. and Meg excused themselves to mingle with the rest of the group. Rick and Amy had come back inside, but they were still talking to each other, so I made the best of my awkward freedom to do some sleuthing.

I moseyed into the living room and found Billy, Bethany, and Todd sitting near the fireplace. Even from where I was standing, I could hear them discussing the prospect of a Beatles reunion. In the four years since the Fab Four had broken up, there had been several rumors about them getting back together. Todd, a die-hard Beatles fan and a sci-fi nerd, held out eternal hope that the rumor mill had it right this time.

Jimmy was sitting alone on the sofa, drinking a beer as he stared into space, obviously not the least bit interested in their conversation.

I seized the moment. "Hi, Jimmy. How's it goin'?" I sat down on the other end of the couch, setting my diet drink on the Niagara Falls coaster on the end table.

"Not bad, and with you? Any progress on the murder investigation?" He hoisted his can in the air and took another drink.

"Not enough, that's for sure. Bob came into Mae's shop the other night and said something about working on Steve Goodright's Fleetwood. Doesn't your dad work on Steve's cars?"

"Yeah, he takes care of all the Goodright family's cars." He thought for a moment and then shook his head. "I don't think I've ever heard him talk about a Fleetwood though."

"I'm sure that's what Bob said. Weird." I lifted my drink to take a sip but stopped midair. "Why would Bob tell Barb that Steve owed him money for car repairs if your dad takes care of all Steve's cars?"

"I don't know. Dad's never mentioned any of the Goodright cars going out for repairs. I mean, why would they send them out? Dad has a top-of-the-line, fully equipped garage on the estate grounds to work in. Wonder what that was all about?"

"Could you do me a favor and ask your dad if he knows anything about a Fleetwood?" I saw a pad of scratch paper and a pencil by the telephone next to my drink. "Here, let me give you my number. If he remembers anything, call me. It's really important."

Amy, followed by Rick, T.J., and Meg, came into the living room, where she proclaimed, "Speaking of *really important*, have I got some news for you."

T.J. and Meg moved closer to Amy. "Betsy came into the diner last night, and Mr. Ladd came in a few minutes later. When I went to take their orders, he said he was in a hurry and wanted something that wouldn't take too long. I suggested the chef's salad, because those are ready to be served. It's really a great salad. It has—"

T.J. threw his arm up and moved his hand in a small circle, signaling to Amy that she needed to keep the story moving.

She rolled her eyes and continued. "Anyway, that's what they both ordered, plus Betsy's usual unsweetened tea and his black coffee." She lowered her voice. "As I was walking to their table with their orders, I overheard Mr. Ladd say, 'I asked you to stay out of it. If anyone saw you coming out of —' Then he saw me and stopped."

"Did you hear anything else?" I asked, leaning over the coffee table.

"No, cook was hitting the bell, so I had to get back to the kitchen because I had more orders up."

As I leaned back into my chair, Amy added, "When I took the order to the table behind Betsy and Mr. Ladd, I noticed Mr. Ladd wasn't at the table, and Betsy looked like she'd been crying. I mean, there were streaks of mascara running down her face. That is so not like Betsy! I mean, I would have thought she wore waterproof mascara—"

T.J. crossed his arms and asked, "*Then* what?"

Unfazed by his impatience, Amy cocked her head and smiled. "What? You don't care about waterproof mascara? I bet Meg does."

This time, T.J. rolled his eyes. "Just tell us what happened next."

"Yeah, Amy, get to the point." Rick shook his head.

She continued, with a twinkle in her eye and smiling like a Cheshire cat. "I asked her if everything was alright, and she said 'No.' Then she whispered, 'Sometimes you try to solve a problem and help someone, and only make more problems for yourself.'" Amy looked around the room and saw she had our undivided attention. "Then the customer in the booth at the end of my section needed more coffee, so I had to go. When I turned around, she was gone. Crazy, but neither one of them touched their salads. What a waste of good food but, at least, she left me a nice tip."

Rick shook his head and followed T.J. and Meg into the kitchen. I sat silently on the couch, replaying the encounter Amy had just described. *I wonder what Betsy meant when she said she tried to solve a problem, but only made it worse? Did Professor Ladd refuse to give Burt a divorce, and Betsy took matters into her own hands? And the audacity of Burt Ladd to go out for dinner with his lover on the same day as his wife's funeral. Disgusting!*

I had to remind myself, "Innocent until proven guilty," but it was hard not to jump to conclusions.

* * *

After grabbing my coat, I stood on Rick's front porch and watched my breath float in the night air. The temperature had dropped again while I had been inside. For once, the weatherman got it right when he'd issued a freeze warning for this evening. I buttoned my coat, stuck my hands in my pockets, and dashed to my car, thankful I hadn't parked any further away. Not having T.J. to talk to had put a damper on the evening and, while I knew I was being silly, I felt very alone without him by my side.

Once inside my car, I turned the defroster on high and pulled my coat closer while I waited for the windows to clear. Thoughts of T.J. and Meg huddled together, Amy luring Rick away, and the puzzle involving Bob, Steve, and the mysterious Fleetwood occupied my mind.

After the windows cleared and my hands regained their feeling, I turned on the lights and headed home. The more I thought about T.J. and Rick, the more depressed I got. Why did T.J. ignore me? It wasn't like I was going to tell Meg all his secrets. I mean, I wasn't in competition with her for his affections, right? Or was I? And then there was Rick. Couldn't he have at least had the decency to finish our conversation? Was Amy that much more interesting than me?

A deer ran across the road, and I slammed on the brakes just in time to avoid hitting it. *Time to slow down, girl, and concentrate on your driving.*

I took a deep breath. I probably shouldn't have left without saying goodbye to T.J. I should have at least tried to act like nothing had changed between us. But, thankfully, there was Monday. Hopefully, I could fix things between us on the way to school. And when it came to Rick, perhaps I got it wrong. He looked sad when I told him I was leaving. Maybe I should have stayed a little longer, but if he wanted to talk, he should have said something. Anyway, if Rick thought of something, I was sure he'd call me or tell me when I saw him at the Commuter Lounge.

As if my life wasn't complicated enough right now—T.J., Rick, and a likely cover-up regarding Anthony Romano's death—there was Craig Miller. For a few moments, I had actually forgotten about him, but now that he was front and center in my mind again, the very thought of him made my blood boil. *He's got some explaining to do!*

chapter sixteen

I pulled into the driveway and noticed the eerie glow from the porch light on the pumpkins and bales of hay on the porch. The harvest decorations provided a pleasant diversion from my problems. Since they weren't there when I left this evening, I figured Mike's wife, Suzie, known for going all out with holiday decorations, must have inspired my mom to decorate.

The living room light was usually left on when I was going to be out late at night, but tonight the room was dark. The departure from what was normal unsettled me.

Then it happened. Something moved, and I froze. *Maybe it was a mouse.* Every so often, one got inside the house. Even though I grew up on the farm, the thought of crossing paths with a field mouse scared the living daylights out of me. I heard it again. Something was definitely moving. I could hear the crunching of paper.

I flipped on the hallway light, but nothing happened, so I made my way in the dark to the lamp next to the couch and turned it on. There sat Gidget on top of the newspaper my father had left on the coffee table.

"You about gave me a heart attack." I started breathing again and walked over and picked her up.

Suddenly, I realized I had two free arms. *Shoot!* I'd left my mom's cake carrier at Rick's. Hopefully, he'd think to bring it with him to school next week.

"Oh, Gidget, I've got way too much on my mind. Let's go get a glass of milk." I chuckled and corrected myself as I patted her head. "How about a glass of milk for me and a saucer of milk for you? And, tell you what, let's take them up to our room. We'll eat up there tonight."

A few minutes later, I was sitting on my bed, head pressed against the pillows I had propped against the headboard. I spread the papers from Keith and all my notes in front of me. Gidget's purring as she sat in the corner of the room lapping up her milk attested to her happiness with our dine-in arrangement.

I'm going to try something different. Instead of thinking of three unrelated mysteries, I'm going to think of them as one mystery with three different parts. I reached for my notebook and made three columns. I labeled them Accident, Missing Money, and Murder. Under each heading, I listed all the facts I had about that category. Since Professor Ladd was investigating the lumber company's finances, I wrote the names of the people in the photographs in the missing money column. *Now, who shows up in all three categories? Mae, Steve, and Bob.* As far as I knew, Barb was not connected to the Peterson household at the time of the accident, but I needed to check that out. Betsy and Craig—my other murder suspects—were not even born yet, so they were off the hook *for the moment.*

I was convinced there was a cover-up regarding Romano's car accident. Neither weather nor alcohol contributed to the accident, so why did the newspaper report that they did? Who would want to publish a false account? Who were they protecting? It had to be somebody important, and from my perspective, there was no one more important at that time than members of the Peterson family. They had money and prestige.

There was also the fact that Bob, the Peterson's chauffeur, had reported the accident. After Chauncey Peterson's death, Bob inherited enough money to open his auto repair shop and had been getting money from Steve through the lumber company—more evidence for my blackmail theory.

It was also interesting that, according to my timeline, when Craig started investigating the lumber company's finances, the checks to Bob increased in amount and the checks to Mae stopped. One possibility was that Bob was the murderer, but why would he kill Professor Ladd? That didn't make any sense, unless he was afraid she would expose his involvement in the accident. But why would he blackmail Steve?

I rubbed my forehead. The pieces didn't fit. Plus, there was still the question of why Steve was giving money to Mae. I needed to talk to Bob like I had planned, but seeing him alone was out of the question, since I had no idea what he was involved in.

* * *

Sunday, October 20th

The next morning, as I peeked out my window, I saw the grass glistening, covered in frost. The trees in the front yard were bare, their leaves scattered on the ground beneath them. I could see T.J.'s car parked in its usual spot in his driveway. I put on my jeans and a gray sweatshirt and wondered if he was up yet. It was Sunday, and he was still probably in bed sleeping, since his family was not the church-going type. I wondered how late he had stayed at Rick's party.

I headed downstairs with my notebook in hand. The family picture hanging in the stairway caught my attention. It was crooked, which was not surprising, considering how many times I ran up and down the stairs every day. The real surprise was that it hadn't fallen down yet.

I gave the photograph a slight nudge to the right and stepped back to survey it. *That's better.* I gazed at the picture and calculated that I must have been about twelve years old when it was taken. Life was so simple then. If only it could be that way now.

I opened the door to the kitchen and saw Mom had already washed the breakfast dishes and put them away. She hated leaving the house with a sink full of dirty dishes. She and my dad had already left for church, and they would be gone for most of the day, except for stopping by the house to pick up their sandwiches. I went with them to church on most Sundays but bowed out today since they were driving to Michigan to spend the day with my grandmother. With so much homework, I couldn't afford to lose a day of studying. Besides, I had some serious business with Craig to tend to.

I turned the radio on, and while Paul Simon sang about the virtues of Kodachrome, I poured a glass of orange juice, fried two eggs, made a piece of toast, and sat down to plan my day. After I finished, I washed and dried my breakfast dishes. I chuckled when I realized that, like my mother, I couldn't leave the kitchen without tidying up first.

I settled down in the recliner in the living room, lying back in it and letting the footrest pop up. As I dialed Craig's number, I reminded myself to remain calm. He deserved the chance to explain himself. "Craig, glad I got you. What all do you know about Anthony Romano?"

There was silence.

"Anything besides the fact he was married to Mae?"

"We need to talk." He paused. "But I think in-person would be better. Can you meet me sometime today?"

"Name the time and place."

* * *

On my way to meet Craig at the Western Steakhouse near campus, I stopped by Mae's Gift Shop to pick up the textbook I had forgotten yesterday. Mae's was closed, but I had my spare key. The light coming through the front windows lit my way to the back room, and I noticed the Sweetest Day card display was almost empty. That would make Mae happy. She disliked storing unsold holiday merchandise. She always grumbled, "It sits in the back room for a year, takes up space, and makes no money." At least this year, leftover Sweetest Day cards would fit in a tiny box. That wouldn't take up too much room!

When I got to the back, I went straight to the table where I thought I had left my book, but it wasn't there. I looked underneath it, in case it had fallen on the floor, but no luck. *Where could it be? Perhaps Mae's desk?* She had a small one in the back of the room that she rarely used. I thought perhaps she moved it there so it wouldn't get lost.

Sure enough, that's where it was. As I picked up my book, I saw a crumbled piece of paper lying close to the garbage can on the floor, so I reached for it, fully intending to throw it away…until curiosity got the better of me.

When I smoothed it out and saw that it was from Professor Ladd, I had to read it. I pulled the chair out from under the desk and sat down. The letter was dated October 1, 1974.

Dearest Mae,

If you are reading this letter, I am no longer on this earth, and my lawyer is following the instructions I have given him. It also means I never corrected a wrong I committed many years ago. For that, I am eternally sorry. I hope you can forgive me.

Growing up in your shadow was difficult. You were always Father's favorite. Where you could do no wrong, I could do no right. When you married Tony, I was jealous and did everything to destroy your marriage. I convinced myself I could love Tony more than you ever could and that he would love me more than he ever loved you. I was wrong. Our affair was wrong.

As you know, the night he died, he came to see me at the family cottage by the lake. I thought he was coming to tell me he was leaving you. In fact, I was so convinced it was over between the two of you that I told Father about our affair. He went into a tirade about how awful I was and blamed me for everything. I, in turn, told him how horrible you were and that you had driven Tony into my arms with all your demanding ways. I wanted him to see that you were not perfect. Yet, rather than blame you for your marriage problems, he blamed me for ruining the family's reputation.

After the accident, I wanted to punish you. I wanted you to believe Tony was leaving you for me. But that was not what happened that evening. Instead, he came to see me and told me he wanted to give his marriage a second chance. He was determined to work things out. I hated you for his decision.

Over the years, I have seen I was wrong. I regret Tony never knew he was going to be a father and that he didn't have the opportunity to know his son. Although I wrote several letters to you over the years, I couldn't mail them to you, because Steve said you had sworn him to secrecy over your address, so I asked him to forward them to you. I do not know if you ever received them, but I know you never responded.

When I moved back to Petersburg, I hoped we could mend our differences. I understand why you wanted nothing to do with me. Perhaps, if I had written this letter sooner, things might have been different. But since you have received this letter, I obviously never apologized to you for everything. I am sorry about the affair with Tony. I am sorry for the lie I let you live with all these years. I am sorry for the pain I have caused you. Please find it in your heart to forgive me. You are my sister. I wish I could have been your friend. Love, Anne

An affair? No wonder Mae wanted nothing to do with her sister. I wondered if Steve ever gave Mae the letters Anne wrote? Was Craig aware that his aunt had an affair with his father and tried to destroy his parents' marriage?

I had been so engrossed in reading the letter, I failed to hear the front door open. With no warning, I heard footsteps coming toward me.

"Who's there?" I shouted. The shakiness in my voice did nothing to disguise my fear. I crumbled the paper and threw it into the garbage can. With my book and purse in hand, I managed to get a few steps away from the desk before the door to the back room opened.

"Michelle? Is that you?" It was Mae. "Are you okay?"

"Yeah, sorry, you scared me. I forgot one of my books for class, so I stopped by to get it," I said as I walked toward the door.

"Did you find it? I put it on my desk in the back."

"Yes, I found it. Thank you." I reached for the doorknob, and as I closed the door, hollered, "See you Tuesday night. Gotta run...got a meeting in a few minutes. Bye."

* * *

Craig was sitting at a booth in the back of the restaurant. Families dressed in their Sunday best sat at table after table, enjoying their steaks and baked potatoes. On most days, the sound of steaks sizzling on the grill would have reminded me it was time to eat, but I was too upset. Food was the last thing on my mind. My great plan to remain calm, however, went out the window as soon as I saw Craig. I wanted answers, and I wanted them now!

I barely sat down before my outburst began. "When were you going to get around to telling me you're Mae's son? Any other secrets? Maybe we should start with your father, Anthony Romano?" Had I not been so angry with Craig, I would have relished that he was speechless.

He looked down at the table. "I...I was going to tell you...

it never seemed like a good time." Finally, he looked up at me. "Why do you think I wanted to see you today? I was going to tell you."

Before I could respond, a perky waitress with a dark blue bib apron tied around her neck and waist stopped at our table. "Have you been here before?"

"Yes," I answered abruptly and then smiled, realizing how gruff I sounded. After all, she was not the one I was angry with. I quickly added, "I mean, I don't know if he has been here or not, but I have."

"Okay, wanted to make sure you knew you had to go through the line to order your meat, and that's where you pay. The plates for your salad and dessert are over there." She pointed to two sets of buffet tables behind her. "And the glasses and drinks are over there," she said, pointing to the corner on the right. "Serve yourself. Just remember to get your receipt first."

Craig sat stone-faced.

"Thank you. We'll get in line in a few minutes," I said.

When she was out of earshot, I picked up where I had left off. "Why should I believe you? You're probably only telling me that now because I found out."

"Anne and my mother had a very complicated relationship."

"That's an understatement." I rolled my eyes. "And you and your mother?"

He looked down. "Sorry to say, we have *no* relationship. We haven't spoken for…I guess it's been five years or so. We had a falling out about the time she moved back to Petersburg with Nathan."

"Nathan?"

"Her husband, Nathan Emerson. She moved here, and I went to NYC and lived with some friends before starting at Columbia."

He looked lost. I almost felt sorry for him, but I needed to keep my guard up. Without a tinge of emotion, I asked, "Why the falling out?"

"It's a long story, and I'll tell you some other time, but, trust me, it has nothing to do with my father's car accident."

"Why should I trust you?" My disgust with him was growing.

"Because it's the truth. Listen, when Anne contacted me, she told me she had suspicions about my father's death. She had a lot of baggage she had been carrying around—"

"Yeah, an affair is pretty heavy to carry around," I said sarcastically.

"Wait, how do you know about the affair? *And*—" he paused, "—come to think of it, how did you find out Mae was my mother?"

"I'm an investigative reporter, remember? You're not the only one who has sources."

"And the affair?" Craig asked.

I pulled the old black-and-white photo out of my bag and placed it in front of him. "Is this your father with Professor Ladd?"

He picked it up and studied it before handing it back to me. "From the few photos I've seen of my father, I would say that's him, and the woman looks like Anne."

"That's what I thought. I also found a letter Professor Ladd had written to your mother, asking for forgiveness for all the trouble she had caused."

"So, you found the infamous letter? My, but you are quite the snoop, aren't you?"

I reared back. "I am not a snoop."

"I know, I know. You're an investigative reporter. Tell me, is there much difference between the two?" he said as he narrowed his eyes. "Never mind, don't answer that. But back to the letter. Anne told me she had left one with her lawyer in case something happened to her."

"You mentioned before that she was worried someone

would come after her. Would you care to elaborate on that…
but this time with no secrets?"

"Shortly after Anne started looking into the accident, there
were so many discrepancies, she felt she was onto something.
Then when she discovered the missing money at the lumber
company, well, one thing led to another. She felt she needed
to get answers before anyone figured out what she was doing.
Anne didn't know who she could trust, so she took a chance
and contacted me. She thought two heads were better than
one, and since it was my father's death she was investigating,
she thought I might want to get to the truth as much as she
did."

"Go on, I'm listening, but first, how did she know you
were Mae's son? I mean, Miller is a common last name."

"After Mae moved away from Petersburg, she stayed in
touch with Bob. Apparently, they had been quite close at one
time. Anyway, when Anne was at Bob's Repair Shop the day I
was on TV, he let it slip that I was Mae's son. He tried to make
it sound like he misspoke and that he only meant I looked so
much like her I could be *mistaken* for her son, but Anne's
curiosity got the better of her. She hired a private investigator
and discovered the truth."

I nodded. "Okay, go on."

"Anne worried, if foul play had been involved in my
father's death, someone could get hurt investigating it if the
guilty party was still alive. She claimed the roads weren't
wet that night, and my father had not been drinking." He sat
up straight, his demeanor becoming more confident as he
talked. "Of course, there was the possibility that he stopped
somewhere on the way home for a drink, or maybe even had
something in the car. That she didn't know. But she knew her
father was furious about the affair and that Bob was in the
vicinity, because he reported the accident. In her mind,
nothing added up to an accident. Flash forward. When she
found out you worked for Mae, she thought you would be

an excellent person to bring on board, but she didn't want you to know the entire story. She thought you would be another set of eyes and ears if something came up involving Mae."

As Craig talked, I noted he was looking me straight in the eyes. He didn't seem fidgety, which led me to believe he was telling the truth.

I pushed my glasses back up the bridge of my nose. "So, Professor Ladd only chose me because she needed a spy, not because she was impressed with my writing abilities. Is that what you're telling me? Wow, this gets better all the time!"

He shook his head. "No, that's not the way it was. She thought you showed a raw talent that needed to be developed. She saw the investigative assignment for the class as having two purposes. The first, to solve the mystery, and the second, to push you to be a better investigative reporter."

"I'm still confused. Why not just tell me the complete story? It sure would have made investigating a lot easier if I knew all the circumstances."

"Valid point. Which is why I was going to tell you everything today. Anne thought the less you knew, the safer you would be. But I realized you were already at risk because of your association with me and our investigation into my father's death. You needed to know what you were up against so you could decide if you wanted to keep working with me."

"I don't understand."

"You don't understand what?"

"What it is I'm up against."

"The unknown," he said as he tugged at his shirt sleeve. "I don't know who, or how many people, were involved in the cover-up about my father. And I don't know if Anne's murder had anything to do with our looking into my father's death. Maybe it was for some other reason. Perhaps the missing money at the lumber company ties into all of this? But until we know who is behind the murder and the missing money, you can trust no one."

"Does that include you?" I asked pointedly.

He leaned over the table. "No. From now on, I will be up-front with you. You can trust me."

I wasn't sure if I could or not. That was going to take some time to figure out, but I still had a nagging question I needed to ask. "If Professor Ladd was so concerned about her safety, why did she write the letter to the board? Wouldn't that give someone a motive to go after her?"

"I agree, and if Anne had asked my opinion, I would have told her not to do it. Which probably is why she didn't tell me about the letter until after she sent it."

I shook my head. "Did she say *why* she felt she needed to alert the board to the financial situation at the lumber company? I mean, I get she wanted to correct a wrong, but with the investigation into your father's death being so risky, why tempt fate even more?"

"Anne said she didn't want to see her father's business ruined. She knew the family's reputation and the family business were intertwined. If the business went down, so would the family name. Reputation was everything. She said she never understood that growing up, but now she did."

As Craig talked, more questions came to mind. "Why didn't Mae have any shares in the company? She said Steve reimbursed her."

"I'm not sure about this reimbursing stuff, but I can speak as to why my mother didn't have any shares in the lumber company. My grandfather was mad because she left and refused to have anything to do with him."

"Do you have any idea why she left when she did, especially when she was pregnant? You'd think she'd want her family nearby."

"For whatever reason, she didn't tell anyone she was pregnant. She kept that to herself and only later told Bob."

"But why cut off communication with her father?"

"After my father's accident, Anne said my grandfather blamed my mother's decision to leave town for creating a lot of gossip about the Peterson family, thereby jeopardizing the family's reputation. I don't think that was her intent. In my opinion, the combination of guilt, grief, and being alone and pregnant was more than she could handle, so she ran and left her past behind her."

"But that doesn't explain why Professor Ladd ended up with shares in the company? Let's face it, she wasn't exactly an innocent party in the affair."

"Yes, but Anne knew how to play the game. She won her father's approval by marrying Burt, a respectable man from a wealthy family. It worked. She got shares in the lumber company, and my mother did not. Pure and simple."

"What about Jonathan Miller?"

"Trust me, that too is a story in and of itself for some other time."

"Really?"

"Yes, but I can tell you he was a kind man who raised me as his son. Unfortunately, his shady business dealings caught up with him and cost him his life, but I digress. I was six when he died, but he left my mother a small fortune, which later helped finance her store, and he left me a sizable trust fund."

I sat there, speechless, reliving finding Professor Ladd's limp body in her office chair and then Bob under the car. Each new piece of information I garnered from Craig made my hunch that Anthony Romano's accident and her death were connected more plausible. Yet, something still did not make sense.

"I don't understand how Burt didn't know you were Anne's nephew."

"Easy." He shrugged. "Anne never told him, and when

she contacted me, she asked Bob not to tell him, or anyone else, including Steve."

I leaned over the table and looked him in the eye. "Promise me that, from now on, you will be honest with me. No holding back. It's not fair that you expect me to tell you everything, but you don't do the same with me."

"Fair enough." He nodded.

I leaned back in my seat and crossed my arms. "I have one more demand."

"What now?" he asked, his brows furrowed.

"I will not do one more thing on this case until we…" I paused for dramatic effect. "Eat. I'm starving."

It took him a minute to get it, and then he laughed. "Fine, but I'm paying."

"You'll get no argument from me."

Craig broke out in a wide grin. "Do my ears deceive me? But I believe that is the first time you have let me have the last word. Could this be the beginning of a trend?"

"I wouldn't count on it." I smiled as I stood up to go get in line.

For the next two hours, we hypothesized about motives and suspects regarding the deaths of Craig's father and Professor Ladd over sirloin tips, salad, and more than a few desserts. We agreed Steve had the best motive for killing Professor Ladd, considering she was about to destroy him with her letter to the board, assuming he was the person embezzling from the lumber company.

I set my fork down. "What about Bob? I don't think we can rule him out. He's the one who reported the accident, and he has been receiving some pretty sizable checks from Steve. I think it's also safe to surmise he knew about Anne's letter to the board."

"Why do you say that?"

"It was something he said one day when he came into the gift shop. He was yelling at Barb about the money Steve owed him for fixing one of his cars. He warned her that Anne didn't mind taking Steve down…even if he was family. I assume he was referring to the letter, but what I don't understand is why someone tried to kill *him*. Was he blackmailing Steve? That's a possibility. The thing is, I need to talk to him, and the sooner the better."

"I agree, but I'm going with you." Craig's tone left no doubt I would not be able to dissuade him. "I called the nurse's station this morning, and they said Bob was going to be moved to a regular room tomorrow. What do you say we go pay him a visit after our class tomorrow?"

chapter seventeen

I had only been home for a few minutes when I heard the garage door open. My parents were home.

It wasn't long before my mom peeked in my room, beaming. "Look what your grandmother gave me—her scrapbook."

As she walked toward my bed, clutching her prized possession, I moved my books and papers to one side, making room for her to sit down. Proudly, she opened the scrapbook, revealing its yellowed pages with newspaper clippings glued on them.

"You'll never believe what she has in here. Newspaper articles about people and things that happened in Petersburg. She started it to create a kind of time capsule to share with her grandchildren and great-grandchildren, but—" she laughed, "—I think she forgot all about it. We were cleaning out her basement, and there it was, under a pile of books. She was just as surprised as I was to find it there."

Mom flipped through the pages. "I think there are some things in here you might be interested in. Look! Here's the wedding announcement for Mae and Anthony."

I leaned over and gazed at the picture. "Wow! Her dress was beautiful."

"Wasn't it, though? And, my goodness, I had forgotten how handsome he was. No wonder she snatched him up."

I turned back to the beginning of the scrapbook and came across Steven Goodright's wedding announcement. My eyes grew wide as I read his bride's name—Barbara Braxton. *Braxton? Are Barb and Betsy related?* I continued reading the article, quickly skimming over the details of Barb's dress and the flowers in the church, until I came across the names of the people in the bridal party. I didn't recognize any of them, but one name caught my attention—Barb's brother, Samuel Braxton.

"She was a beautiful bride, wasn't she?" My mother sighed, pointing at Barb's photo. "I worked with her once on a fundraiser for the Women's League of Voters. I'll never forget how good she was at raising money. But I guess that should be no surprise, considering all her connections with the businesses in town. It helps when your family is rich, and everyone knows your name." Mom laughed.

I hopped off the bed and walked toward my vanity.

Mom continued reminiscing as I opened the drawer and pulled out a pen. "I never had any run-ins with her, but one woman on the committee warned me that, when it came to the Goodright children, Barb was like a lioness protecting her cubs." She stopped. "Everything alright?" she asked as I sat back down on the bed and started writing.

"Everything's fine. I realized a girl I know at school might be related to Barb Goodright, and I don't want to forget to ask her about it. Small world, isn't it?"

"Yes, it is."

I could tell from her puzzled look that she knew I had something on my mind, but she didn't ask me about it, and I pretended not to notice her gaze. After we finished looking through Grandma's scrapbook, the phone rang, and she went downstairs to answer it.

"Michelle," she hollered, "it's for you."

"Is it T.J.?"

She handed me the receiver and whispered, "No. Somebody named Jimmy." She took a few steps back.

A feeling of sadness came over me, but I quickly pulled myself together, hoping my mom didn't notice my disappointment. "Hi, Jimmy! What's up?"

Not one for idle chitchat, he got right to the point. "I talked to my dad about the Fleetwood, and he said he doesn't remember Steve ever owning one."

"That's weird. I thought for sure Bob said he had been working on Steve's Fleetwood. I don't know how I got it so wrong."

"Not so fast. Dad said that, about twenty-two years ago, Chauncey Peterson owned one. My father remembers because he was working part time on the estate when Old Man Peterson was getting rid of the Fleetwood. Dad wanted to buy it, but he wouldn't sell it to him because he never wanted to see it again. Hope that helps."

"Oh, it does. It does." I smiled. "Thank you, and tell your dad thanks too!"

"Good news?" Mom asked.

"Yeah, I think so."

She smiled and went into the kitchen, and I quickly dialed Craig's number.

"You'll never believe what I just found out!" I excitedly told him about the Fleetwood and my grandmother's old scrapbook. "And guess what? Betsy and Barb Goodright might be related."

"You're kidding," he gasped. "How?"

I told him about the wedding announcement and then asked, "Would you be able to find out anything on Betsy's family? I won't be able to get into town before class tomorrow, and since we're planning to go to the hospital to see Bob…"

"Let me see what I can do."

"Great. See you tomorrow."

I put the receiver down and ran upstairs. I wrote the info about the Fleetwood in my notebook and put a question mark by it, since I wasn't sure how it fit into the puzzle, although I had my suspicions.

As I plopped on my bed and cracked open my journalism law textbook, I felt a calmness I hadn't felt since finding Professor Ladd's body. The pieces of the puzzle were coming together, finally. The big unknown was whose face I was going to see when it was finished.

* * *

Monday, October 21st

The morning sun blinded me as I hit around the nightstand, trying to turn the clock radio off. I knocked a book onto the floor and realized I had fallen asleep while studying. A pile of books was still on the bed, and my notebook was open with my pen sitting on it.

Gidget, sleeping at the foot of the bed, glared at me through her slivered eyes as I gathered the books. She barely moved, letting me know she was not ready to start her day. Getting out of bed on this Monday morning was solely my responsibility. She was in no mood to help.

"I take it you're a little miffed with me?" I gently stroked her head, but she didn't purr. "What if I give you a few kitty treats? Would you forgive me then?"

With Jefferson Starship's "Ride the Tiger" playing in the background, I got the treats out of my vanity drawer and laid a few in front of her face, which was resting on her paws. She sniffed each one and then daintily started eating.

Before leaving my room, I quickly checked to ensure I had everything. Books? Check. Notebook and pens? Check.

Check. Money for a can of diet pop, because I was sure going to need a caffeine fix to get through this day. Check.

As I got to the bottom of the stairs, I looked out the small window at the top of the front door and saw T.J. pulling into the driveway. I ran into the kitchen, where Mom had a banana nut muffin wrapped in a paper towel, ready to go.

"Remember, if that nasty ol' detective gives you any trouble, call Crystal's brother-in-law. You have his number, right?"

I nodded.

"Good. Call David if you need him." She sounded worried as she handed me a cup of milk and my muffin.

"Thank you?" I said, puzzled why there was now a plastic child's training cup in my hand.

"What?" she said defensively. "It's the only thing I had that I thought you could drink from without spilling it in T.J.'s car. I thought you might need some protein in the morning. You've been looking a little pale lately."

I smiled, appreciative of her thoughtfulness, but not sure how I would explain drinking out of a kid's cup to T.J.

After I grabbed my coat, I opened the door and rushed down the porch steps to T.J.'s car, parked with its motor running and music playing.

How does he not go deaf? I shook my head and chuckled. As much as I liked Deep Purple's "Smoke on the Water," I had a strange desire to still have my hearing when I was old and gray—a wish T.J. obviously did not share.

I balanced the cup with its lid on my lap as I buckled my seat belt.

"Reliving your childhood, I see?" He laughed as he picked up the kiddie cup and swished the milk around.

"My mother's idea, so I won't mess up your car."

"Nice of her to be so concerned." He grinned.

It was good being with T.J. again—going to school, listening to music, and laughing. Just like old times. I wanted to forget how he'd acted at Rick's house, and I almost did, until he asked, "So, what did you think of Meg? Pretty incredible, isn't she?"

I turned and looked out the passenger window. "Yeah, she seems really nice."

"Yep, she's a keeper."

I turned back in time to see him grinning as he continued.

"We're planning to go to the Jefferson Starship concert this weekend. It's gonna be one cool week! That is, if I can get tickets."

I said nothing. Suddenly, my hopes for a good week were dashed.

After our investigative journalism class, Craig and I headed to his office so he could drop off his book.

"I talked to Burt last night," he said.

"Really? Did you find out anything?"

"He dropped this off this morning. I thought you might like to see it." He pulled a newspaper clipping out of his coat pocket.

I read the first sentence and stopped. "Betsy's father was Samuel Braxton. That means she is Barb's niece. How did we not know that?"

"I guess because we never asked." He shrugged. "Burt also told me he's Betsy's godfather and has been helping her with her finances."

My mouth dropped open. "That means Betsy has a connection to both families—the Goodrights *and* the Petersons."

"That's right." Craig unlocked the door to his office. Deep in thought, he walked to the front of his desk and sat down. "In the end, it might mean nothing, but I find it interesting that, in all the times I've talked to her, she never mentioned her connection to Anne."

"I guess she didn't think it was important."

He looked perplexed. "I still find it strange."

"Did Burt say anything else about Betsy?"

"This is your lucky day!" Craig smiled mischievously. "Burt told me Betsy received a sizable trust fund from her father's estate when she turned twenty-one, which is why he's giving her financial advice. He also told me her father had invested heavily in the Peterson Lumber Company."

"Wow, the two families just keep getting more intertwined, don't they? It's kind of like a real-life soap opera."

"Even better." His green eyes twinkled. "After Betsy's father died, her mother began receiving monthly dividend checks from her husband's investment in the lumber company."

"So, let me get this straight. You're telling me that if the lumber company went belly-up, Betsy's mother would lose a source of income?"

"You got it," he said, leaning back slightly while clasping his hands behind his head.

"So, if Burt is Betsy's godfather, and he's been giving her financial advice, that explains why they were meeting...but why in Watertown? It seems out of the way."

"Good observation. I asked him about that. Turns out he's been helping the manager at the new bank branch in Watertown."

I thought for a second. "Guess that rules out the affair angle of their relationship. At least, I hope so 'cause that would be really gross."

Craig grinned as he stood up. "After talking to Burt, I think we can safely say they were not having an affair." He buttoned his coat, grabbed a scarf, and slipped his gloves on. "Sorry, Sherlock, but the Betsy-Burt affair theory is a dead end." He held open the door. "But don't despair, we've still got Bob. Ready? We can take my car, but I need to run upstairs and let Betsy know I'll be out for a while."

Once upstairs, I stood in the hall as Craig opened the door to the journalism office and yelled, "Betsy, if anyone comes looking for me, tell them I'm gone for a few hours. I'll be back later this afternoon."

The sound of her nails rapidly dancing on the typewriter stopped. "Are you still teaching today?"

"Yeah, I'll be back by then."

Betsy muttered something I didn't catch. The clacking of the typewriter keys resumed as the door to the office swung shut.

Craig led the way to his Jaguar, and I slid onto the red leather seats, ready to enjoy a bit of luxury for a few minutes. He pulled a cassette out and asked, "You like the Doobie Brothers? I've got their new tape. Well, I guess it came out the first of the year, but…it's new to me. He smiled as he pushed the cassette into the tape player and turned up the volume.

I sat back and enjoyed the good life.

* * *

The last time I had been inside St. James General Hospital was when my brother was about ten and had surgery on his broken arm. That was in 1962. I was only seven years old at the time, but I remember how cold and sterile everything looked. Today, although the lobby still had the same white walls, the addition of blue leather-like sofas and teal chairs on the multicolored rug made the room look cheerful. Not homey, but definitely better than how I remembered it.

Our first stop was the reception desk, where Craig inquired about Bob's room number. The receptionist pressed a button on her phone and asked for Bob Lane's room number.

"He's out of intensive care," the receptionist said as she

hung up the receiver, her reading glasses dangling on the chain around her neck. She smiled. "And he's in good condition."

I breathed a sigh of relief. "He's going to be okay."

She continued. "Are you family?"

Craig and I shook our heads.

"The police are limiting visitors to only family members. Maybe check back in a few days."

Craig again asked for Bob's room number so we could send flowers.

"Room 525."

As we neared the exit, he quickly grabbed my arm and pulled me into the hallway leading to the elevators.

"What are you doing?" I asked.

"Don't you want to talk to Bob?"

"Of course, I do, but you heard what she said. Only family."

"Yeah, I heard her." He grinned as he pushed the up button for the elevator.

Soon I found myself on the fifth floor, but when we turned the corner to go to Bob's room, we quickly retreated. A policeman was sitting in the hallway.

"They've got an officer posted outside his door," Craig whispered.

"Looks that way. Now what?" I asked.

He started pacing back and forth. "Let me think a minute."

I peeked around the corner and saw Mae leaving Bob's room and coming in our direction. I grabbed Craig's arm and pulled him into a nearby patient's room, where a nurse was taking an elderly woman's blood pressure and temperature.

The patient turned her head toward us, but, fortunately, with a thermometer in her mouth, she couldn't speak. The nurse, misinterpreting the woman's stare, thought her patient knew us.

"I'm almost done here," said the nurse, in her crisp white dress and hat. "She's doing much better today. She ate her lunch and even sat up in bed for about an hour this morning."

I nodded and smiled as Mae passed by the room. Once she was out of sight, I said, "Tell you what, we'll let you finish, and come back later."

We exited the room as the nurse removed the thermometer. I glanced back into the room and saw the bewildered look on the older woman's face.

"That was close." I sighed. "Why do you think Mae was here and how in the world was she allowed to see Bob? She's not related to him."

"I have no idea, but I'm glad she didn't see us. I'm not ready to talk to my mother…not here…not now," Craig said, looking downcast. "Unless you've got a foolproof idea, I don't think we can get past that police officer."

"I hate to admit you're right, but I don't think we can either. Besides, Douglas probably has us on some kind of a watch-list." I paused. "Guess it's back to the drawing board."

As we waited with a group of people for the elevator door to open, I saw Barb Goodright coming out of the elevator. I grabbed Craig's arm and spun him around.

"What—" he uttered, as I put my hand over his mouth.

I whispered, "Barb."

Out of the corner of my eye, I saw her take off toward Bob's room.

Finally, the door to the down elevator opened and we dashed inside.

"Two close calls in one day are way too much for me. Let's get out of here." I stepped into the elevator with Craig close behind.

He laughed. "One popular guy, that's all I can say. Two women visiting him in one day! He's lucky they didn't show up at the same time. He wouldn't know who to pay more attention to."

The elevator jerked as it came to a stop. I turned to Craig. "Why do you think Barb and Mae went to see Bob? Do you think they're just concerned about him, or do you think there's another reason?"

"I honestly don't know." He shrugged.

As the elevator door opened, I saw we were across from the hospital gift shop.

"Let's find out," I said.

He looked at me, puzzled.

"You implied to the receptionist we were going to send flowers to Bob, right? Well, let's get him some flowers." I grinned as I pulled him into the small shop.

"What are you thinking?" he asked with eyes narrowed.

"I think I know how I can get into Bob's room. We just need to make sure Barb is nowhere around."

With a vase of flowers in hand, we went up the stairs to Bob's floor. I stayed out of view as Craig asked the officer outside Bob's room if Barb Goodright was still there. Craig shot me a look that told me the coast was clear. Now it was my turn.

I walked down the hall, acting like I was trying to find a room, and stopped in front of #525. With his notepad in hand, Craig was taking notes as he asked the officer questions about crimes and weapons. I heard Craig say something about doing research for his new book.

The officer seemed agitated when I interrupted their conversation.

"I have some flowers for Bob Lane."

"Yeah, sure, go on in. Just make it quick." He turned back to Craig, who continued asking him more questions.

Bob had his bandage-wrapped head propped up and an IV in his arm. His voice was barely above a whisper when he greeted me, but the smile on his face told me he was happy to see me.

"How are you doing?" I cheerfully asked.

"I've seen better days." He rubbed his forehead. "I'm glad you found me when you did. Who knows what would have happened if I had been out there much longer?"

I put the vase next to the telephone on the table. "Do you have any idea who did this to you?"

Bob's face went blank, and he turned away from me as I stood by his bed.

"Bob, I know something is going on, and I want to help. This is all connected to Anthony Romano's accident, isn't it?" I was going out on a limb, but it was worth taking a chance. I figured I could gauge how close I was to the truth by his reaction.

He quickly turned and stared at me without saying a word.

"Bob? What is it?"

"Stay out of it, Michelle. These people are too dangerous, and it's not worth it. Trust me. I should know."

"Is that who hurt you—these people? Who are they?"

He reached over and grabbed my hand. "I've said too much already. They're powerful, and they'll do anything to save their precious way of life." He squeezed my hand. "I poked the beast one too many times, and it turned on me. Don't get near the beast."

The door opened, and Detective Douglas walked in. "Ms. Kilpatrick. What a pleasant surprise," he said sarcastically. "Moonlighting as a florist these days?"

"I…I just wanted to see how Bob was doing? Isn't it wonderful that he's doing so much better?" I knew I was talking fast, but I couldn't slow down. There was no hiding I was nervous. My best defensive move was to get out of Bob's room and as far away from the detective as possible. I flashed a broad smile in the detective's direction and then turned to Bob. "Well, I'll see you later, and get well soon, okay?"

Detective Douglas followed me into the hallway, where I found Craig standing exactly where I had left him. Except now, instead of looking like a man in charge of the situation, he looked like the kid who got his hand caught in the cookie jar.

"What exactly are the two of you up to?" Detective Douglas looked sternly at Craig and me.

"Like I said, we just wanted to make sure Bob was okay. We were worried about him," I explained.

"Uh, huh?" After a moment of silence, Detective Douglas continued. "I must ask *again* that the two of you not interfere with our investigation into the murder of Professor Ladd or the attack against Mr. Lane. This is police business only."

"Yeah, I know, but—"

"No excuses. There is a murderer out there who may also have tried to kill again. Do you understand?" His eyes widened as he stared at me. He looked dead serious.

"Yes, but you've got to understand that I need to find Professor Ladd's killer, so I can clear my name—" I looked at Craig, "—*our* names."

"Ms. Kilpatrick, for your information, you and Mr. Miller are no longer suspects. I don't believe either of you had anything to do with Professor Ladd's murder. Let me level with you. If you continue to meddle in this case…either case…it may be *your* murder I'm investigating next. Do I make myself clear?"

"Yes, sir." I took a deep breath. "May we go now?"

"Yes, please. Go. Get out of here."

Before we turned the corner, I looked back and saw Detective Douglas talking to the officer outside Bob's room. From the look on the guy's face, I'd say the detective was giving him quite a verbal thrashing. *Poor guy! I didn't mean to get him into trouble.*

"So, what did you find out?" Craig whispered as we walked to the elevator.

"I'm not sure." I shrugged. "Bob said the people who hurt him were powerful and would stop at nothing."

"Did he say who they were?"

"No, he just referred to them as 'the beast.'"

Despondent, Craig uttered, "Not much to go on."

After the elevator door closed, I nudged him. "No, but at least we know we're dealing with more than one person."

"And that's supposed to make me feel better?"

I thought about it for a moment. "Yeah, I guess you're right."

He smiled. His green eyes twinkling. "Music to my ears."

Confused, I asked, "What?"

"You said I'm right." He grinned while I rolled my eyes.

"You, dear sir, are incorrigible!"

chapter eighteen

Craig parked his Jag in the faculty parking lot on campus. With dark clouds gathering in the distance, we knew rain would soon be upon us. I buttoned the top of my coat and scrunched my shoulders as if that would keep the warmth from the car with me until I reached the building.

"We better get a move on if we want to avoid getting wet," Craig said as he pulled his scarf around his neck.

"Looks like that storm they've been promising us for the past couple of days is finally getting here." I looked at the ever-darkening sky above us and was thankful the faculty parking lot was behind Sheffield Hall, enabling us to make it to the building as the rain started.

"Guess we timed that right," Craig said as he held the door open.

"Thanks for helping me today." Craig could be many things, but today he had been kind and helpful—traits I wish he showed more often.

"Sure, no problem. I'm only sorry you didn't get to talk to Bob longer. Maybe he'll be able to go home soon, and then we can try again." He glanced at his watch. "Just enough time to get to my class. Where are you off to?"

"The second floor, but first I'm going to stop by the journalism office and see if Betsy is in."

Craig looked confused. "Why?"

"I want to interview her for my article on Professor Ladd. You know, the one I'm writing for the *Daily News*?"

"I forgot about that. How's that going?"

"Pretty good. I hope to turn it in to Keith tomorrow... which is why I need to talk to Betsy today. If I find out anything, I'll let you know. Where's your class at?"

"Third floor...room #315."

"Well, have a good one!" We parted ways as Craig continued up the stairs and I headed down the hallway.

As I opened the door to the journalism office, Betsy was at her desk, sorting through a stack of papers. She looked up and smiled. "May I help you?"

"I'm writing an article about Professor Ladd for the *Daily News,* and I was wondering if you would have a few minutes to answer some questions."

Betsy looked down at the papers on her desk and then back at the clock on the wall. She shrugged. "Sure, if it won't take too long. Dean Brown is out for the rest of the day." She turned and looked behind her and then back at me. "Why don't you come back here, and we can use his office? It'll be more comfortable. I'll leave the door open so I can see if anyone comes in."

Betsy moved one of the chairs in the office closer to the door so she could see the counter while I settled into the other chair.

I pulled my notebook and pen out of my bag and took a deep breath before beginning the interview. "How long have you known Professor Ladd?"

She gave a little laugh. "My whole life, actually. Her husband, Burt, is my godfather. Of course, I didn't really get to know them until they moved here a couple of years ago."

"I didn't realize Professor Ladd had only been in Petersburg for such a short time. Somehow, I had the feeling she had been at the university forever."

Betsy laughed. "She gave off that vibe, didn't she? But they moved here in 1972."

"Why did Professor Ladd want to move here?"

"She was tired of being on the road all the time for assignments and wanted something a little slower paced."

"I guess you got to know her quite well by working with her five days a week."

She twisted a blond strand of hair around her finger. "You could say that. Although I'm not sure you ever really know a person. Burt was the one closer to my family."

"Do you think Professor Ladd was happily married?"

The smile on her face disappeared as she sat straight up in her chair. "That's a personal question. Why do you need to know that?"

I lowered my voice. "The rumor mill says she and Craig Miller were having an affair. Do you think they were?"

"What a horrible thing to say!"

"I'm sorry, I don't mean to speak ill of the dead, but the rumor is still out there. I'd like to put things straight if it isn't true. What do you think?"

"As far as I know, she was *not* having an affair with Craig, or anyone else, for that matter." She leaned back in her chair and crossed her arms and legs as tears welled up in her eyes.

"Do you know that for sure? I mean, did you ever ask her?"

"Yes. Yes, I did. The morning she died, she came in early. She and Craig were working together...again."

From her defensive body language, I knew I was onto something, so, using my best Perry Mason approach, I started asking her a series of questions in quick succession.

"And how did she take that—being accused of an affair? Did she think you were overstepping your bounds? Did Burt put you up to talking to her?"

"No," Betsy said, leaning forward in her chair. "He had nothing to do with it. We had met the night before to go over my investments, and he was quite upset about Anne and Craig. He believed they were having an affair. So, the next morning when Craig and Anne were using the copy machine in the office, I heard Craig say he was going to go work out at the gym. When they were finished, I followed Anne to her office and confronted her about their affair."

"What did she say?"

"Anne was furious and blamed me for spreading the rumors about her and Craig and getting Burt so upset. She threatened to have me fired. That's when I left and went back to the office. I was so upset, I spilled coffee all over my skirt."

"But she was alive when you left the office?"

"Yes, very much alive." Betsy looked distraught. "We both said some things that should not have been said. I'd give anything to undo everything."

"Everything?"

"I got so many people upset for no reason." She pulled a tissue from the tissue box on the table by her chair and dabbed her eyes.

"What do you mean?" I quit writing and leaned forward.

"I called my Aunt Barb and told her Anne was going to get me fired."

"Barb Goodright?"

"Yes. She said she and Uncle Steve would be right over to talk to her."

"I don't remember anyone saying Barb and Steve were in the building that morning."

"That's probably because no one saw them in the building. They used Dean Brown's private entrance that goes to the elevator to his office."

"A private elevator?" I couldn't believe my ears.

Betsy pointed at the door on the wall behind us. "Climbing stairs is hard for Uncle Steve...something about his knees. Anyway, he and Dean Brown have some projects they've been working on for the past year, so Dean Brown gave him a key to his entrance door."

I twisted the charm around my neck. "Okay…so, tell me what happened when Steve and Barb got here that morning."

"It was around 8:00 a.m. when they got here. Aunt Barb stayed with me, while Uncle Steve went to talk to Anne. He returned in a few minutes, saying there was no reasoning with her. Uncle Steve and Aunt Barb went into the dean's office for a few minutes. When they came out, Barb told me not to worry, that everything would be alright. She said they needed to leave for a meeting, but suggested I try to get the spot out of my skirt. I left a note on the counter that I would be back in a few minutes and went to the restroom. On my way back to the office, I ran into you."

"Did you see Steve or Barb leave?"

"No, when I got back, they were gone." She dabbed her eyes again.

"Did you tell the police any of this?"

"No. I knew they had nothing to do with Anne's murder, and I didn't want to get them into any trouble because of me. I mean, if it hadn't been for me confronting Anne and then calling them, they never would have been here."

"You know, you need to tell the police."

Betsy abruptly stood up. "No. And if you say anything about it, I'll deny everything." She walked toward the door to the main office. "I think we're done. I need to get back to work."

She headed straight for her desk, where she immediately began typing. I turned to say goodbye, but she avoided looking at me.

Once in the hallway, I took a few steps, leaned against the wall, and ran through the timeline of the morning of Professor Ladd's murder. *Craig said he was at the gym by 7:30 a.m. That means he probably left the building by 7:15. So, let's say*

Betsy went to Professor Ladd's office around that time. They argued, and she then calls Barb, who gets to the office with Steve by 8:00. I paced back and forth. *Okay, think. What next? Steve goes to talk to Professor Ladd while Barb stays with Betsy. When he gets back to the office, he and Barb talk. Betsy leaves the office to wash her skirt and, when she returns, Barb and Steve are gone.*

The timeline suggested Professor Ladd had been murdered sometime between 7:30 a.m. when Betsy last saw her and 8:35 a.m. when I got to her office. Who had motive and opportunity? *Steve!*

I debated going to the police station to tell Detective Douglas what I suspected, but then I remembered Stacy saying Mae and Steve had been having a lot of meetings. Mae's safety was my top priority. I needed to warn her about Steve.

I ran down the stairs, only to realize I didn't have a car. T.J. drove today.

What am I going to do?

I thought for a moment and then ran upstairs to the third floor. Frantically, I pounded on the door to room #315.

Craig opened the door. His eyes widened when he saw me. "What's wrong?"

Winded, my words came out in brief spurts. "No...time to...explain. I have to...warn Mae...about Steve. Can I...borrow...your car? Please?"

He reached into his pocket and pulled out his keys. "Can you drive a stick?"

I nodded.

He removed the car key from the key chain and handed it to me. "Be careful."

"I will...I'll take good care...of your car."

"I didn't mean the car. I meant you."

After adjusting the seat in Craig's car, I drove to the commuter parking lot and placed a note under the windshield wipers on T.J.'s car: "I borrowed Craig's car. Going to Mae's—no need to wait for me. Will call you later."

* * *

Stacy was standing behind the counter holding a new roll of cash register tape when I walked through the door into Mae's Gift Shop. "Somebody got caught in the rainstorm."

"Yeah, forgot my umbrella." I forced a laugh.

She glanced at her watch. "It's not five o'clock yet, is it? Whatcha doin' here so early? Class get canceled?"

"No, but I had some errands to do before work. Is Mae here?"

"No. She said something about stopping by the cemetery and doing something she should have done a long time ago. I really wasn't listening." She paused and then added, "Oh, I remember, she said to tell you that, if she wasn't back by 8:00, for you to close up and go home early."

"That doesn't sound like Mae."

Stacy wrinkled her nose. "I thought it was strange, too, but I'm not one to argue with Mae when she says to go home early." Stacy smiled and went back to unwrapping the cash register tape.

I watched as she held the tape up to the open slot on the cash register. She shrugged and shook her head in defeat.

"Want some help?" I asked.

"Would you mind? I don't know what I'm doing. Mae always changes the tape when I'm here."

Stacy handed me the roll of register tape, and I slid it over the spool and threaded the tape through the register.

"Thanks," Stacy said with a huge smile. "I don't know what I would've done if you hadn't shown up."

"Glad I could help. Just ring up a sale of $0.00, and you should be ready to go." I stepped away from the register, pivoted, and headed for the door. I shouted to Stacy, "I'll be back, but if I'm running late and you can't stay, just lock up, and I'll reopen the store when I get back."

Stacy's mouth hung open. "Where are you going?"

"I need to find Mae. I'm going to the cemetery and see if she's still there."

"You and Steve both."

I stopped with my hand on the open door. "What?"

"Yeah, Steve was here a little bit ago, and he was looking for Mae too. I told him the same thing, that she was at the cemetery. You'll probably run into him there."

I ran to the parking lot, slid into the driver's seat in Craig's car, and peeled out of the lot. The one and only cemetery in town was about twenty minutes away, on the other side of campus. Once I got there, I didn't know where I would find Mae…or Steve.

After driving through the cemetery for a few minutes, I saw two cars parked in front of a mausoleum. One was Mae's. The other one I didn't recognize. I left the car door slightly ajar as I closed it, in the hope of not alerting anyone to my arrival.

From the road, I could hear muffled voices coming from the gray stone building. They grew louder the closer I got. I darted to the side of the mausoleum, so I could hear what they were saying without being spotted.

Mae was shouting. "Bob told me everything! How my father had him sideswipe Tony's car that night. How, when it went off the road, you went down to Tony's car, and when he crawled out of it, you hit him. You hit him! Again and again."

A man's voice pleaded, "I can explain. Just put the gun down."

"No, I don't want to hear anything you have to say. You've lied to me all these years."

I peeked around the corner and saw Steve backed against the wall. Mae was waving a gun at him, her back toward me. Her rage continued. "Bob saw you pour alcohol all over

217

Tony's clothes and into his mouth. How could you? You killed him. You killed Tony!"

"It was for the good of the family," Steve yelled.

"The good of the family? Killing my husband? My baby's father? And...the letters from my sister? She said she wrote me, and you were supposed to forward them to me, but you didn't. Why? I trusted you!"

"Mae, give me a chance to—"

I lost track of Steve's words when I suddenly felt something hard and cold pressing against the back of my head.

"Stand up," a woman's voice commanded. "And get moving." She pushed the object harder into my head as I stood from my crouched position.

"Okay, okay," I said, shaking. "What—"

"Shut up and get inside."

My knees felt like they would give out under me as I struggled to walk up the steps leading to the mausoleum.

Once inside, the person holding me hostage shouted, "Mae, put the gun down, or I'm going to blow this pretty little thing's brains out!"

As Mae turned to see who was behind her, Steve lunged toward her. After a brief struggle, he took control of the gun. The woman behind me shoved me down to the cement floor.

I looked up and saw Steve and Barb pointing their guns toward Mae and me.

Mae started crying. "Michelle, what are you doing here?"

"Shut up, Mae, before I shoot you both! Now move over there and sit down!" Barb shouted as she motioned to the stone bench in the center of the mausoleum.

Steve's hand shook as he waved the gun in the air. "What do we do? Mae knows about Tony. She'll go to the police."

"If you had killed Bob like you were supposed to, I wouldn't have to be cleaning up your mess now," she snapped.

"You don't have to kill us," I pleaded, standing up. "Steve, you can tell the police what happened. It was a long time ago."

"Sit down or, so help me, I'm going to shoot you!" Barb took a step forward, her gun pointed at me.

Without hesitation, I sat down. "Surely there's another way. If Steve would just talk to the police."

"Murder is murder, sweetheart, no matter how long ago it was. But nice try," Barb said. "Now shut up!"

"We can't shoot them here," Steve said.

"Fine. Where do you suggest we shoot them?" she impatiently asked, never once moving her eyes off Mae and me.

For a moment, Steve said nothing as he stared at us until he stated in a matter-of-fact tone, "Let's take them out to the pond. We can shoot them there and then push their bodies into the water."

"Like you did Tony," Mae said in disgust.

I looked at Steve and asked, "Why did you kill Anne? She was your cousin."

"I didn't kill Anne," Steve protested.

"I don't believe you!" Mae yelled.

"Well, you should, because I'm the one who shot her—family or not—and I'm glad I did it," boasted Barb. "The big troublemaker. Snooping where she shouldn't have been."

"Looking into Tony's murder?" I asked.

"That and the money at the lumber company. She just couldn't keep her nose out of the family business. Then she was going to fire dear, sweet Betsy. Enough was enough. I wasn't going to let some has-been journalist ruin my family or my way of life."

I looked at Steve. "Why steal from your company? Were Mae and Bob blackmailing you?"

"I did no such thing!" Mae said.

Steve explained. "I was trying to make up for the past."

"Stop with your lies!" Mae shouted.

"Didn't you ever wonder why you started getting checks after Nathan died?"

"You said it was to reimburse me for the shares in the company, that my father never should have cut me out of his will."

"That wasn't really the reason. I did it because I felt guilty for everything I had done, and I wanted to make things right."

"And you thought *money* would do that?" Mae said, her eyes shooting daggers.

"No. I knew it wouldn't change the past, but I thought I could make the future better."

"What about the money for Bob? What was that for?" I asked.

"Not that it's any of your business," he said, glaring at me, "but Mae has a right to know." He turned his attention back to Mae. "Your father paid Bob off in the beginning, in exchange for his silence over the whole Tony matter. That's how he got the money to open his garage. After Chauncey died, Bob demanded more money, not a lot, just enough to help him live more comfortably. But when he heard about Anne digging around about the past, he upped his demand. I had no choice but to stop paying you, so I could pay him, at least until I could get my hands on more money. Don't you see? By keeping him silent, I was protecting you."

"Protecting me from what?"

"From reliving the past and all its hurts. I did it for *you*."

"You did it to protect *yourself*," I said, glaring at Steve.

Barb waved dismissively. "Oh, shut up, all of you— enough of the excuses. I'm not going down because of Tony or Anne or the money my dear, misguided husband thinks he owes you," Barb said. "I will not lose everything because you two couldn't leave well enough alone. Now, get up, and let's go for a little walk, shall we?"

As Barb motioned for Mae and me to get up, five squad

cars pulled into the cemetery and drove past the mausoleum. I didn't know where they had gone, but I wasn't sure Mae and I could survive a shootout on the stairs, if that's what the police had in mind. I had to do something fast before Barb and Steve led us out of the mausoleum. If I could keep Steve and Barb talking long enough, maybe the police would hear enough to arrest them for murder *before* they led us to the stairs at gunpoint. If I was going to die, I didn't want to die in vain. I wanted the police to know who killed Anne.

I looked at Barb squarely in her eyes. "Before you kill us, at least tell me how you got into Anne's office? Nobody ever saw you in the building."

Barb started laughing. "That's my little secret. You might say it helps to have friends in high places, or maybe—" she laughed again, "—low places would be more accurate. What's it matter? I got in. I shot her. I got out. End of story."

Trying to stall for more time, I looked at Steve. "But why try to kill Bob after Anne was out of the picture? Wasn't he scared he'd be next?"

"You kidding? He wanted even *more* money after Anne's death. He threatened to go to the police and tell them everything if I didn't come up with the money."

Barb's impatience had reached its limit. Without taking her eyes off us, she rebuked Steve. "Enough! We did what we had to do. Now, you two, we're going to take a little walk."

At that moment, Detective Douglas appeared in the doorway to the mausoleum and motioned for Mae and me to drop to the ground as he shouted, "Police! Drop your weapons and turn around slowly."

Steve and Barb whipped around with their guns still in hand. Mae and I scooted behind the stone bench and crouched as low as we could.

"I said, drop your guns!" Detective Douglas yelled.

Peering around the bench, Mae and I watched as several

police officers rushed up the steps with their guns pointed and ready to fire.

Barb and Steve looked at each other. Although I couldn't see their faces, I deduced they each hoped the other had a solution for getting out of their predicament, but there was no way out.

Steve lowered his head and dropped his gun. Barb shrugged and followed suit.

As Detective Douglas and Lieutenant Grogan handcuffed Steve and Barb, Craig came running up the steps.

He rushed to Mae and me. Out of breath, he gasped, "Are you two okay? I was so worried."

He reached out to take Mae's hand to help her stand up, and as soon as their hands met, Mae broke down in tears. "Craig, I'm so sorry, so sorry."

"I know, Mother, sit down. It's all over now."

After helping Mae sit down on the bench, Craig sat between us. He reached over, grasped Mae's hand, and then turned toward me. "Are you sure you're okay?"

"I'm fine."

"You're shaking."

"It's not every day someone points a gun at you." I laughed nervously. "But what are you doing here? How did you know—?"

"After you got my car keys, I knew something was up, so I wrapped up my lecture as fast as I could and went to the journalism office, because I remembered you said you were going to talk to Betsy, and I thought she might know what was up. When I got there, she was crying. Barb had been by and told her not to tell anyone that she and Steve had seen Anne the morning of the murder." He paused. "After Barb left, Betsy feared the worse— that Steve or Barb killed Anne. She wanted to believe they didn't do it, but I could tell she had her doubts. I told her she needed to call the police, and she said that's exactly what you had told her."

"But how did you end up here?"

"I ran over to the Commuter Lounge. Nobody knew where you might be, but someone at a nearby table overheard me talking and offered to drive me over to the gift shop. The girl working there—"

"Stacy."

"She said you had gone to the cemetery to find Mae and that Barb had been by looking for Steve. I knew something was up, so I had Daryl, I think that was his name, drive me over here."

"My goodness. You went to a lot of work to find us!" I looked at the police cars along the street. "But how did the police know to come here? Did you call them?"

"Yeah…before I left Mae's."

"I wonder if Betsy ever called the police? Do you think she's going to be in a lot of trouble?"

Detective Douglas, who had been nearby talking to another officer, joined our conversation. "Betsy withheld valuable information in a murder investigation. That's something she's going to be held accountable for."

"But why did she cover for them?" I asked.

"I suppose love, family, loyalty." He looked at Craig and Mae. "Speaking of family, I guess the two of you have a lot to talk about."

"Yes, we do." Craig patted his mother's hand and then whispered something in her ear. She smiled, stood up, and took his arm. As they walked down the stairs, I saw Mae lay her head on Craig's shoulder.

"I still can't believe Barb killed Professor Ladd. So many people look up to her in the community. She seemed to have everything."

Detective Douglas sat down next to me on the bench. "People do strange things over money. Barb's way of life was in jeopardy. If Anne uncovered Steve's phony invoices, she would have had the paper trail to prove Steve guilty of embezzling funds from the lumber company."

"And the money wasn't even for Steve's lifestyle, per se. He was using the funds so he could give Mae money out of guilt and to Bob because he was being blackmailed by him." I shook my head. "It's so sad. All the lives ruined over lies. Tony wasn't leaving Mae for Anne, and Anne and Craig weren't having an affair."

"Yes, indeed." He looked around. "Chauncey Peterson was so intent on not having his family's reputation ruined by Anthony leaving Mae, he set into motion a series of events that led to his family being broken beyond repair and two—almost three—murders. One of which was his own daughter."

"That reminds me. How is Bob? Are you going to arrest him?"

"Yes. He is being charged with withholding evidence in the case of Anthony Romano's death and for blackmailing Steve Goodright. There's also the possibility we could charge him with contributing to Romano's death by causing the accident."

"I have a question."

"Just one?" His eyes twinkled.

"Maybe." I smiled. "How did Mae get a gun? I thought the police confiscated hers the other day, or did she have another one you didn't know about?"

"When the revolvers we got from Mae's safe and your house didn't match what the medical examiner found, we released the guns to their owners. Mae picked hers up a couple of hours ago, and your father said he'd be in tomorrow morning."

All the talk about guns made me relive how close I came to being shot. "Thank you for getting here. I don't know what would have happened if you hadn't gotten here when you did."

"It's a good thing Craig called us and we were able to get here before anyone got hurt." His face grew more severe, and I braced myself for a lecture as he continued. "Now, didn't I say to let the police do their job?"

"Yeah, you did, but I kind of helped you solve two murders at one time." I smiled and stood up to leave. "I can go, right?"

"Yeah, just—"

"I know, don't leave town." I shrugged.

"No, go get some rest. You've had quite the day." He grinned.

I took a few steps toward the stairs but turned around and yelled, "Detective Douglas…thanks again!"

He nodded and smiled.

As I walked to the road, a black limo pulled out from behind the row of police cars and slowly drove past me. I looked for the license plate, but there was none. Curious, I started to run to my car so I could follow it, but then I remembered I didn't have a car. I had driven Craig's.

Shoot! Not only can I not chase after that limo, but I need a ride home.

I looked over my shoulder, and Craig was still talking to his mother off in the distance. I couldn't bring myself to interrupt them. When I turned back around, I saw T.J.'s car speeding around the corner. He parked behind the line of police cars, and he and Rick flung their doors open.

"Michelle, you're alright!" T.J. yelled as they ran toward me. He gave me a big hug.

"What in the world are you doing here?" I asked.

"When I found the note on my car, I went back to the Commuter Lounge to see if anyone knew what was going on. Rick offered to come with me, and we went to Mae's and—"

"Let me guess. Stacy sent you…poor Stacy probably thinks we're all having a party here, and no one invited her."

"Yeah, probably." He sighed, "But I...I mean, we...needed to make sure you were okay."

"Thanks for coming to check on me." I smiled, impressed they too had gone to all that trouble to find me.

"What happened?" T.J. looked at the significant police presence around us. "What are all the police cars doing here?" He pointed to one of the squad cars. "Is that Barb Goodright in the back of that car?"

"Yeah, and Steve is in another one. It's a long story. Can you give me a ride home and when we get there, I'll fill you and my parents in on all the details?" I paused. "And, maybe, with you guys there, my mom and dad won't freak out so much."

T.J., knowing my parents, laughed. "That's never going to happen. But, hey, we're game if you are."

chapter nineteen

Tuesday, October 22nd

The following morning could have been any Tuesday morning this quarter for all intents and purposes. My alarm went off. I hurriedly got dressed, grabbed the English muffin my mom had for me on the counter, and kissed her goodbye. I threw on my coat, ran out the door, and hopped into T.J.'s waiting car. Nothing out of the ordinary, except this was not like any other Tuesday.

The day before, I had looked death square in the eye and had lived to talk about it. Today, I had a new lease on life, and no matter how overcast the October sky or how stressful my life, the world was beautiful, and my hope for a better tomorrow had returned.

I ran out the front door to T.J.'s car where I was greeted by the sounds of Three Dog Night and T.J. singing "Shambala."

As I tugged on my seat belt, he turned the volume down, looked at me, and sternly said, "Promise me you'll never do anything like that again. Ever. You about got yourself killed."

I smiled mischievously. "But I didn't."

He did not look amused. "Michelle!"

"I know, I know. I'll be more careful next time."

"Next time? What are you talking about?"

"Think about it. With everyone's help, we solved two cases—the murders of Professor Ladd *and* Anthony Romano. Maybe we should join forces and start the Commuter Lounge Detective Agency. What we accomplished blows me away."

"Yeah, and you just about got yourself blown away," he said, still annoyed.

I gently slapped him on his arm. "But thanks to you and Rick and Craig and Stacy and—"

"Detective Douglas. Don't forget the guy with the gun and all his backup," T.J. added. He was quiet for a moment. "But I don't know what I did. When you needed me, I wasn't there. I never would have forgiven—"

"T.J., you and Lawrence and Yash, and even Jimmy and Amy, helped solve this mystery. It took all of us to put the puzzle together. We made a good team. I have to admit, though, I'm glad it's over." I looked out the passenger window. "I think I could really get into investigative reporting." Turning back, I saw the scowl on T.J.'s face, so I quickly changed the subject. "Still taking Meg to the concert this weekend?" Mentally, I crossed my fingers, hoping the concert was sold out, but when he flashed a big smile, I knew my hopes were in vain.

"Yeah, got the tickets yesterday."

"Great," I said, trying not to sound disappointed. I reached over to the radio and turned up Lynyrd Skynyrd's "Freebird."

With a glimmer in his eye, he turned the volume up so high I feared the speakers were going to blow. I teasingly elbowed him, and he turned it down a little. As we sang at the top of our lungs, the conversation about Meg and the concert faded away.

After parking, we grabbed our books and walked toward campus.

Before going our separate ways, T.J. asked, "Got anything exciting planned for today?" He laughed. "Hopefully, nothing more exciting than yesterday."

"No." I smiled. "Should be a rather dull day. Classes…and then turning in my article to Keith for the *Daily News*. They canceled my poli sci class for today, so Craig and I are going to work on—"

T.J.'s eyes grew wide and his jaw dropped. "I thought your investigative work together was over."

"It is, but we still have our journalism project to finish."

He sighed. "I forgot about that."

"Wish I could. I just want to get it finished and put this whole Ladd / Romano thing behind me."

T.J.'s demeanor relaxed. "Yeah, it'll be good for you to be finished with your project, and then you won't have to deal with Craig anymore." He paused and added, "I mean, I know how he gets on your nerves."

I nodded. Craig annoyed me at times, but at others, he could be unbelievably nice. Now, I decided, was not the time to mention that to T.J.

Instead, I replied, "He called me last night, and he thinks we have a good chance of getting our story published in the *New York Times*, since Professor Ladd used to work there, but we have to get it to them before their own reporters snap up the story. Craig may be an arrogant snob, but his connections in the publishing world can come in handy."

T.J. smiled. "Here's hoping you get it done today. The sooner the better. See you tonight!"

* * *

It was hard for me to concentrate on Professor Knight's lecture in my journalism law class. The emotional roller coaster of trying to keep up with classes while looking for

Professor Ladd's murderer had caught up with me. I spent more time looking at my watch than listening to the him.

As soon as the professor closed his notebook and said, "Class dismissed," I jumped out of my seat and put on my coat.

"In a hurry much?" Melody laughed.

"Guess I wasn't in the mood for class today."

"That was obvious. Every time I looked your way, you were looking at your watch or out the window. Did you even take any notes?"

With slumped shoulders, I sighed. "Busted. Can I borrow your notes tonight?"

She smiled as she handed me her notebook. "Sure, what are friends for?"

On my way out of the building, I stopped by the journalism office to check on Betsy, but she wasn't at her desk. There was no blazer hanging over her chair nor any papers lying on her desk. Did Dean Brown fire or suspend her because of her involvement with Professor Ladd's murder? I was thankful she'd told me what happened the morning of the murder, or who knows what would have happened between Mae and Steve? An icy shiver went down my spine as I headed for the stairs.

When I opened the door to the *Wildcats' Daily News* office, Rachel looked up from her typewriter. "Hi, Michelle. Heard you had quite the day yesterday!"

"Yeah, it was one to remember, that's for sure." I smiled. "Is Keith in?"

"No, he's in class. Can I help?"

I pulled my four typewritten pages out of my bag and handed them to her. "Can you see he gets this? It's my piece on Professor Ladd." I waited as she flipped through the papers. "It might be a little long, depending on how much space he has, but I think it'll be easy to divide it into two or three sections. At least, that's how I envisioned it."

She smiled. "I know he'll be happy to get this!"

"I certainly hope so. My phone number is on the front page if he has questions. Well, gotta run. See you later."

I headed down the hall to Craig's office. After tapping on his door, I heard him shout, "Come in!"

As I walked into his office, he was standing in the middle of the room, surrounded by papers scattered on the floor.

"Is this how you always work?" I laughed as I closed the door behind me.

He walked to his desk and laid a stack of papers on it. "Now you know my secret for success. The messier it is—" he waved his hands over strewn papers, "—the better the writing."

"Can I quote you on that?" I tilted my head and smiled.

"No one would ever believe you if you did." He laughed. "Pull up a chair. We've got a lot of work to do."

As I unfolded a chair stashed in the corner, I asked, "Do you know where Betsy is? Is she okay?"

"She's on administrative leave for the time being, while the department investigates her involvement with Anne's murder."

"I hope she doesn't lose her job."

"Don't worry. I'll put in a good word for her, and I'm sure Burt will do the same. What she did was wrong, but I think she learned her lesson. Blind trust can be costly."

For the next four and a half hours, we put the story of Anthony Romano's death on paper. We both felt we had an amazing serial investigative piece. Craig wrote about the Peterson family's history in Petersburg, Ohio, to give the readers insight into our cast of characters. My assignment was to piece together what happened to Tony that fateful night and the cover-up that followed. The first part of my assignment was straightforward, but I still had questions about the cover-up.

"I know Bob blackmailed Steve, but how did the newspaper get it so wrong? I mean, reporting rain and alcohol. None of that came from the police report."

"You're right." Craig peered over his glasses. "I talked to Detective Douglas this morning, and he filled me in on some details he got from questioning Bob and Steve. It seems my grandfather, Chauncey Peterson, who was the mayor of Petersburg at the time, told Sam Winston, the newspaper editor, what to print. Of course—" he grinned, "—it didn't hurt that dear ol' Grandpa gave Sam a sizable cash gift for following orders." He handed me a copy of an old accounting ledger for Sam Winston from that year. He had highlighted the line with the monetary amount from Peterson to the editor in yellow.

"How did you get this?"

"While doing research on the Peterson family, I remembered seeing that the Winston family had donated a lot of Sam's personal correspondence and memorabilia to the museum's room devoted to the history of Petersburg."

"I never would have thought to look there." I shook my head, amazed.

"I wish I had thought about it sooner." Craig shrugged. "I must say, the detective might be a rather good contact."

I cocked my head. "What do you mean?"

"He called me this morning and asked me to stop by the station. He gave me this." Craig handed me a paper.

"What's this?"

"It's a copy of Steve's confession. Not only does it confirm that the information was false in the newspaper articles, but that Chauncey paid the police chief to keep quiet. That explains why no one from the police department ever disputed the story printed in the paper. The chief even promoted and relocated the officers who responded to the crash that night. Convenient, huh?"

"Wow, deception everywhere!" Saying the word *deception* reminded me of the many times Craig had not been honest with me. It was hard to trust him when I felt he was still harboring secrets. I had just seen what misplaced trust could lead to, and I didn't want to go down that path. Yet, I felt sorry for him and his broken relationship with his mother. "How is Mae doing? You know she closed the shop for the rest of the week?"

"Yes, I know. She's doing okay," he said as he sat down in front of his typewriter. "Dealing with a lot of emotions. She was angry with her father for putting the family's reputation above everything and everyone...and with Steve for his part in my father's death. But, honestly, I think the hardest thing for her right now is realizing her sister is gone, and that she can never bring her back. They can never resolve their differences. They can never start over."

"And...what about...the two of you?" I asked.

"We're talking. It's going to take time. When I moved to NYC to become a writer, it reminded her too much of the sister she blamed for destroying her life. In my mother's mind, Anne and I became the same person, and she shut me out. There's a lot of hurt on both sides, but I think we'll make it." He sighed. "Anne would have liked that. She hoped that, if she could get my mother's forgiveness, my mother and I could repair our relationship as well. Maybe through Anne's death, we can move forward." He smiled wistfully, looked at his papers, and started typing.

I also got to work. Craig had concocted a makeshift desk for me in the corner. After writing and rewriting several paragraphs, I looked at the clock on the wall and saw it was 3:30. I moved my neck around to get the kinks out. "Time sure flew by fast. I didn't know it was so late." I started packing up my things. "Best be going. I've got to meet T.J. in a few minutes, or else I'll be walking home." I laughed.

"I could give you a ride home later. That would give us a chance to finish this paper tonight." He lifted an eyebrow. "It would be to our advantage if I could call the story in to the editor tonight."

What he said made sense. "Okay…let me run to the commuter lot and tell T.J. and—" I paused and took a breath, "—can I use your phone to call my parents?" It was far better to be embarrassed about having to call home than deal with my parents' wrath for not telling them I was going to be late.

"No problem." He smiled and pointed to the black rotary phone on his desk.

At 7:30, we finished our article. According to Professor Ladd's syllabus for the class, if any student got an investigative journalism piece published during the quarter, they got an automatic A. Although Craig couldn't care less about the grade, I was thrilled with the prospect.

I sat patiently in my metal fold-up chair and listened as Craig called his editor friend at the *New York Times*. After being transferred to another department, Craig read the article, and then reread it at a much slower pace, stopping to spell the names of people and places.

After what seemed like an eternity, he smiled as he put the receiver down. "Great news! Our article will run in Thursday morning's edition. How 'bout we celebrate the two of us getting our first byline in a national newspaper by going out to eat? My treat." Craig slipped on his black pea coat and buttoned it.

"Sounds good. I'm starving." I put the cover over the typewriter and handed a stack of papers to Craig.

When I brushed against my coat hanging on the wall hook, it fell to the floor. As I bent over to pick up my coat, I found several papers Craig had missed picking up. Scrawled across the top of one of them were the words "family business." I started to ask him about it, but the sound of the howling wind outside diverted my attention and reminded me how cold it was outside.

"Do you mind if I pick the place?" Craig asked.

"No, whatever is fine with me. I'm not picky," I answered.

"Good. Let's go."

* * *

After a thirty-minute drive, Craig pulled into Grayson's parking lot.

"Uh, you know this place is on the pricey end, right?" I asked.

"Tonight, we celebrate!" Craig's eyes sparkled as he flashed his pearly white smile.

When the maître d' greeted Craig by name, I regretted having mentioned the priciness of the restaurant. Of course, Craig could afford a place like this. Sometimes I forgot that not everyone counted their pennies like I did. I thought about the life Craig must be used to living in the big city and shook my head as the maître d' led us to an elegantly set table by the window overlooking the Maumee River. Although not usually known for its beauty, tonight the river was nothing short of breathtaking with an array of colored lights shining on it.

"Have you ever been here before?" Craig asked.

I mustered my best nonchalant, "No." Having already given away that I thought it was an expensive restaurant, I didn't want to add to my humiliation by acting too impressed with the place. Maybe he would think I was concerned about his finances, since he was the one paying. In the end, it didn't really matter what he thought. I was going to savor every moment at Grayson's, in case I never got to come back.

"You know," Craig began, "I wasn't happy about working with you on this assignment in the beginning."

"Yeah, I know." I nodded, feeling a bit upset he would bring that up right now.

"Even with all your inexperience, though, you surprised me."

I wasn't sure that was a compliment and uttered, "Thanks?"

"No, I mean it. Nice job. You pulled it off." He set his glass down. "I'm glad you went to look for my mother yesterday at the cemetery, but why did you go?"

"When Betsy told me Steve and Barb had been in the building that morning, I had a bad feeling. I knew Mae had been meeting a lot with Steve, and I wanted to let her know he might be her sister's killer. I didn't want her to be alone with him anymore. When I found out Steve was looking for her, too, I really got worried. I never expected to find Mae holding Steve at gunpoint, and I certainly didn't expect Barb to pull a gun on me and throw me into the mix. That was a little more than I had planned on."

"What a reporter does for a story," Craig said, raising his glass. "Speaking of being a reporter, are you still interested in that internship this summer with the *Chicago Tribune*?"

"I was, but I needed a letter of recommendation from Professor Ladd."

"Would one from Craig Miller suffice?"

"Really? You would write one for me?"

"It's the least I could do. I mean, you did just risk your life to get me material for my next book. I know I'm not a professor, but would a mystery-writing grad student work?"

"That would be great! I'll drop off the paperwork tomorrow." I smiled at the unexpected turn of events. My thoughts, however, soon returned to everything that had happened the past several days. "What do you think is going to happen to the Peterson Lumber Company now that the police arrested Steve?" I took a bite of my Caesar salad.

"That, Sherlock, is the other thing we're celebrating tonight. I've been asked to sit on the board. Also, my lawyers are looking into my grandfather's will and whether the company is mine."

"I thought he left it to Steve in his will."

"The will Steve knew about did, but there was a second one that my grandfather wrote a week before he died. In it, the lumber company only went to Steve in the event there was not a direct male descendant. Steve knew nothing about that one. In fact, the only people who knew about it besides Grandfather were his lawyers and Anne. She kept a copy in her safe deposit box. Burt told me about it when I talked to him the other day, and he brought it over last night."

"Wow, I didn't see that coming!" I paused. "But why do you think your aunt didn't tell you about the second will?"

"I've thought about that. Perhaps she was concerned that, if Steve found out that I was Chauncey's grandson, he would try to get me out of the way—legally or literally." He stopped and took a few bites of his steak.

"And there's more. Besides my spot on the board, and possibly the ownership of the Peterson Lumber Company, it seems I have inherited a rather large house—the Peterson Manor."

"That's incredible. So...will you be staying in town?" I asked, almost choking on my broccoli floret.

He nodded and took another sip from his wineglass. "Are you okay with that?" he asked. "Didn't mean to make you choke on your food."

"No...no...that's a great idea. I'm sure your mother will be happy to have you nearby and..."

"And...?" He smiled.

"And you'll do a great job with the lumber company and..." I stopped mid-sentence again. I rather liked the idea of Craig staying in town, but I wasn't exactly sure why. I noticed he was waiting for me to finish my thought, but I couldn't. The words wouldn't come.

Breaking the uncomfortable silence, he simply said, "I agree."

I finished my salad and realized life had suddenly gotten more complicated.

* * *

Three days later, another week of school ended. I was looking forward to a party at Rick's that night. It was just what I needed. Good friends, good food, and good music. The perfect ending to a crazy couple weeks.

As I carried a plate of millionaire shortbread cookies on a platter into Rick's house, a group of smiling faces and a banner with "Congratulations, Michelle!" hanging across the archway into the kitchen greeted me.

Amy came up and gave me a hug. "Michelle, we're so proud of you! You should think about being a detective."

Before I could think of something to say, Yash pushed Amy away and wrapped his arms around me in a big bear hug. "Sexy lady, you're all they are talking about at the lumber company. With Steve out of the way, there's talk of a loan to hold the company over until things get squared away. That means—" he pretended to do a drum roll, "—there's a good chance they will not be laying off anyone."

My face started to get hot from all the unexpected attention.

Jimmy and Todd both gave me a thumbs up, with Todd adding, "Like I told you the other day, you did good work. Glad you got your name cleared and found the killer. Maybe they'll put your face on a cereal box!"

After chatting with a few friends I hadn't seen at the Commuter Lounge since the big run-in with Steve and Barb, I made my way into the kitchen, where I set the platter on the counter.

"Those look good," Rick said as he grabbed three of them. "You make these?"

"Yeah, when I got home last night. After all the excitement this week, I wanted to make something extra special tonight."

"I like the way you think." He grinned.

"Nice banner, but rumor has it congratulations are in order for you and your mom too."

"How'd you know?" Rick took another cookie.

"Word travels fast in the Commuter Lounge." I laughed. "So, when is the grand opening?"

"Mom's meeting with the shopping center representative this weekend in Columbus. She's going to sign the lease on her space, and—" he crossed his fingers, "—we'll start renovating November 1st."

"That's exciting!"

"She's going to let me work with the architect on the remodel. I'll get some real hands-on experience."

"That's wonderful. I can't wait to go see the fitness center."

Rick beamed as he took two more cookies. "It would be great if you could come to the grand opening. Everybody's invited. It's going to be December 14th, and it's going to be a killer of a party!"

"I wouldn't miss it for the world!"

about sharon kay

SHARON KAY grew up in Ohio and earned a photojournalism degree from Bowling Green State University. The *Michelle Kilpatrick Mystery* series is inspired by her life in the 70s as a commuting college student who worked at her parents' gift shop. She is the proud mother of three children who all graduated from the University of Michigan and served in the Army National Guard. Her hobbies include drinking iced tea, working in her garden, and keeping up with the British royal family.

If you enjoyed, The Peculiar Case of the Petersburg Professor, please take a few moments to leave a review. Thanks!

Visit www.thesharonkay.com for information on new releases, events, special promotions, Book Club Discussion Questions, Michelle's recipes, and playlists for the series.

Coming Spring 2024: Book Two—"Fashionably Fit, Fatally Flawed."
You can also find SHARON KAY on

facebook.com/thesharonkay
instagram.com/thesharonkay

Made in the USA
Monee, IL
04 December 2024